THE BOOTLEGGER

One wants to save the family farm so he turns to bootlegging.

The mobster needs his gin to save his business.

That's not how it's going to turn out.

First published in UK

by

The Mobster

Sean "Lucky" O'Leary grew up in Ireland; a republican who hates the British. As a youth, he has spent time in a British jail for being picked up as a look-out for a gunrunner. The truth is, he was in the wrong place at the wrong time but the real accomplice had set him up and fingered him to the police.

After a couple of years inside, on release O'Leary tracks down and murders the "snitch" with his bare hands, slowly choking him to death. With a substantial reward for his capture, it is decided by sympathisers that he should be shipped off to the States to shelter with previous emigrants. It isn't an easy escape; he parties too long, oversleeps and misses his berth on the S.S. Titanic, watching her from the quayside at Queenstown as she sets sail for the USA. He would have been the 114th third class passenger from Ireland, meaning only 113 boarded as well as the 7 second class.
Hence his nickname.

When he finally lands in New York, he finds the city controlled by the Italians and the Jews, the Irish mob continually squeezed in the Protection and gambling rackets by the Black Hand gangs of Italians in particular, and struggling. Unable to find a role that suits him, he is pushed on by contacts to Pennsylvania. A couple of months mining gives him money to get away and a distaste for working underground. Instead, he becomes a union fixer. Six feet (tall for the times), red fiery hair, he applies his muscles to getting respect and his brains to gain position. Too successful and noticeable, he has to flee to Chicago to escape the bounty put on his head by the mine owners.

The story begins ……

1914

Henry Ford pays his workforce a minimum of $5 per day for an 8-hour day as he mechanises production using new "scientific management" methods and adopts the production line as seen in the meat industry.

Chicago White Sox and New York Giants play an exhibition game in Cairo, part of a world tour.

US Congress approves a new law – the Burnett Anti-Immigration Law

Charlie Chaplin's The Tramp is seen by movie audiences for the first time, in "Kid Auto Races at Venice".

Firestone patent a non-skid tyre pattern.

Babe Ruth plays professional for the first time, but as a pitcher.

Franz Ferdinand, Archduke of Austria is assassinated in Sarajevo.

War in Europe.

Sean O'Leary arrives in Chicago

CHAPTER 1

Chicago

Chicago is one of the most venal and corrupt cities in the United States. Fire off a full belt of a machine gun in City Hall and it would be a miracle to hit an honest politician. A melting pot of immigrants from over the world but mostly Europe, it is where people climbed out of the gutter and poverty by offsetting any morals and a willingness to do anything (or almost anything) to get on and only a brave and high-minded few are willing to try and change that. For a poor Irish immigrant with ferocity and courage, it is an opportunity.

Sean "Lucky" O'Leary arrives in the Windy City with ten dollars in his pocket and the clothes on his back. He'd zigzagged a route away from Pennsylvania to confuse any enemies, of whom he has a few. Along the way, narrow escapes meant leaving possessions behind as he jumped out of boarding house windows to escape murder squads. Where's the best place to hide a tree? In a forest. So, Lucky made his way to Chicago with its high Irish populace among others.

Finding his way to an Irish bar isn't hard, the city has evolved into ethnic zones and he heads to the North Side, an emerald heartland. It was settled in the 1880s by immigrants, Germans and Swedes alongside the Irish. Sean is part of a new wave of immigrants arriving. He pauses to look at the Water Tower, a utility building posing as some Gothic castle, and wonders who thought to do that and why. Equally puzzled by the Queen Anne style of the Archbishop's residence. Mimicking English architectural styles was not what he expected. The city and surrounding lands could so easily have been Canadian and gone for French styling after its founding by Jean Baptiste Point du Sable. That was shortly after the American War of Independence, in which the French had been allies of the rebels. How things turn. Sean had done some checking in libraries on his way here. Intention was to keep warm but he chose to read books to pass the time.

In a downtown area, he comes across a bar that looks promising, a bit more stand out than others, not upmarket, a working man's bar with peeling paint around the door and windows, something that says we don't put on airs, we are the genuine article. The bar is named the Blarney Stone and, inside, hung with fake shamrocks and a colour scheme that was once green but which has darkened over time from nicotine, which is still contributing to the effect from the pipes and cigarettes of drinkers. A weak light comes through the dirty windows and shines half-heartedly over the crowd within as if it doesn't want to identify them, providing a sanctuary of anonymity. Sawdust is liberally sprinkled over the wooden floor – the smell of fresh pine mingles with spillages of old stale beer and a heavy fug of tobacco smoke, but not strongly enough to hide the hard-set aromas.

Lucky enters with care, stands just inside the entrance and looks around, taking in the set up and the customers. Seeing no threats and deciding he fits right in, he walks over to the bar and buys a beer. The desire is to gulp it down and have a second, but he can't afford that. The ale hits a stomach empty except for some stale crusts eaten that morning. As he sips, he looks over the rim of his glass, more intensely studying the room, not acting too hasty or desperate to make contact. If he doesn't want to be sleeping in a park or under a bridge, he needs to make this work for him. Resting an elbow on the counter and hooking his heel over the brass footrest, he sizes up the clientele as low class, low skilled men, who earn their wages by brawn not brain. Here is their companionship in life's struggles, numbed by cheap booze. Men he has known all his life, in one way or another, only one step out of the gutter and teetering on a kerb, ready at any unfavourable incident to fall down. As he slows his drinking and even takes pretend glugs of his beer, making it last, he notices a number of men have started to loudly disappear, as if a plug in a bath of humanity has been pulled and they are swirling into the plughole, actually a door into a back room. Casually, he asks the bartender, a tall streak of a man with a cast in one eye, what is on.

"What's happening that I'm missing, fella?"

The bartender looks the questioner over – probably early twenties, six-foot, which makes him taller than any of the customers, flame red hair curling over a collar, scarred knuckles, needing a shave- and decides that O'Leary is a fellow Irishman and obviously not a cop, answers.

"The boys like a bit of a fight. We've got Crazy Cavanaugh tonight. He'll take on all-comers, five dollars a time. Winner takes a purse of fifty dollars."

"Fifty! That's a lot of cash."

"Has to be," replies the barman as he dries glasses with a dirty cloth, holding one glass up to check for smears, as if he could tell in the dingy light. "He's unbeaten, so it takes a desperate man to get in the ring with him; you have to need the money badly to take that risk."

"I think I'll have a look-see," and Sean, first draining the last of beer in his glass, casually walks away from the bar and through the door.

The back room is bigger than the bar room. Empty of furniture except for a table and chair, where a bookkeeper sits to take the bets, a billy-club on the table top next to a cashbox and a desklamp, which illuminates a ledger where he records bets. No windows let daylight into the room but a couple of overhead lamps shine a yellow light, making the spectators look jaundiced. Ring is a misnomer, except for the shape; a circle drawn on the floor in chalk, around which the spectators stand, beer glasses in hand. At the back of the room, Cavanaugh is stripped to the waist, a big man carrying a bit too much weight but still powerful. His eyes suggest he is taking something or else he really is crazy. Facing him, his opponent is a young worker from the meat-packing factory; handsome in a rugged sort of way. Stripped to the waist, he looks fit and a possible contender; working in the meat factory has put muscles on him. No doubt, cuts of meat leave the factory under a coat and he dines on red meat at home.

Into the circle steps a portly man, with a huge moustache that swirls from his upper lip to cover his cheeks, wearing a fancy waistcoat with a gold watch and chain, who is the referee and master of ceremonies. Strutting around, thumbs hooked into his armpits like some exotic rooster, he waits for the crowd to filter in. An unlit cigar sticks out from the corner of his mouth, almost as a piece of organic jewellery for the lips.

Sean recognises the set up. This is a bareknuckle fight to the finish. No rounds. If a man goes down, he is given a chance to get up then the fight will continue. The referee does not have much to do except to rouse the crowd. Time for action, removing the cigar he calls out.

"Gentlemen, Gentlemen. Place your bets before the bout starts. We have Mr Cavanaugh challenged by Shamus Flynn. Now, Mr Cavanaugh says he's been under the weather this week as his kitten died so he may not have his mind fully on the fight."

This gets a laugh from the crowd and the referee smirks at the success of his joke.

"Shamus looks a fit young man. He's got youth on his side and the strength of a Hercules."

Letting the crowd take a longer look at the contender, his beady eyes take in the money changing hands. Many are considering Cavanaugh a safe bet, despite the poor odds. Gamblers and friends of the contender are betting heavily, believing the time has come for Cavanaugh's reign to end or they are just tempted by the faint chance of a big win. A nod from the bookkeeper that enough bets have been taken and the referee speaks again.

"Gentlemen, up to the mark if you please."

The murmur of the crowd ceases as both fighters walk up to the ring centre and face each other. A palpable tension from gamblers who desire winning and fear losing their cash. This close, young Flynn looks nervous, the bravado evaporating now the booze is wearing off and he is removed from the mates who have encouraged him. Engaged to be married, he'd been keen on the prize money to set up home with his intended. Crazy – and it is obvious no one calls him that to his face – glares.

The bookkeeper, having closed and locked the cashbox, takes a quick dram of whiskey before he strikes a bell on his table.

O'Leary watches with interest. Back in the "old country" he'd done some fairground boxing and has proved proficient punching out farmboys on the circuit. In the mines, fistfights are toe-to-toe until a man goes down and Sean had had a share of these. Young Flynn gets some punches in to the body of Cavanaugh, but the big man seems

11

oblivious, responding with a right hook, which the younger man blocks. The kid is not exactly a novice after all. O'Leary notices that Crazy is open to left hooks – maybe the sight in his right eye is not so good.

No one has yet gone down on the floor, when Cavanaugh drops his guard and Flynn sees his chance...or thinks he does. As he opens his stance to get his punch in, a steamroller of an uppercut slams in to his chin, his eyes roll up, blood sprays from his mouth, followed by a couple of teeth and Flynn goes down like a felled tree with a crash, raising clouds of sawdust. Cheers from the Cavanaugh supporters; groans from Flynn devotees.

The referee stoops over the supine meat packer, can see the kid is unconscious and breathing.

"And out by a knockout. The winner... King Cavanaugh!"

The meatpacker's friends throw a bucket of mop water over him. The dirty water dilutes the blood from his mouth, runs down his face and puddles in the sawdust. A few happy gamblers collect their winnings from the table while losers start back to the barroom to drown their sorrows. O'Leary's voice cuts through the clamour.

"Any chance of a fight, or does he only do the one?"

The momentum of bodies stops immediately and a couple of dozen faces turn toward him. Slowly, the referee comes over from the bookkeeper, the crowd parting to make way, and he looks the new arrival up and down.

"A new face. And what might your name be?"

"Sean O'Leary. I've got five dollars."

"Now then, boyo. Mr Cavanaugh needs to enjoy his moment of glory, so join me at the bar and we'll see what we can do." Turning to the crowd who have lingered to follow the new development, "Don't go away yet, lads. We might have some more entertainment for you. Follow me, Mr O'Leary. I'm Padraig Hennessey, the owner of this fine establishment."

Those who have lost money and are thinking of leaving decide to stay and have another beer, even if no money to bet, there could be free entertainment.

At the bar, Hennessey orders a whiskey for himself and has a pint of beer put before O'Leary.

"Tell me about yourself, Sean. You don't mind me calling you Sean, do you."

"It's my name."

"Fine, fine. So, when did you arrive in our fair city and where are you from?"

"In today. From Limerick, via New York and Pennsylvania. I'll be looking for work but the fifty dollars will tide me over until I find it."

Hennessey laughs. "You're confident you'll win the fifty? You might end up losing five and needing a surgeon."

"I'll take that chance."

Hennessey turns to the crowd of drinkers. "Gentlemen! We have a contender!"

Hennessey has calculated and sees the chance to take more money off the punters and to sell more beer and whiskey. No skin off his nose if this fresh big, dumb ox of a young man is to take a hiding. Business might be better than average today. It isn't always easy to find contenders willing to go up against Crazy.

In the backroom, O'Leary strips to the waist after handing over five dollars. Onlookers, on seeing his physique, previously disguised by baggy coat, and thinking that Crazy might be less than 100% having had a bout, especially those who like longshots, start to lay money on the newcomer. Sean is considering his options. In the fairgrounds he might let his opponent tire himself a bit before going in to trade punches. Here, the ring is too small and the crowd will push at his back should he try to work the edges. Gut punches might not be effective – Crazy has some fat over his muscles and it will be hard to wind him. It will have to be head shots; get left hooks to the side of the head – ear and temple – keep pounding, while avoiding that killer uppercut, so keep his guard up. Move fast, in and out – no standing still. Losing five dollars will almost wipe him out. Winning fifty will tide him over nicely.

Hennessey struts into the ring like a fighting bantam cock released from a basket.

"Gentlemen! Gentlemen! We have a contender. As Mr Cavanaugh

has had a fight already, we are only offering evens on Mr O'Leary."

A moan from the crowd. It is only worth a longshot bet if the odds are good. Some of the betting moves back to Crazy. Hennessey has considered the physique and the confidence of the challenger, whom he realises has a height and reach advantage. Before too much money shifts across, he gives a nod to the bookkeeper. The bell sounds and Crazy launches an attack, eager to get the contest over. Sean receives a pounding on both arms held up before his body, then takes an opportunity to step back and aside and sweep a left hook in. Crazy takes it on the jaw, shakes his head slightly and comes back with a left right combo of jabs.

Sean decides to pedal clockwise around the other man, be a moving target always to what he hopes is a blindside. He manages a couple of hooks to Crazy's left ear. He can see an effect as his opponent pauses ever so slightly after taking a hit. Then Crazy gets a right hook back and Sean feels it, a buzzing in his ears. Shaking his head to clear it he sees Crazy's grin, confident this would not take long. Sean feints with a right hook, Crazy responds defensively and Sean gets him with two rapid left jabs, one on the ear and one on the jaw hinge. The fighter's eyes widen at the shock of pain. His hesitation allows Sean to slap him over the ear with an open palm, creating a pressure wave to burst the eardrum if possible. It certainly is painful. Sean's turn with left right combos, as fast as he can, hammering Crazy who starts to wobble. Seeing the opening he wants, Sean gets one good left hook to connect with the jaw hinge again and breaks it. The fight goes out of the big man, his jaw hangs lopsided, he puts his arms up for protection and takes blow after blow before falling to his knees.

The crowd shouts, even those who have bet on Cavanaugh: "Finish him!"

Sean looks at Hennessey and shakes his head.

Afterwards, in the bar, with the winning punters slapping him on the back and placing whiskey shots in front of him, Sean is approached by Hennessey.

"Why don't we go into my office, where it's quieter?"

"Why would I want to go in there?" asks Sean. "It's nice out here, with all these people."

"You're smart. Not just tough, but smart as well. I have a proposition for you."

Hennessey turns away and walks over to his office, entering and leaving the door open as an invitation or temptation. Sean weighs up his options. He's beaten up the money-maker that is Crazy Cavanaugh and he'll be taking fifty dollars off Hennessey. The office could be a trap for the man's minions to take him out back, recover the money and beat the crap out of him. On the other hand, sometimes you have to gamble to make opportunities and today Sean feels lucky. Pointing at the row of shot glasses paid for by his admirers, he says to the barman:

"Pour them back in the bottle. I'll take it with me when I leave."

Only pausing to see his instructions obeyed, he walks over to the office and enters, leaving the door ajar. Not only will he have something to drink later, people might question why the bottle is still there if he never comes out of the office; not that he really believes anyone would care.

"Why didn't you finish Crazy off? You had him at your mercy." Hennessey's small eyes pierce Sean, who shrugs.

"Waste of effort. The man was beaten. I'd won. Nothing more to prove. And maybe one last hit might have bust my hand. It is a lose-lose choice to carry on."

"So not an act of mercy, then?"

"Had you held up twenty dollars as a bonus, he'd be laid out good and cold."

"Yup. Smart. I saw that by the way you fought. The usual mugs just go wading in, but you spotted his weakness and took him. I can use a man like you. I need muscle but I don't need gorillas. A hundred a week and bonuses." Hennessey is all business.

"What do I have to do to earn that?"

"Anything I say. Is that going to be a problem for you?"

"I guess not."

"Good. Come back tomorrow first thing." Passes over a note. "Meantime you go to this address and tell Mary I sent you. You'll have a room to yourself. Then go to Rafferty's the tailors on 22nd Street. Choose a suit and shoes, nothing flashy. He'll send the bill to me. Finally, get a haircut and a bath. See you in the morning."

"Before I go..."

"What?"

"My winnings."

Pocketing the fifty dollars as he leaves, Sean can hear Hennessey laughing uproariously behind him. On the way out, he swoops up the bottle of whiskey from the counter and nods to the barman, Dougal, who returns a big smile.

CHAPTER 2

Sean "Lucky" O'Leary starts working for Hennessey the next day. He has found his lodgings, a single bed room, shared bathroom and dining room, with Mrs Mary O'Shea, a childless widow in her middle thirties, who is an attractive woman, brunette and sparkling green eyes, who looks much younger than her years. Two other lodgers are workmen for the City, doing repairs to roads and the like. They are quiet when Sean is around.

Rafferty the tailor has fitted him with an off-the-peg suit, a bit baggy because he has to take a size large for his muscular frame, a couple of shirts and a pair of black shoes. Sean buys a green tie and some cufflinks to set himself off. Rafferty says "come back and let me adjust the suit for a better fit, no charge". Sean replies, "I'll be back to have a couple made soon."

Lucky again, Sean has walked into the bar of Padraig Hennessey. Hennessey has been around a while. His big chance had come several years earlier, in 1905, when Jacob "Mont" Tennes, king of the gamblers, obtained control of the horse racing results coming over the wire. In the gambling dens, the results would come in by tickertape and be announced by the bookie. To have the knowledge before anyone else allowed the chance to place a bet after the race was run and the winner known. Cutting out the other bookmakers unless they paid him handsomely, had created a turf war. Tennes, made allies with John Condon, Tom McGinnis and John O'Malley from the Loop district and they fought with a group led by John O'Leary (no known connection to Sean) and won. Hennessey earned his reward for successes in various fights and bombings and now rules his own patch, earning well as long as he pays up the line to the top boss, which is a fee for political protection and corrupt law enforcement payoffs.

Arriving back at the Blarney Stone, Sean is given the once over by Hennessey.

"You'll do. Things work out, we can improve on this." Sean nods and Hennessey continues, "I'll show you round my district. We keep strict boundaries. We have our lines and we don't cross over without permission. Nor does anyone come into ours without invitation. Some of our neighbours are allies, some potential enemies. I'll need you as my bodyguard, which won't be onerous unless the balloon goes up. Your work will be more about enforcement. People who don't pay their debts. Drunks who get out of hand." Hennessey opens the drawer of his desk and produces a Colt .38, ammunition, and brass knuckles. Pointing at the gun, "You know how to use this?"

"I've used a gun before. Might be useful to have some practice though."

"I'll have Dougal take you into the country and you can shoot up

20

some trees. You met Dougal last night. He's the bartender. He's waiting out back with the car."

Sean nods and pockets the knuckles and ammo and sticks the gun in his waistband. Hennessey leads the way through the rear exit of the bar to where Dougal is indeed waiting with a car, the new 1914 Packard 48 Tourer, a symbol of Hennessey's status that he can afford a new motor. Dougal nods to Sean and gets a nod back.

Hennessey gives instructions, "We'll just drive round. We might stop to check a few places. Easy on the pedal, Dougal. Let the people see us," and sits back comfortably to enjoy the ride.

As they motor around, Hennessey nods to people whom they pass and lets them see Sean, the word of the fight having spread like wildfire.

He explains the set-up to his new hired hand. "The boxing matches are entertainment for the bar customers, something to bring in trade and a little extra earner. More for fun than profit but it brings people in. I'm not wasting you in the ring, that's chickenfeed. Our income comes from collecting bets for the lottery and sports events, enforcing payment of loans for those who lost and are slow in paying. I've ensured your reputation is spreading. Anyone who can knock out Cavanaugh is a man to be feared and respected but you'll need to smack a few heads quickly to reinforce the message, first chance you get."

The Bootlegger

They soon arrive in the Levee, the notorious red-light district of Chicago, south of the Loop, consisting of the bottom end of the trade with cheap whores. They drive down South Dearborn, Hennessey acknowledging recognition with a casual wave, sometimes getting Dougal to pull into the kerb so he can make small talk with people of slightly higher standing than the usual customers. Sean is taking it all in, seeing opportunities for himself under the patronage of his new boss.

"I've got financial interests in five brothels here. There are around one hundred in total, owned by various interests. There's enough business to go round. In and around Twenty Second street, many of the buildings are connected by tunnels, useful for avoiding police raids or the occasional customer too well known who does not want to be seen entering an establishment. Hey, Dougal, pull over!"

Two men are fighting on the sidewalk outside of one of Hennessey's brothels. Sensing an opportunity to confirm his enlarged entourage publicly, he looks at Sean, "OK, son. Sort them out."

Sean climbs out of the car and walks over, sizing them up as worse for drink and unlikely to be carrying firearms. Sensing some entertainment, people on the opposite side of the street pause to watch.

"Now then, boys. What's this about?" Sean tries the friendly approach as an opener.

"Fuck off and mind your own business." Drunk enough to brawl but too drunk to understand what he is up against.

"I thought you might say that. Well, this is my business."

With speed, Sean grabs each guy and pulls them together so their heads smack. Releasing them to let them fall on to the ground, Sean walks back to the car to the cheering of onlookers and overhearing: "That must be the guy who beat Crazy. They say he is a redhead."

Hennessey smiles at Sean as he settles in the back seat again. "Lovely. Lovely."

The two men lay stunned on the ground as the car drives away.

The success of the red-light district fails later this same year. The Vice Commission manage to effectively close the Levee as a centre for prostitution, after a number of inept attempts before. A few brothels, with high end attraction, continue but the sex trade becomes one of smaller bordellos and individual "soiled doves" working out of home or hotel. Most of the women in the trade, young, are selling their bodies as an economic necessity to get by.

Sean thinks he has a solution and makes a proposition to Hennessey. "We should move some of the girls into the suburbs. Spread them around instead of concentrated in one district. For customers who don't travel out, use the rooms upstairs in the bars and put a couple of girls in each – the three-dollar tricks. The girls work for themselves and you take a cut. That will encourage them to do more punters."

"I like it. Takes the heat off and overheads. You'll make a good businessman, Sean."

After a while, the assumption that Sean is the second-in-command grows and eventually he takes on more work off Hennessey's shoulders. Under his supervision, the money rolls in from vice and gambling. The workforce of the fairly new Western Electric Company at the Hawthorne Works Plant providing a lot of customers for both services.

1917

The US is warned by Germany that U-boats will attack neutral merchant ships. The next day Admiral Alfred von Tirpitz announces the policy of unrestricted submarine warfare against allied shipping. Two days later, the US liner Housatonic is sunk.

"Dixie Jazz Band One Step/Livery Stable Blues" becomes the first jazz recording released on a 78.

US merchant ship "Algonquin" is sunk. President Wilson orders the arming of US merchant ships.

US declares war on Germany (April 6).

The Selective Service Act is passed to raise an army through compulsory enlistment and the first units of the American Expeditionary Force (AEF) are ordered to France under the command of General John J. Pershing. The register for the Draft begins (June 4).

The 18th Amendment to the US Constitution, authorising prohibition of alcohol, is distributed to the states for ratification after approval by the US Congress. A move to stop grain needed for food being used by the large brewing industries. It encourages the Temperance movement.

CHAPTER 3

Over the previous three years, Sean "Lucky" O'Leary has made himself indispensable to Hennessey, who has increased his kingdom and is now a serious player rather than an underlord. Lucky is no longer a bodyguard and enforcer – though he still serves in those roles – he is now firmly established as Number 2 in the organisation. Hennessey respects his intelligence, growing the business, as well as his ruthlessness in dealing with problems. Leaving work to Lucky gives the older boss time for other things in life, and he drinks more, spends more time in his restaurant than working the district. Hennessey enjoys working in the kitchen, cooking up huge meals. His favourite is rare sirloin steak, which he drenches in hot butter, heated to nut-brown then poured liberally over the meat, a sprinkle of sea salt crystals, roast potatoes in goose fat, and tender green beans followed by a large dish of ice cream to which he adds a liqueur and whipped cream. No one is surprised when he keels over with a heart attack, just when.

Sean is in the office at The Blarney Stone checking betting slips when Dougal comes bursting in.

"Lucky! Padraig's dead!"

Sean immediately thinks an assassination by rivals, the usual death for a mobster in Chicago, and the start of a territory war. There'd been no rumbles but the Italians were getting feisty and the border between the two factions is contested, with frequent squabbles over collecting protection money from the businesses there.

"How'd it happen?" His mind already working on strategies to meet any threat.

Dougal, in his shock and anxiety, sees that he hasn't made it clear and quickly informs Sean how Hennessey met his demise. "He choked on a piece of steak and that gave him a heart attack. He was dead before the ambulance got there".

A sense of relief that gang war is not happening yet, but there is still the need to consolidate the succession. "Who else knows?"

Dougal shrugs. "The word will be out soon enough. The restaurant was packed."

"Get everyone tooled up and out on the streets. I want our men seen everywhere. All our bars and brothels. Have them driving around so they can be seen. We have to show strength before anyone gets an idea they can muscle in and take over. Send my car round to the front with a couple of guys. Time to tour our businesses."

The orders given, he takes two pistols from the desk drawer, checks they are working and loaded and sticks them in his belt under his coat. So it isn't an assassination but rivals will be circling and eyeing up an opportunity. Sean has to act fast to protect his interests and his role. Opening a safe, he grabs handfuls of money without counting and stuffs his pockets. He has only hours to stamp his authority over his district before the other mob bosses come looking. The King is dead – long live ….who?

This is a crux time. Districts have their gangs – Italians in the South Side, Irish and Polish in the North, Jews and Negroes taking smaller districts in between. Seeing a boss fall has the vultures gathering to feast on the pieces; one eye on opportunities, the other on the competition. Sean knows he has to show strength before anyone acts. He is employing tactics to demonstrate control and preparedness to act: his own men to drive slowly up and down streets, shotguns on laps, making eye contact and smiling. Overtly showing firearms by tucking back their coats, men stand outside the bars, giving gimlet eyes at any stranger and, more importantly, known rivals.

Sean tours and shakes hands like a politician. Indeed, he has had Dougal drive him to pick up a couple of aldermen, stuffed cash in their pockets, reminded them of the favourable arrangement, and driven them around publicly. His messengers track down the police chief and several captains and each is now hundreds of dollars richer this day, likewise having wads of cash shoved in a pocket and brought to meet Sean to receive a firm handshake and a long look in their eyes. In return, police officers are sent out to O'Leary's establishments and told to stand outside with Sean's men until relieved. The district is locked down for the coronation of the new king.

With the police and the politicians sorted, Sean pulls up at each of his bars, walks in and shouts, "Who'll have a drink with me?" and when glasses are loaded, "Here's to Padraig! May angels carry him to heaven." A joke and laugh with people, reminding some of the favours they have enjoyed and can continuing enjoying. Feeling on top of everything, he sends Dougal off to make funeral arrangements – nothing too small, plenty of flowers, a choir. Invitations to the high and mighty of Chicago. Get the word out.

The next day, O'Leary hosts the top men from the Irish gangs. They come in, ostentatiously to pay respects but their eyes and ears take everything in. All are quietly questioning whether the district is secure from takeover by the Italians and whether they should step in first. Sean takes them to Hennessey's restaurant and courts them, seating in view of the windows. A lot of cigars are smoked, a lot of whiskey drunk and toasts to Padhraig Hennessey given. Mentally, Sean checks the guests. Each a mob boss or lieutenant. Blood on their hands and still sleep tight at night. They grew up in a dog eats dog world and know nothing different. Any sign of weakness on his part and they would devour him. If he can't be seen as a useful ally, then they would want him gone and someone who can control the district in place. Leave no door open for the Italians, the biggest competitors to the Irish, to enter. He reads their expressions with limited success. He knows he is being auditioned and hopes his reputation is good enough to win them over. They surely know that he was running the gang, that Hennessey had unofficially retired and left everything in his hands?

He wipes his palms down his trouser legs and takes a drink to cure his dry mouth. All the food consumed and bottles empty; time for the guests to go. Cars are parked up in the street, ready to take them back to their districts. Sean stands in the doorway to thank them for attending. On the way out, back slaps and handshakes. The senior Irish gangster, lord of the North Side, takes Sean to one side.

"Lucky. A sad loss. Padraig was always the life and soul of any party. Never any trouble to his pals and never a weakling to his enemies."

Sean knows how he is expected to respond. "My friend... and my teacher."

Lucky, once alone that evening, breathes a huge sigh of relief. He now owns his own district. The King is in his court, even if it is a small one. Carefully, he will work to make it a big one.

During the day a car driven by Italians from Colosimo's mob had come into the district and got the message to leave quickly, being noticed as they passed the restaurant. They took in the view of all the big players and the respect and friendship being shown to O'Leary. They go back to report back to Big Jim Colosimo: "The cat died but a lion now rules." Colosimo thinks about what this means and is part worried about how the Irish syndicates have been strengthened and part happy that not too much has changed. There is stability still, for the moment.

The day of Hennessey's funeral comes and the late Spring is unusually warm, as if suggesting Hennessey's final destination beyond the grave. The scent from the floral tributes, paid for by Sean but also many from the other gang leaders, hide the usual urban smells that linger in the old quarters of the city, as if disguising a fetid truth, like a whore overusing perfume. Crowds are already lining the streets to see the procession of limousines and the powerful men of Chicago arriving to pay tribute to Padraig. This is a display of wealth and power that they can only imagine. Hennessey has not had that much clout, really just a single brick in a wall of green, but no one wants to be noticed by absence, so the turnout is nothing short of spectacular. Even the Italians show up, having agreed protocols for the day. They want to see how things lie and also it's an opportunity to do deals. In the church, John Torrio, lieutenant, sits quietly next to Big Jim Colosimo, his boss. Colosimo had made a quick rise to gang boss and makes his money from gambling, brothels and racketeering. Like Hennessey, he has a fondness for the better things in life, especially food and wines.

The priest holds a good service, neither too short or too long, and expects overflowing collection plates. O'Leary has already paid a bonus to the choir, with a word to sing to the heavens. The service ends and Sean stands at the doors of the church and personally thanks everyone for coming. The Irish will be going to the Wake; the Italians will go back to their districts. Standing eye to eye, as six feet tall himself, Colosimo is loud, "Good funeral, O'Leary. I'll have to have mine like this when the Lord calls me."

Sean responds. "Not too soon I hope."

Torrio, about 12 years older than Lucky and of unprepossessing appearance, gives a weak handshake and hurries on after his boss. Sean is unaware they had followed his rise from the day news reached them of his victory over Crazy Cavanaugh – both men keen boxing fans.

At the moment, the troubles in Europe don't concern many of the citizens of America, let alone the gangsters. But times are a'changing and will soon send shockwaves across the Atlantic and some people will find opportunities to prosper. Away from Chicago, in the Illinois countryside, life changing events for one person that he can't foresee.

CHAPTER 4

THE GREAT WAR

The call to arms comes for men to enlist and fight the Germans. For farmworkers, the essential need to get the harvests in to feed the troops as well as the nation gives a special exemption to those in this vital work. The Hakermans have a farm in Illinois. Joshuah and Emily and their only son, Jesse, work the land with a foreman, Moses, and his wife, Molly, who live on the farm, and the seasonal workforce they hire.

To avoid being conscripted and having to go off without Jesse, it is arranged that Tom Buckley Jr, the son of the sheriff and the town schoolteacher, will be a farmhand for the Hakermans that summer and the two friends can join the army in autumn and be part of the two million doughboys under the command of General Pershing.

Secretly, Tom Jr's parents, Buck and Agnes, are relieved.

"Perhaps the war will be over before the boys get there."

"I hope so, Agnes. I do hope so."

The Buckleys are not unpatriotic but war is a terrible thing and this is a European war, America is not being invaded. Tom Jr is special to them. They'd tried for a child and had almost lost hope when a doctor eventually told Agnes she was pregnant. It hadn't been an easy pregnancy but eventually they had a boy. In the maternity ward, another boy was born. His name is Jesse and his parents are farmers. It is as if a bond is formed there and then. The two boys become best friends. It is some compensation that Tom Jr will be with Jesse if they get sent to fight in France.

The two pals are glad when the harvest is finally over and they can go to the "great adventure." They'd been worried it would all be over before they got there. Having spent their first two decades in a small midwest town, the idea of first going to a city, then overseas to Europe is beyond simple excitement.

"Well, Tom. Reckon we need to get going."

Now there is no excuse to stay, Tom Jr is experiencing some doubts about having to go and kill people. The travel out of the country, heck, even out of the state, is alluring but the purpose of the travel is not attractive. He was always the more cautious of the two boys, perhaps having a mother who fussed over him and worried over every childhood illness or fall, the consequence of the difficulty of having a child and only being able to fall pregnant once, had made him unwilling to put her through any torment. Yet, Jesse's excitement is infectious and he hides his doubts. He'll never desert his pal. Once, when around ten years old and influenced by a story of Red Indians, they had each made a cut on a hand, grasped wound to wound, and swore as "blood brothers" undying loyalty. Jesse can't imagine having doubts. This was an opportunity not to be missed. To have some momentous event before taking up farming as his life, it was inconceivable that Tom Jr did not feel it too, although his adult life might be as a teacher like his mother or lawman like his father.

At the train station, waiting for the ride to Springfield, two young men and four parents huddle from a cold wind. A discarded newspaper blows around their legs then gets free to disappear ahead, as if to send news before them. The adults put a brave face on it but are scared at sending their only sons into danger. The mothers are both determined they won't cry, at least not until the train has left the station and they've finished waving. The fathers hide their concerns that this might be the last time they see their son. Jesse and Tom Jr are keen for the train to arrive, the strained atmosphere playing on their nerves.

Buck speaks. "You boys take care of each other. Remember, only two people over there won't let you down. Yourself and your best friend."

Joshuah joins in. "You've looked after each other since you crawled. It's a comfort you'll be together. Just come back safe. Come back safe." He chokes and has to turn away. Emily and Agnes grab their boys into tight hugs and the tears flow.

"Now, ma. We'll be alright. Nothing bad is going to happen to us."

"Yeah, ma. Through thick and thin, I couldn't be safer if'n I were with pa."

In the near distance, a train whistle announces the approaching transport coming to take them away from their little midwest town, a haunting sound. Somewhere it is answered by a whip-poor-will, an omen of death according to native tribes, an inauspicious farewell message. The loco pulls up with a burst of steam that swirls around the six of them as they do their last hugs and handshakes. Jesse and Tom Jr climb into a carriage and choose seats on the side where they can still see their parents, two couples, four lonely people. The bell and the guard's whistle sound and the loco takes off slowly, with a jerk and a clang, then gathers speed. Unable to open a window, the young men quickly lose sight of their parents and settle down for the journey. In facing seats, they look at each and burst out laughing – each seeing a mirror image of himself with lipstick smears on both cheeks.

At the depot, Buck turns to Joshuah and Emily. "Let's grab some coffee at Sid's. We all need warming up."

The men walk ahead of their wives, so as not to notice their tears. Truth is, both are close to crying themselves. This is the first time either youth has left home and instead of a celebration it is like a wake, not knowing if they would see either child ever again.

Behind the men, the women have been conferring and Emily speaks. "Agnes and I are going to the Church. We'll see you at Sid's later." The mothers have decided that a prayer is more necessary than coffee. The two men, walking with the weight of the world on their shoulders, continue to the Diner on Main Street.

Sid, owner of the Diner, lugubrious which is his default appearance and suits today particularly well, welcomes them in. "Hi there. What will it be?"

Buck answers. "Two strong coffees, cream and sugar." To Joshuah, "Anything to eat?"

"No thanks, Buck. Just the coffee."

A bit early for the usual trade, they have the place to themselves and sit at window seats in order to keep a watchful eye for the wives. Sid brings the coffee over, hot vapour rising from the cups held in one hand and cream in a jug in the other. Joshuah idly spins a sugar bowl already on the table.

"Today is the day, then? Boys left." Sid places the cups and jug down,

"Yes. Hard on the girls." Buck pushes payment for the coffee over, which Sid pushes back with a shake of his head, before speaking.

"Hard on any parent. Seeing their sons off to a war, and it being so far away. I'm sure they'll come back. Those two never separate. They'll look out for each other."

"Thanks, Sid."

The Diner owner goes back behind his counter and starts to clean up, wiping a cloth over the surfaces for something to do. Buck takes a fifth of bourbon from his coat pocket and holds it up to Joshuah, who nods, and Buck pours generously into each cup.

"Buck?"

"Yeah?"

"I've never fought. Not a war or conflict. Scrapped in the playground of course, but never a life-or-death fight." Joshuah confesses to a life not visited by violence.

"Should only ever be a last resort." Buck shrugs. "I was taught that early on. Had to draw my gun a few times. Often that is enough. A few times I had to pull the trigger. Always told myself the other guy deserved it."

"I guess the Germans are just lads like ours though. Sent by politicians to kill or die."

"Maybe they're all fed up after four years. Time to end it. Our boys might never fire a gun in anger."

Joshuah raises his cup in a toast. "Amen to that."

The bell on the door rings as it opens and Agnes and Emily enter, allowing a cold draught to make an attempt too. Agnes, first in, calls over to Sid as they sit with their husbands.

"A pot of tea for two please, Sid."

"Coming right up," and he attends to the task of making the beverage.

The ladies have not only prayed at the church, they'd mended their makeup, but a redness of the eyes is an indicator of their sorrow and distress.

Buck asks Joshuah about the farm. "How you going to manage without Jesse?"

"Moses is doubling up and Molly pitching in more. Those two are the hardest workers you could find."

"Good people." Buck nods in confirmation of his words.

"Yes, they are."

Agnes speaks up as Sid arrives with their tea on a tray. "Emily and I are going shopping after. You men can wait in a bar if you want. Are you going to share some of that bourbon I see in your pocket, Tom Buckley?"

CHAPTER 5

Arriving in Springfield, the state capital, Jesse and Tom Jr ask for directions and go directly to the Army Recruiting Office. It's not so cold here but still a wind pierces their clothing and their hands chill carrying their small suitcases. They stand nervously in front of the building, where Uncle Sam points a finger at them and says "I want you for U.S. Army" from the wall. A confirmatory look at each other and they step inside, appreciating some warmth. In a hall with benches down the side and a table and a chair at one end, they are met by a grizzled veteran of the conflicts with Mexico, an eye patch over his right eye. He greets them warmly with handshakes that threaten to pull their arms from their shoulders.

"What do we have here? Two brave young men ready to fight for their country?"

"Yessir. We want to join the Army." Jesse speaks for them both.

"Right this way. Let's get the paperwork done then the docs can do a medical."

The paperwork is uncomplicated – their names, addresses, date of birth, next of kin, faith. They find the medical more difficult, or rather, more embarrassing. Behind a makeshift screen, the doctor listens to their chests, looks in their mouths as if they are horses, then handles their genitals, inviting a cough, and lastly an inspection of their rears. Finally, they are measured and weighed and the data recorded on their forms.

"OK, boys. Get dressed. An officer will be by to swear you in. The Army welcomes you."

After a night's accommodation in Springfield, they travel with a dozen other new recruits to the training camp, nervous conversation passing the time. None of the young men have ever been out of the States and a lot of guesswork about their destination fills most of the exchanges. Arriving at the camp, they are billeted in tents as not enough permanent buildings exist to cope with the huge effort to increase army numbers which still continues. Their civilian clothes are exchanged for uniforms and instructions how to maintain. Jesse and Tom Jr accept an offer from another recruit, who has a camera, to have a photo taken that they can send home. They fit in easily to the routines and disciplines. Doing exercises, physical fitness isn't a problem for two young men who have spent a long hard summer on a farm and have an advantage over the city dwellers, clerks and the like, who have spent their working days at desks or standing behind counters. Their instructors are impressed. They are also not unused to rifle shooting, having hunted game for the pot at home, and are among the best shots of the intake. Urgency to send troops to Europe mean they never have a chance to go home on leave. They have to rely on phone calls, which they come to do less and less as they usually end with a mother in tears and they feel homesick.

The day soon comes when basic training, which included how to salute an officer and how to march, is over and the men pack their kit ready to move out. A parade through town (the lessons in marching coming into play) to the rail station, modest crowds waving and the families of local recruits crying and cheering intermittently. Jesse and Tom Jr have no one to see them off and although they would have liked to have seen their parents one more time, they had to be satisfied with a phone call home the previous evening. Jesse's parents had been advised by mail of the move and had gone to the Buckleys to receive their phone call, not being connected at the farm, after Tom had spoken to his mother and father.

A troop train takes them to the New York docks for a carrier ship across the Atlantic. This is a new experience for the country boys and they are awed by the size of New York and their first ever trip on a ship. The sailing is a dangerous journey, as the Germans have their U-boats on alert for all shipping and it is the success of the submarines on American shipping that has brought the States into the War. The journey is varied for the recruits by daytime watch duties, more physical fitness training, and target practice on objects thrown overboard. Jesse earns some money from bets placed on his marksmanship but loses it on dice games. Tom Jr makes a little cash on card games, knowing how to play the odds better than many of the other soldiers, as a result of lessons from his father who is a mean poker player. A life lesson for both that it is better to back one's own skill rather than random chance.

Seven days of sailing pass and out of a morning mist a shoreline emerges as the ship navigates the English Channel. Many crowd the rails for their first look at a foreign country. The ship sails up the Solent and they can see shores on both sides, one the English mainland and the other the Isle of Wight. They disembark at Southampton, on the south coast of England, the city where the ill-fated Titanic sailed from in 1912, only five years earlier. There is no time for exploring as they still have a way to go and NCOs maintain control and discipline. Jesse and Tom Jr are captivated by the surroundings and English voices but no time to mingle. As they form ranks on the docks, another ship has started to disembark soldiers returning from the Western Front. A solemness falls over the Americans as pale shadows of men shuffle down the gangplank, followed by a line of men with bandaged eyes, each holding the shoulder of the man in front, like a line of elephants who grip the tail of another with their trunks so they stay in single formation. Someone says, "Gas." The NCOs quickly move their men straight to the train station to commence a long slow journey to another training camp, this one in the southern county of Kent. Now an early winter sun has risen and the landscape reveals itself as the train passes through. When a railway guard walks through the carriage, Jesse has one question for him.

"I've never seen farms like these. What are they growing and what are those strange pointed roof buildings?"

"Those are hop farms and the buildings are oast houses."

"Hop farms?"

"For beer."

Jesse is impressed just how green England is. The fields separated by hedgerows. It looks so prosperous. Farming must be easy here.

The camp has a couple of wooden buildings but again all the troops are under canvas. It's a holding area until transport is available to France. Just two weeks of lectures about warfare, plus how to dig trenches, then a ship from Dover to deliver the soldiers to the Western Front with all its horrors.

A repeat of the Southampton experience, seeing the sheer numbers of British soldiers disembarking from the home trip, bandaged eyes from gas damage, missing limbs, grey-faced, brings a realisation to the young Americans that the war has neither gone well nor is truly an adventure. They board the ship, which seems to cling to its cloak of misery that has soaked into its hull from its damaged homeward passengers. The adventure is beginning to lose its glamour and minds wonder if this would be their fate, to come home like one of the young British soldiers, or not to come home at all. There is little chatter among the doughboys.

1918

Mississippi is the first state to ratify the 18th Amendment.

US Food Administrator, Herbert Hoover, appeals for "meatless" and "wheatless" days to help the war effort.

A weekly armed forces newspaper – "Stars and Stripes" - is published.

President Wilson authorises the Distinguished Service Medal.
the continent.

Sunday baseball is legalised in Washington D.C.

Amendment allowing women to vote is passed by the House of Representatives.

US and French forces launch an offensive at Aisne-Marne, followed a month later by the Hundred Days Offensive.

Chicago Cubs and Boston Red Sox players threaten to boycott the World Series unless guaranteed prize money of $2500 for winners and $1000 each to losers.

GI Alvin York single-handedly kills 25 Germans and captures 132.

CHAPTER 6
France

Jesse is incensed at orders to attend a SOS course with the British; he'd come to fight Germans, not go on a "Supply and Service" course. The only good news is that Tom is also going on the course. They pack panniers with basics, hang rifles on their slings over their backs and on a borrowed British Triumph motorbike, they set off for Linghem, Pas-de-Calais. In a twist of irony, Triumphs have links to Germany, as the company had been started by a German immigrant called Siegfried Bettman in Coventry in the English Midlands. Ignorant of that historical fact, Jesse and Tom Jr find that the bike compares favourably to the Harley-Davisons they'd learned on back home.

Only getting lost a couple of times, meaning the day is passing, they arrive to find it a surprise how remote the place is, nothing more than a quiet French village, above which is a high plateau where lays an old civilian shooting range, now with some huts and tents. A British NCO is taking a smoke outside one of the larger huts when Jesse and Tom Jr roar up on the motorbike. Stubbing his cigarette out, he growls, "Who are you two?"

"Hakerman and Buckley, US Army, 23rd Infantry, 2nd Division. We've got papers."

Jesse pulls the orders from his pocket and passes them over for the NCO to read.

"Yanks, eh? OK. Your tent is the fourth along that line. The rest of the guys have settled in for the night, busy day tomorrow. Go round the back and the cook will give you sandwiches and a brew. Leave the bike here." As Jesse and Tom Jr start to walk away, "and you address me as Corporal."

"Yes, corporal."

Sandwiches eaten and something hot, described as tea, drunk, they unpack and take a walk round the site in the fading light. Snores from some tents; glows like fireflies from cigarettes in others.

"This is a rum place, Jesse."

"I guess the Limeys are making do. It's a good thing we're here to help them out the mess."

It is late and the ride to Linghem has been a long one. Tired, both men lie down in the tent and are soon asleep.

The next morning, after a surprisingly decent breakfast which included fresh laid eggs, mushrooms and boar sausages, much sourced from local farms and woodlands, there is to be a briefing, where they meet other soldiers on the course. Twenty men, mostly British with a few French, and the two Americans are seated in what also doubles as the dining room, which had been cleared while they did their ablutions. A British Officer walks in, the men snap to attention, chairs scraping back noisily on the wooden floor. He walks to centre front then faces the men. On an unspoken signal, an NOC calls "At ease." The officer stands erect, his clear gaze taking in the assembly before he introduces himself as Major Hesketh-Prichard and "You are here to learn the arts of Sniping, Observation and Scouting".

Jesse and Tom, mouths agape, look at each other. Had they recognised the name, they might have realised they were in the presence of a man of reputation, big-game hunter, marksman, and cricketer, assuming they even knew what that sport was.

After instructing the soldiers to resume their seats, the lecture commences.

"The Germans have been excellent in their use of snipers from the beginning of the war. Our casualties to their efficiency are too high. In reply, this school was set up so we could take back the advantage. You men have been sent here as your company commanders deem you to be excellent shots. We'll see if you have what it takes to be a sniper – not a blunt instrument but a surgeon with a rifle.

"Sniping is one, finding your mark. Two, defining your mark. Three, hitting your mark.

"What is your mark? You will not shoot at everything that moves. You will watch for the officer directing men, especially the artillery spotter. You will be pitched against their snipers – take them out of the picture and your comrades will be safer. Sometimes you won't shoot at all. You may see something that a single rifleman cannot deal with. The importance of the Observer then is to note all he can and direct artillery on to a target." The major has a tendency to march up and down the room, then pause to deliver a key statement.

"You will work in two-man teams. Your roles will be reversible. One to shoot, one to direct and record. First things first. Report to the range with your own rifle and ammo. Let's see if your commanders spoke truly. Dismiss."

A couple of hours are spent on the old civilian range. There is an embankment at one end, in front of which boards hold targets. The soldiers, five at a time, lie down at the opposite end and on command, empty a magazine of rounds at their individual target.

"Weapons down!" screams the range instructor, who watches vigorously that his orders are obeyed. One soldier who had closed the bolt on his rifle gets a reprimand. "Show me you don't have a round loaded in the breech, you moron!"

Everyone, not just those who had shot, walk down to the targets to see the results. Some are more pleased than others. The same five repeat the process three times more before a new set of five take over, with fresh targets. The process goes on until all men have shot the same number of rounds. The NCOs in charge are checking for consistency and not luck, meticulously recording the scores against each name. Shooting done, the last job is to have the rifles cleaned and inspected; some soldiers told off for shoddy maintenance. "Fuck me, tommy. It's darker down your rifle barrel than it is down the pit when the candle blows out."

After a break for a midday meal of cold cuts and bread and more of the brew the Brits call tea, they are back in the classroom, although four fewer than earlier; already men are sent back to regiments as not up to the standard required, having failed at marksmanship and maintenance.

While the Major goes over the scorecards from the Range NCOs, a British Sergeant takes the briefing: "You've showed the ability to hit a big target at 100 yards. As a sniper, you have to hit a visible target no bigger than your fist at up to 400 yards; that may be all you can see of your enemy. To do that you need the right rifle, not one that has been banged off hundreds of times – that ruins the quality of the barrel for accuracy. That rifle will be your wife. You will treat her with respect, coddle her, and never, ever lend her to another man.

"To see your target, you will use an Evans telescopic sight. This will improve your view. Again, it is to be loved and cherished and maintained. For observation, a telescope is preferable over binoculars. We have some of the best for you - the brass extending telescope made by Ross of London. For these three pieces of kit, you will be shown how to keep in tiptop condition.

"The rest of the course deals with your ability to stay unnoticed. How to use the land to blend in. How to be invisible to the enemy.

"Sergeant Hicks will school you in the use of the compass. You will need to know where you are and to accurately map reference the enemy so that artillery support can be called in, or aerial reconnaissance to see what is happening behind the Huns' line.

"Physical fitness every day with Sergeant-Major Betts – you need to be fitter than most for the arduous tasks of crawling distances into position and maybe running away from danger. If it comes to hand-to-hand, you will also learn some ju-jitsu combat.

"Corporal Cameron from the Lovatt Scouts will instruct in use of the telescope and how to read terrain tomorrow. But for now, gentlemen. Outside."

The class forms a line outside the hut, a bit stunned by the staccato delivery of the course purpose and structure. A ramrod-straight Sergeant-Major Betts inspects the men, his eyes like gimlets, before barking an order. "Double time. Over the field until I say stop."

Double time it is, until they reach some broken ground, with scrub and grasses.

"Halt" and while the men catch their breath, "tell me what you see." Pointing at one man then another. Various answers of "trees", "bushes", "hill" from the group. Jesse suspects more is required but can't see anything different from the others; it's just French countryside of bushes, scrub and grasses.

Betts has a smile on his face. "OK, chaps. Stand up."

The trainees are astonished when the ground moves and three soldiers stand up next to them. They'd gone completely unnoticed, disguised as they are with some kind of netting, sacking and vegetation that has totally blended them into the landscape. The troopers have big smiles on their faces at their success.

"You will learn to do this. Being good with the rifle is no good if the enemy can see you and pour fire on your position. Gentlemen, this will save your lives."

*   *   *

The training is intense. Little by little the numbers are whittled down as men are returned to unit, not deemed to have met the high standards required of a first-class sniper or observer. Jesse and Tom take to it – it is exciting. Both have experience of guns, being raised in the rural midwest of America, unlike many of the British troops from towns. The best Brits are ex-gamekeepers (or poachers) and make the best tutors, passing on their skills and knowledge.

No detail is overlooked. From maintenance of kit to physical fitness. Consistency at 400 yards is the goal for the sniper; accurate recording and map-reading from the observer, although, in theory, both roles are to be reversible, so everyone receives the same full training.

Jesse finds a natural affinity for the ju-jitsu, maybe from some local success at school and college as a wrestler. Tom finds he could never beat his friend but he holds his own against other trainees.

Eventually, they return to their unit, taking their new kit with them, excited to have a specific role. Not many understand what that role and they soon come up against a junior captain from Chicago named McAvoy.

"Hakerman! What are you doing with that rifle? That's too good for you. Hand it over."

"Stand down, captain. These boys have some work to do." The CO then speaks to the duo.

"Hakerman, Buckley. You're back just in time. We've taken casualties from a Hun sniper and we're a bit pinned down and not getting any observation done. The Brits promised us this SOS course you've been on is a game changer. Tell me what you need."

They are excused normal duties, much to the disgust of McAvoy, angry at being reprimanded in front of privates. Jesse and Tom Jr are ready, knowing what they want and are quickly provided with whatever they ask for and let loose to do what they could do. Putting their newly learned skills into action, the German sniper lasts two days before Jesse gets him. In the weeks following, the Americans dominate the trenches, the enemy afraid to stick their heads up. Even using periscopes is not successful for them, as Jesse can just as easily shoot them to pieces. From a fair shot, hunting game at home for the pot, Jesse is now a crackshot, having been taught techniques and provided with a high-class rifle and scope. Tom Jr is nearly as good but has the better eye for observation, so they fall easily into their roles of sniper and spotter. This length of the American lines feels safer now, no longer sitting ducks. US Command, in co-ordination with the British and French, begin preparation for a big push that summer. The Americans face the German Fifth Army along their sector of the front.

CHAPTER 7

"Now, Youth, the hour of thy dread passion comes
Thy lovely things must all be laid away;
And thou, as others, must face the riven day."

Ivor Gurney 'To the poet before the battle'

This day, it starts with the same captain who wanted Jesse's rifle, ordering them to return to the copse where they have been working the last three times. McAvoy is not respected by the men, having gotten his rank through influence as the son of a Chicago politician, and not through competence. He is also a bully to those of lower rank than himself and a sucker-up to those higher, though they only tolerate him because of his connections back in the USA. Back home used to getting his own way, he is petty when thwarted.

"Sir. It's not safe to use the same spot again. The Hun will be watching and ready."

But to no avail and no senior officer to hear Jesse's doubts and overrule the captain, who threatens the two if they refuse an order. Jesse and Tom Jr take the line of least resistance, figuring one more excursion then the senior officer will be back and listen to reason. They'll be super careful today.

They set off at first light, before the sun has even hit the eastern horizon but when there is a subtle illumination. Like ghosts, they move through the trenches. Men notice the rifle and realise this is a sniping team, patting both Jesse and Tom Jr on the back. "Give 'em hell." "Kill a few for me."

If Allied snipers are dominant, the risk to soldiers is greatly reduced. It helps the lads' mood to realise how useful they are and how appreciated.

By way of the trenches, they can get a few hundred yards from their destination, a copse of trees. At that point, before exiting the cover, they pause, surveying the ground for movement, until they are certain they are not under enemy observation, the early hour and weak light providing some level of security. They crawl, bellyhugging the ground, the remaining distance into the trees and, once there, set up their camouflage. Everything is done at a snail's pace, no hurried movement to draw attention. The copse has taken some damage from fights but as it is impossible to hold, it sits in No Man's Land between the lines.

Jesse uses the telescope first, to understand the layout of the Huns' positions, check for any changes. There is a line of trenches, uneven parapets, and some campfire smoke as breakfasts are cooked. The smoke is helpful; going straight up, it indicates no wind. Passing the 'scope to Tom Jr, he checks his weapon carefully. The outline of the rifle is broken by sacking, dyed green and brown. The telescopic site has its hood extended, so that no light can reflect off the front lens.

Tom Jr takes a more detailed examination of the enemy position, talking quietly to Tom as to what he can see. Jesse writes some notes down for the Intelligence boys at base. The only difference to their previous observations of this part of the German line is the increase in height of the trench parapet, a response to Jesse's effective sniping. That would be another reason to give the commander as to why the copse has lost its use, a shortage of targets, let alone probably zoned by minenwerfers, the Germans' heavy trench mortars, ready to unleash hell.

Unbeknown to the pair, a patrol of three men in field grey uniforms is making its way to the copse equally as carefully. 'Volunteered' by their sergeant, their mission is to find and capture or kill the American sniper that has taken out two officers and one spotter in the last four days. Carrying only rifles with bayonets fixed, bayonets blackened in campfire smoke so as not to shine, and grenades on their belts, the men are expected to move quickly and unencumbered. No one doubts the importance of their mission. Success could result in an Iron Cross for taking out a serious threat and saving countless lives of comrades.

Jesse has a bead on a special part of the enemy parapet. Experience tells him, it is the likely place for a spotter to use. Even if the soldier uses a periscope, it is still worth shooting that down – one less piece of equipment and a warning to "keep your head down", meaning the enemy will be less efficient. Jesse is in focused mode. Light breathing, slowed heart rate, the crosshairs barely moving on this tiny gap between sandbags. This is what sniping is. Choose a potential reveal of a target and wait until one shows. His patience is eventually rewarded – something has moved and he is confident that an enemy soldier is peering through the gap, the light changing between the sandbags that can indicate something there. The shot fired; rifle reloaded for a quick second shot if necessary. All smooth, calm movements. He's either killed one, or the enemy will have got the message to keep their heads down. What he doesn't know is that the German soldier has used a helmet on a stick to draw fire, to help his comrades out there on the sniper hunt. The soldier is glad it is his helmet with the hole in it and not his head.

Having crawled to the edge of the copse and waited, the German patrol hears the gunshot. With a quick check that each man is ready, rather than take risks of approaching an unseen enemy, they decide to throw several grenades in a scatter pattern along the line of trees and bushes facing their lines. The intention is to flush the Americans out or, better, kill them at little danger to themselves. No one wants to be a dead hero.

Tom Jr reacts as the first grenade explodes off to his right. Looking round he sees figures rising from the ground and, importantly, a second grenade coming close. Without hesitation he throws himself over Jesse as it explodes, shrapnel shredding branches and leaves above them. Ears ringing, Jesse pushes Tom Jr off himself, turns to face the attack.

He can see three men running in their general direction, Tom's movement alerting the enemy to their approximate location. Lifting his rifle and firing from the hip while still supine, he sees the nearest man go down with a bloody hole in his chest and a surprised look on his face. That is enough to create a pause by his comrades before they resume the attack, now knowing exactly where the Americans are. That hesitation allows Jesse to reload, fire and wound another. Unable to move quickly, with Tom Jr's semi-conscious body over his legs, there isn't time to reload a third time before the last man is standing over him, about to plunge his bayonet, teeth bared in a snarl, their eyes locked. Jesse accepts his fate, unable to fight back, when there is an explosion and the soldier topples over, his bayonet missing by inches and sticking in the ground. Tom Jr, with gritted determination to overcome his failing strength, has drawn his pistol and fired straight up, through the thigh and into the belly.

The grenade explosions and gunfire have drawn attention from the German trenches and bullets are buzzing through the trees like deadly hornets. The troops had been ready since setting the lure and now want to join in to ensure the 'American Devil Sniper' is finished once and for all. Since the first explosions, the enemy was looking over the parapet and been ready to open fire. The two Americans are now in a shooting gallery. Keeping low, Jesse turns to his friend to say "Let's get out of here" but notices Tom Jr is wounded in several places from grenade shrapnel, bloody shredded uniform across his body. He hangs his rifle on its sling over his shoulder and, himself with shrapnel wounds, drags his comrade until clearer of the fusillade. Only when he feels it safe to do so, he pitches Tom Jr on his back and carries him to their own lines. The US troops, also hearing the commotion, have put down covering fire for Jesse and Tom, Lewis guns particularly stitching the enemy parapets, encouraging the Huns to stay low.

Gasping for breath, Jesse reaches the safety of the line and, tumbling into their own trenches, he slumps to recover while Tom Jr is placed on a stretcher and medics carry him away. Not to be parted, Jesse makes the effort to rise and limps behind, blood leaking from his wounds.

"Easy mate. You've been hit too," says one of the medics, and he takes Jesse's arm and supports him to the casualty station. Seeing Tom Jr laid on a table, he immediately goes to his pal and calls to the doctors treating others.

"He's been hit by grenade shrapnel. He's got several wounds." A desperate cry for attention.

The senior Field Medic takes one look at Tom Jr and barks at Jesse, "Out of my way, son. He's bleeding too much." Then to others, "Let's have some help here. Pronto."

The medics quickly work on Tom Jr, but his blood loss is too great and he dies on the makeshift operating table. His last words "I love you, Jesse." Jesse is consumed with grief and sobs heavily while his own wounds are attended to. The adrenaline had blinded him to his own injuries but given him the strength to bring his pal back to their lines. Now he needs surgery.

Away from the Casualty Station, taken back to a Field Hospital, Jesse is operated on to remove the several pieces of shrapnel he took in the fight. The surgeon is impressed when he is told how Jesse carried his buddy while so wounded himself and commiserates with Jesse that his pal did not survive. "War is shit. Just be grateful you survived and can honour the memory of your friend."

Their CO recommends Jesse for the Distinguished Service Medal and Tom Jr gets a posthumous award. Unable to resume duties, Jesse misses the failed push from the Germans with their last offensive of the war and the concerted attack of the Allies to repel them, eventually to force a surrender. This July, over 300,000 men had prepared to take the initiative, men and armaments from Soissons to Rheims were in position to finish the stalemate and herald what would be the end of the war. Jesse could only hear about it while he recovered from his surgery. Greater than the physical wounds were the mental wounds of the waste of Tom Jr's life and the bitter regret that he hadn't refused the order to return to the copse. He tried to write the facts to Sheriff and Mrs Buckley but has only been able to say they were on a special operation and he had been with their son at the end.

1919

President Wilson vetoes the Volstead Act but it is passed by Congress (October 28), having been ratified by all states by January 16.

Gasoline is taxed (1 cent per gallon) for the first time.

Congress passes the 19th Amendment to the Constitution – the Women's Suffrage Bill.

Jack Dempsey defeats Jess Willard to become the new World Heavyweight Champion.

A dirigible crashes in Chicago, resulting in 13 deaths.

28 people (15 white/23 black) die and 500 are injured in Chicago race riot.

Anti-Cigarette League of America forms in Chicago.

Communist Party of America organises in Chicago.

Chicago White Sox lose to Cincinnati Red in baseball's World Series.

General John J. Pershing and 25000 soldiers return to the USA

CHAPTER 8

France

Finally, Jesse has to bid farewell to the French farmer and his family. The orders have come to return to America for demob.

"Au revoir. Thank you for looking after me and teaching me so much."

"Non. Thank you, Jesse. For coming here to rid us of the Germans. I wish you well. Please give our love to your family when you get home."

It is an emotional parting. Rather than be an invalid resting in a chateau commandeered for the purpose of hospital and convalescence, Jesse has joined in the work of a farm. At first, easy tasks, then, as his strength returned and his wounds healed, he worked tirelessly alongside the farmworkers and the farmer. His schoolboy French has improved to conversational standards and he has helped with the English homework of the farmer's children, although they criticised his spelling, it being American and not English English as their schoolbooks. The surrender of Germany the previous November meant he never returned to his unit and was allowed to stay on the farm until transport home was organised for the troops no longer needed.

He travels first to Paris, where he has three days to explore before an onward trip to Calais to catch a ship home. During the train journey, Jesse attempts to read Germinal by Emile Zola with the help of a French-English dictionary the children have given him.

Paris is an experience. Just on arrival, Jesse is awestruck by the city, the largest he has ever stayed in. He finds a small hotel in Montmartre owned by Madame Gilbert, a widow. It is clean and reasonable and a good place to explore from. Jesse particularly wants to visit Notre Dame cathedral, having read a translation of Victor Hugo's "The Hunchback of Notre Dame". There are also the museums to see and even just walking round the streets and seeing the artists is a revelation to the country boy from Illinois.

On the second day of his stay in the capital, Jesse visits the Louvre (cannot understand the fuss over the Mona Lisa, a smaller painting than he expected and the strangeness that she has no eyebrows), dines at the Le Chat Rouge, a modest establishment but the chef a master with seafood, and returns to the hotel. Approaching, he is curious about onlookers trying to peer into the foyer and a gendarme on the steps, keeping them back.

"Excuse me, monsieur, but I am staying in this hotel."

"Wait here." Over his shoulder, the gendarme shouts, "Inspector!"

A thin man in a bowler hat and thin raincoat comes out of the hotel, looking annoyed.

"The gentleman says he is a guest of the hotel."

"Your name, monsieur?"

"Jesse Hakerman. I am in room 8."

"Please follow me."

The inspector leads Jesse into the foyer, where more police are milling about and a man in a suit, well-groomed hair and a neatly trimmed moustache, is looking over the counter. He turns and casts an enquiring eye over Jesse while the Inspector asks questions.

"When did you arrive?"

"I came yesterday. I've been here for one night. Can you tell me what is going on?"

The inspector stands aside and indicates that Jesse should look over the counter. Jesse moves forward and leans over. He gasps as he sees Madame Gilbert on the floor with a bullet hole in her chest.

"My God. What's happened?"

"Where have you been today, monsieur?" The Inspector continues his interrogation.

"I, I. I've been at the Louvre and on the way back I had dinner at Le Chat Rouge. I've just left there."

"We shall check, of course."

"This is terrible, Poor Madame Gilbert. Who did this?"

"We shall find out. Have no doubt. May we see your room?

"My room? Why?"

"It is just to establish who is staying here and why. We shall inspect all the rooms of guests."

"Room 8. The key is on the board behind the desk."

One of the police cautiously steps round the counter and retrieves the key. In doing so, he cannot avoid stepping in Madame Gilbert's blood. The smartly dressed man speaks sharply.

"Be careful. Don't go anywhere until you have thoroughly cleaned your shoe. Take it off and go outside." Turning to Jesse, "Allow me to introduce myself, I am Edmond Locard, consultant to the police."

"Jesse Hakerman. I'm just passing through. Catching a ship home in a couple of days."

"Well, shall we get this over with? Let's follow the officers."

The inspector and a couple of officers have already gone ahead to room 8 and when Jesse and Locard arrive, they have tipped Jesse's belongings on the bed. One officer is excitedly holding up Jesse's rifle, having opened the gun case as if to say "Voila!". The Inspector gives Jesse a keen and piercing look but Locard takes the rifle, opens the breech, sniffs it then sniffs the barrel end.

"We can rule this out as the murder weapon. It has not been fired recently."

Jesse speaks. "Madame Gilbert is shot with a handgun."

"Oh, how do you know that?"

"I've seen what guns can do. Plus, Madame Gilbert is not a tall lady. The killer would have had to be close to the desk to shoot her. That would be difficult with a rifle or he would have taken a headshot."

Jesse has recovered from the initial shock, and continues. "Close up, it is normal to hold a handgun with the arm bent at right angles. At arm's length, again, it would have been a headshot. Looking at the wound, taking account of her height, and where the bullet passed through into the wall behind, that looks like a straight trajectory and you can estimate the height of the killer, a taller person than myself."

The Inspector does not give up easily.

"And who exactly are you, monsieur?"

"I've been fighting on the front. I was wounded and I spent my recovery at a farm. I'm now on my way home."

"Most Americans left some time ago. The ones remaining are mostly deserters. Perhaps Madame Gilbert was going to report you."

Edmond Locard, who has been examining Jesse's belonging, especially the paperwork, has heard enough.

"Inspector. You are barking up the wrong tree. Monsieur Hakerman is not our killer. The evidence speaks for itself."

The Inspector bridles slightly and puts on a challenging face.

Locard continues. "The rifle has not been fired. If it were the murder weapon, and I agree entirely with Monsieur Hakerman's explanation of the murder, he could not have returned it to his room as obtaining or returning the key would have required him to step in the victim's blood. You saw how the officer did just that. If he had shot Madame Gilbert, I doubt he would have stayed around to be caught but cleared off immediately. Yes, a cold-blooded killer might try a bluff, but you have suggested our American guest is a deserter. As a motive, it is disproved by these papers – an official order to return to the United States and a mention that he is a decorated war hero. His alibi is dining at Le Chat Rouge, which can easily be verified. Possibly, Monsieur Hakerman can show you a receipt and a waiter will identify him. That would rule out shooting with a pistol and going out to dispose of it. Plus, I do agree with the killer being taller or shorter, depending how he held his weapon. We can measure the height of the bullet entry as if Madame Gilbert is standing and the height to the wall where it ended having passed through her. If they align on the horizontal, we can calculate the height of the shooter as if he held the weapon with bent arm or straight. Either rules out Monsieur Hakerman."

The Inspector lets out a heavy sigh, shrugs and indicates to the officers to follow him out of the room. Locard speaks approvingly.

"Impressive deductions."

"My godfather is a Sheriff back home. He would tell his son and me stories from his career. Also...."

"Please. Go on."

Jesse expects a laugh.

"I've read all the Sherlock Holmes stories several times."

He does get a laugh, but in good way.

"So have I. So have I. Please, let us find a cafe and have coffee and cognac and talk some more."

Seated with cups of strong coffee and large cognacs, Jesse and Locard enjoy a pleasant conversation. Locard explains his methods, pleased to have a receptive audience.

"We are moving to more scientific examination of crime. It was in 1858 a magistrate in India had a contract signed with a handprint, the idea of uniqueness overcoming any potential forgery of signatures. Barely 30 years ago, the first method of recording fingerprints and keeping them on files was tried in Argentina by a police chief. I believe the US military take fingerprints and the police forces adopted the procedures soon after. There have been successful prosecutions on fingerprint evidence. I noticed that Madame Gilbert kept a very clean establishment. Hopefully, there will not be too many fingerprints on the counter but some that belong to our killer.

"When we retrieve the bullet from the wall, we can ascertain the calibre of the gun. If it is not too damaged, we may even be able to match it to a weapon, if the police find one, by the markings made on it from the rifling in the barrel. Hopefully, we find the gun in the possession of the person whose fingerprints are at the scene. You see, the crime scene is like a silent witness. The perpetrator of the crime leaves evidence, no matter how small, there will be always be something. In return, the scene transfers evidence to the criminal. It may be fibres, dust, blood. There will be something if we look hard enough.

"Thankfully, our killer does not set fire to the hotel. Fire is a big destroyer of evidence. We might not even have realised Madame Gilbert had been shot."

Jesse finds an afternoon in a cafe with Monsieur Locard much more interesting than museums. The consultant is keen to learn more about Sheriff Buckley and the American law system and investigative methods.

CHAPTER 9

Illinois

The funeral of Jesse's father is well attended. Joshuah Hakerman had been a good neighbour, a church stalwart and a damn fine banjo player. As the mourners troop down from the ridge to the farmhouse, where Molly has prepared refreshments, Buck hands a letter to Jesse.

"This arrived at the office. It's been around a bit before it got to me."

Jesse sees that the postmark is Paris and dated several months earlier.

"Go ahead. I'll read this before I come down."

To Mr Jesse Hakerman
care of Sheriff Thomas Buckley, Illinois, USA

My dear young friend,

I hope the American postal service is good enough to find you and deliver this letter. I am of the opinion you would have wondered about the outcome of the investigation into the murder of Mde Gilbert. Forgive me if I ramble a bit but I wish to lay the path to the conclusion, just as we followed the evidence to discovering the murderer and the motive. It is a tale of woe.

As you know, we returned to the hotel and you collected your belongings and went to another hotel. I stayed and assisted the police with their search. It is in the cellar that I unearthed, literally, the first clues. There is nothing untoward that could be seen, the officers had done a cursory check but did not stay too long due to an infestation of flies. If you had read "Les faune des cadavres" by my compatriot Jean Pierre Megnin, you would say Aha! at this. The flies are particularly interested in a long wooden table and more around floorboards in the corner, which has various items piled on it but nothing organic with which to attracted the insects. So let me relate a little story to you.

In the 13th century in China, an official named Song Ci has the duty to investigate a murder by stabbing. A diligent man, he carried out stabbings with various instruments and tools on the carcase of a cow. By this method, he deduced that the murder weapon was a sickle, a common farm instrument. This is where it gets clever. Song Ci has the men of the village put their sickles on the ground and stand by them. It is not long before one blade attracts a fly, then another and soon more. Although any blood on the blade was invisible to the human eye, the smell is alluring to flies. The owner of the blade confesses to the murder.

With this knowledge it is apparent to me that the table in the cellar has had blood, although now clean. Of course, this might be animal blood if food is prepared here but there is also the matter of the flies in the corner. In the meantime, our Lestrade, actually Inspector Bernard, had been making enquiries among the neighbours. The gossip is that Mde Gilbert had a secret trade, that of an abortionist. The horror of what we might find is sinking in on me and telling my fears to the Inspector he has his men move the items from the corner then prise up the floorboards. Quelle horreur! Wrapped in sheets, the body of a young woman and the foetus of an unborn child lay there. The decomposition is not far along but the flies had smelt it before we humans could.

The bodies were removed to the morgue for an autopsy and, as it seemed to me in the cellar, an abortion has gone wrong and the mother bled out. Mde Gilbert had made an effort to hide the bodies, possibly temporarily until she could move them but is herself murdered. This, as such is not necessarily the motive for her murder. It might be totally unrelated, so Bernard continued his enquiries. In the meantime, the bullet had been retrieved from the wall and is found to be a 7.63 x 25mm, the most likely gun being a Mauser pistol. We also have a collection of prints from the desk. I particularly liked a left-hand palm and fingers print where someone had rested their hand.

Bernard came round to see me for my findings and he had another piece of gossip about a young woman who had gone missing earlier that month. We had an address and I went along with the Inspector and two officers. At home is Mr Berger, who went white as a sheet when he answered the door to us. Inside the home, we found empty bottles strewn around and, from the state he was in, it looked as if Berger had been drinking non-stop for several days.

Here I must refer back to your assessment of the crime scene, where you described how a pistol might be held. The result must be that, if the murderer of Mde Gilbert is Berger, he held the gun at arm's length, being a small man, shorter than yourself or me. I instructed the Inspector that we should obtain hand and finger prints but before we do, Berger confessed and told us a sad tale.

In the new year, an Irish American soldier, thought to be a captain, had courted Julie Berger. Mlle Berger believed they would marry and she would go with him to America. The man seduced the innocent girl and left the country without a message. Later, Mlle Berger confided in her father that she is pregnant. He said he would send her to an aunt in the country and they could have the baby adopted. But Mlle Berger sought out an abortionist rather than leave Paris and give birth to an illegitimate child. She left a note for her father but not an address. When she doesn't return, he searched for her and a conversation in a bar led him to Mde Gilbert. She denied everything, so he came home and got his Mauser pistol, a weapon he had taken off a dead German while serving in the Army. Threatened by the gun, Mde Gilbert admitted to carrying out an abortion but said that his daughter had left. In his grief he pulled the trigger. Looking over the desk and seeing that she was dead, he ran back to his home and had been there drinking ever since.

We matched his prints, the Mauser to the bullet, and with his confession he is convicted. Remember what I told you – every criminal leaves something of himself at the scene – every scene leaves something on the criminal.

Personally, I am glad to say a death sentence is not passed but I fear the poor man has enough sadness in his life that he may not consider living a mercy.

Well, that is the story and outcome. I trust you have been interested and not bored. I have no Watson and I wanted to tell someone other than the court of what occurred.

Your good friend
  Edmond Locard

1920

Midnight Friday 16th January 1920

The Volstead Act comes into force, forbidding any drink containing more than ½% of alcohol.

[It will last for nearly 14 years.]

The US government gives the job of enforcement to fewer than 1,500 federal agents.

It is a golden opportunity for the gangsters...

...and entrepreneurs

CHAPTER 10

PROHIBITION OF INTOXICATING BEVERAGES.

SEC. 3. No person shall on or after the date when the eighteenth amendment to the Constitution of the United States goes into effect, manufacture, sell, barter, transport import, export, deliver, furnish or possess any intoxicating liquor except as authorized in this Act, and all the provisions of this Act shall be liberally construed to the end that the use of intoxicating liquor as a beverage may be prevented.

The Volstead Act 1920

The Volstead Act, named after the Minnesota congressman who proposed it, is the means intended to enforce a wartime emergency measure to divert the resources needed for brewing and distilling into food production. The abolitionists for a "Dry" nation pushed this 18th Amendment to the Constitution to a successful result in 1919, calling for a national, rather than regional (some states are already Dry) Prohibition. In Chicago, the citizens voted 3 to 1 against it, so they are ready when the Volstead Act comes into force, to ignore it. Chicago has been a massive manufacturer of pure alcohol – for making liquor but also in pharmaceutical needs – that the bootleggers will take advantage of.

There is enough demand for gambling and vice to go round and not until the Act do the rival gangs start eyeing each other's territory. Bootlegging becomes where the money is at and an entry level crime for the younger hoodlums. Prices rocket even for poorer quality booze. Chicago still has its own distilleries, taking pure alcohol from legitimate business and mixing it for substitute spirits and to give the third-rate beer being brewed illegally a bit of a kick. Cocktails are invented purely to disguise the poor-quality homemade gin. The government responds by deliberating tainting industrial alcohol to make it undrinkable but that leads to deaths as crooks mix it in, a brew known as "bathtub gin".

Competition for supplies means smuggled imports are often hijacked. Premises are raided by bought police on behalf of rivals and the booze "confiscated" only to appear elsewhere. Some police officers are in business for themselves, such as detective sergeant Eddie Smales, already into gambling. Smales has a talent for intercepting whisky consignments assisted by similarly crooked cops. Another problem for the mobsters is incorruptible Prohibition Agents, ones like Bruce Armstrong. Armstrong cannot be bought, turning down larger and larger amounts of money, and he closes 93% of the city's illegal breweries. Fortunately for the gangsters, there are those higher up the chain who take dirty money and Armstrong is transferred away to where he would not be a problem. The general feeling is "if the public want it, let them have it," be that gambling, vice or booze.

Overall, Sean O'Leary takes a slowly slowly approach. He has a reputation for keeping the Hennessey mob together and with a business acumen, he has maintained the gambling, adding slot machines to the bars, girls upstairs as well as the brothels out of the city boundaries where they aren't bothered.

He has numerous mini-breweries set up in domestic houses to keep him supplied but quality varies. Bathtub gin is almost literally that – any large basin into which neat alcohol, obtained from the perfumery and medical supplies, is mixed with whatever is thought will add flavour. Rarely is it distilled and, when it is, sometimes the poisonous first distillations containing methanol are not discarded and cause blindness or death. The Italians are doing a better job of organising brewing by concentrating on beer, the drink of the working classes, and importing spirits for the speakeasies, which keep profits for the Irish mob down. A deal is done with the Italians to sell their beer, as they have cleverly bought up real breweries and kept their production going behind closed doors and by bribing officials to turn a blind eye. Smuggling of spirits is from Canada, some getting back in to the States by bribing border guards, others by hidden compartments in vehicles.

Sean is always alert for talent and recruited men who would be loyal to him. The Irish mobs are recruiters of fellow countrymen, whereas the Italians, although hard centred on their own, particularly family members, are far from adverse on an ethnic mix, taking in Russians,

Bulgarians and the like. Italians are the chief competitors to the Irish gangs. They also have a better network than the Irish – connections between Chicago and New York are strong and faithful and New York is also another smuggling route, taking in supplies from Europe and distributing them.

Hughie peels his orange and tosses the result at the one-legged boy selling papers on the street corner. "Hey, Leftie. Did you forget something?" The fifteen-year-old is amused at his own wit when the size 10 boot of Sean O'Leary connects with his rear and sends him flying down the road. He spins on the ground, despite the pain of a sore arse and pulls a switchblade. Turning and realising who has kicked him has him dropping his arm to conceal his weapon, fearing the consequences of pulling a blade on the big man.

Sean looks down at the newspaper seller, one folded trouser leg where his right leg should be and a homemade crutch. "Hey, kid. What's your name?"

"Johnny Miller, sir."

"How'd you lose the leg?"

"Hitching a ride on a tramcar. I fell off and the wheels went over my leg."

"Who's your da?"

"He's dead, Died of tuberculosis"

"And your ma?"

"She does laundry at a hotel. It doesn't pay enough, so I sell papers."

Sean turns his attention to Hughie. "Hey, kid. Johnny here is my pal. If he wants a drink, you get it for him. If he wants an apple, you get it for him. Anything he wants, you get it for him. I hear good about you, you get ten dollars a month. You got that?"

"Yessir. I got that."

"Good. OK, Johnny, nice talking to you. Now I want you to do things for me. Keep your eyes and ears open. You think I should know something, you come in the bar and tell the bartender. You're on twenty a month to keep a lookout for me. You OK with that?"

"Yessir. Thank you, sir."

"OK, then. Collect the first of the month from the bar."

Sean walks over to the Club and calls Dougal to the doorway.

"See that kid down there?"

"The one selling papers? That's Bobby Miller's boy."

"What do you know about him?"

"I went to school with Bobby. Straight guy. Died of the lung disease. Rosie, Bobby's wife, has to take in laundry to make ends meet."

"That squares with what the kid told me. I've put him on the payroll – twenty a month. I want you to do something, Dougal."

"Yeah, boss."

"For now, give him a lift home and ask his ma if she would do our laundry from the Club. Offer her good rates," Sean pauses and considers the business upstairs, "and say that some of the sheets might be messier than she is used to."

Sean enters the Ace of Clubs. He'd moved out of the Blarney Stone only the previous year, feeling the need to demonstrate the new level of power and status the gang had extended under his rule. When the Volstead Act was passed, he had had the frontage changed to indicate that this was a Sports Club for working men and nothing about what went on inside was obvious to an uninformed passer-by. Regular payoffs to politicians and police, which had previously protected the gambling and vice now include the booze trade. The front entrance was simplified to only allow access to a vestibule beyond which are the desired entertainment areas but which can only be reached past a couple of doormen. There is a long bar along a back wall and the rest of the room is spaced out with gaming tables for blackjack, craps and roulette. Poker games are held in individual rooms for high stake players. Hostesses work the bar area to encourage the punters and anyone in need of some intimate entertainment can pay them to use a room upstairs or go up to visit one of the girls already up there. A bar-gated yard behind allows access to unload from vehicles and has a door into a storeroom, beyond which is Sean's office.

As it is still morning, the only activity is from cleaners and barmen restocking. Sean likes to take personal interest in these matters although he knows he can rely on Dougal, who came with him from the Blarney Stone. Dougal had been offered management of the Stone but had asked to come with Sean, which pleased the big man. The old bar is boarded up but the interior still functions as a pub and bookmakers for those in the know, which is generally everyone in the vicinity. The new manager, one of the brighter of Hennessey's goons, runs a couple of girls upstairs there, in the old accommodation. It's a money maker but not on the scale that the Ace has become. Quickly showing profits, they rose under Prohibition as prices could increase for illicit drinks.

The city is divided into factions, usually by ethnicity, and each area has its own quirks. Some of the Irish gangs do not go for vice, a result of Catholic upbringing, and stay with gambling and racketeering. Their new interest is in providing beer to a working-class customer. The Italians, on the other hand are happy to provide girls, on top of gambling and racketeering but not all are interested in bootlegging. As the Chinese say, "May you live in interesting times."

CHAPTER 11

Chicago (the Italians)

"Never take anything big. Stick to the little stuff. It's safer."
Senator William Mason to "Bathhouse" John Coughlin

John Torrio had been working for Big Jim Colosimo for a few years, managing the vice, gambling and rackets as businesses. When the politicians make a genuine business illegal, he spots an opportunity that many are overlooking, inspired by Frankie Vale in New York. Early entry would put him ahead as there is no existing competition of any size in Chicago and if he acts fast, he can run a monopoly, every businessman's secret desire. One problem – the new National Prohibition Act is a federal law and would be enforced by federal agents and not the local law, easily corruptible. His boss, Colosimo, doesn't like the risk and prefers the safety of his existing lines of income. Torrio gains confidence when he sees that there is no real effort by law agencies to provide enforcement, in the naïve belief that the public would quickly inform on lawbreakers and the agents could just roll in and make arrests. That ignorance means that too few agents are employed, many incompetent and do not perform well. Others, with pay lower than garbagemen earn, are willing to look the other way for bribes. Big Jim is not convinced still, with a sort of contented laziness added to his discomfort at taking on risk of any size. He is happy in his new life as the owner of a popular Café, entertaining the well-to-do and celebrities, stepping away from the daily tasks of his empire and leaving them to Torrio. Torrio is unhappy they are missing a huge opportunity and, if it is left ungrasped, others will benefit, leaving them in the wilderness.

Big Jim Colosimo is recently wed, just turned 42, having divorced his first wife, Victoria Moresco. Three weeks earlier, this crime boss, owner of an upmarket brothel in the Levee district and a cabaret restaurant, married his "angel", Dale Winter, 29, a singer in his cafe. The ceremony took place at French Lick, Indiana – it was the go-to place for a quick marriage. Colosimo had hired a circus for entertainment of their guests, so it was no quiet affair.

Dale Winter has softened Colosimo from the tough mobster into a more civilised businessman. He was already enjoying the more legal side of his business and the A-list guests who give their custom to Colosimo's Cafe at 2126 South Wabash Avenue. The food and entertainment are first class and politicians, police chiefs and gangsters frequent the establishment where no bad behaviour is tolerated and discretion assured. Big Jim is happy with his empire and quashes Torrio's plans to go into bootlegging, which upsets his lieutenant, who understands the fortunes that can be made under Prohibition. Buying what he needs for his café is fine, providing booze for others is too risky, he thinks.

This May 11, Colosimo is looking forward to a dinner for himself and his new bride in a top restaurant overlooking Lake Michigan, having planned a romantic evening, when John Torrio phones him.

"Boss. I've got a guy desperate to meet you. He's got two truckloads of good whiskey, pre-war stuff. If we don't meet him, he may go to the Irish."

Colosimo hates for the Irish to get anything and he does want good booze for his customers.

"Okay. I'll meet him at my place. I'll leave now as Angel and I have a dinner date later. Make sure he's there."

"Sure, boss. No worries. I'll phone him now."

Big Jim apologises to Dale. "You go shopping with your mother. I'll send the car back for you after Woolfson drops me off at the café." He's frustrated at the change of plans but business is business.

What Colosimo doesn't know is that Torrio has planned with his new aide, Alphonse Capone, to eliminate the problem, him. Bumping off the boss can bring a heap of trouble down on their heads if done wrong and Capone has called in a favour from his old boss, Frankie Vale, in New York.

Big Jim has his driver, Woolfson, bring round his Pierce-Arrow to take him to his own restaurant. During the drive over, he admires a diamond bracelet he has bought as a surprise for his new wife. Colosimo has a weakness for gems, hence another nickname,

Diamond Jim. Things are never better for him, a new young bride, restaurant doing well, life is quiet. He'll wait until dessert then pass the gift over and watch her reaction. He smiles in satisfaction at the image he conjures up.

Colosimo's restaurant is closed – it doesn't do trade in the afternoon, being a popular night spot for the cabaret and private dining options. The porter, Joe Gabrela, is mopping the floor and looks up when Big Jim arrives unexpectedly, thankful the boss caught him working and not smoking and sneaking a drink.

"Hey, Joe. Anyone asking for me?"

"No, boss."

"Well, if they do, send them to my office."

He checks on his bookkeeper, Frank Camilla, who is at the back running through the accounts.

"Hi, Frank. Anyone looking for me?"

"No, boss."

"I'll be in my office."

There, Colosimo first calls his lawyer for a social chat, catching up on news. Nothing to excite him, hanging up, he takes a cigar from his desk humidor and smokes it while waiting. His mind is on the dinner date later and what he expects to follow, his planned perfect evening. Eventually, impatient, with the cigar nearly all smoked and time to be leaving soon for his engagement, he goes into the foyer to look out the window. No one is about and Big Jim is angry and decides he will leave. He intends to tear a strip off Torrio for the time-wasting. The café has two doors, roughly 50 feet apart, and Colosimo chooses the swing doors, which is an unfortunate choice as it is nearest the cloakroom.

Frankie Vale, having arrived earlier and secreted himself in the cloakroom thanks his luck for the good fortune of his target being so easily offered up. Colosimo is standing with his back to him as he creeps from cover, his pistol ready in his hand. He plans a double tap in the back of the head so that Big Jim doesn't have a chance to defend himself. He raises his weapon and can't resist whispering "Johnny says goodbye" as he fires his .38 into the base of Colosimo's brain, killing him instantly. A second shot, meant for security but unnecessary now, misses as the big man falls to the ground, blood flowing across the floor, slowly as no pulse to pump it, just a leak from a cadaver. Satisfied he has performed the execution, a quick, unnoticed departure for Vale and away in a car parked ready around the corner. He'll head straight back to New York and no one other than Torrio and Capone, having a meal in public to establish alibis, will know he was ever in Chicago.

In the back office, the sound of the gunshot arouses curiosity. Camilla goes out by the second front door to the street and sees nothing but when the door has automatically closed and locked behind him, he has to return by the swing doors which is where he finds the unmistakeable body of his employer. The last inch of a cigar is rolling across the floor where Colosimo dropped it and extinguishes with an inaudible hiss as it rolls into the blood pool.

The Police swarm over the café, making the sort of investigation that Torrio had anticipated, knowing that an attempt to buy them off from being too conscientious would backfire. Immediately suspected are the brothers, Jose and Louis, of the ex-wife but who are able to produce verifiable alibis. Torrio would have liked that distraction and curses he never thought to have them engaged where there would be no witnesses as to their whereabouts. There are statements that a man was seen hanging around the café earlier. Mid to late twenties, fat-faced with a dark complexion, wearing a black derby and a black overcoat, with patent leather shoes but no one knows who he was. The description fits Frankie Yale but no one makes the match to a New York gangster. When the Press move on to make suggestions of an internal hit, Torrio denies involvement with a show of anger at such ideas and organises a huge over-the-top funeral for Big Jim, the biggest yet to be seen in Chicago.

Torrio faces a hiccough when plans for the funeral to be held in any Catholic church, or burial in their grounds, are denied by the Archbishop, George Mundelstein. He sees Colosimo as a "sinner", who rarely attended church, was a divorcee and had a dubious marriage, not having the requisite time gap between divorce and new nuptial. Torrie will not let that stop the popular respects and books an alternative church immediately.

On the day, a crowd has formed outside the home early for the free entertainment. Fifty-three pallbearers to attend the casket. Alongside three judges and a Congressman, are most of the aldermen of the city. Outside of the politicians are representatives of the culture side of Chicago, restauranteurs, members of Chicago Opera, plus many crime families leading players.

The floral tributes are magnificently large and will set the standard for mob funerals that follow, making the efforts for Padraig Hennessey a few years earlier seem no more than a posey. Several cars are needed for the bouquets and wreaths alone. Colosimo is buried in a $7,500 casket and the hearse is followed by around 5,000 people, a lot of them Union members associated with the mobster. First Ward Alderman, Michael "Hinky Dink" Kenna, gives Torrio a ride to the church. People watching recognise who now holds the power - Big Jim's right hand, Johnny Torrio. Kenna, a crooked politician as ever there is, has handled the rise of Colosimo from street kid to the city's premier pimp. In return, he gets support from the Italians at election time, payoffs and free "perks". Now Kenna is backing Torrio. Torrio makes his headquarters at the saloon he owns – The Four Deuces – which also provides whores and gambling – with his righthand man and protege, Al Capone, who despite only being 21 is seen as an upcoming force.

From now on, Torrio and Capone are in the booze business. Torrio applies the flair of a businessman. They are the first to buy up breweries cheaply as the legitimate businesses have to close. Within months they own six professional breweries, having started with Standard Brewing, and are putting out over one thousand bottles a week. As honest law enforcement closes the breweries eventually, they switch to small breweries but mainly smuggling in or hijacking shipments, notably those belonging the Irish mobs. This causes a backlash of violence.

John Torrio and Sean O'Leary are alike. Intelligent men with business acumen but also not afraid to use harsh methods of intimidation, from beatings to murder. Sean has expanded his territory by absorbing other small Irish districts and by allying with others more powerful. There is an uneasy truce on the surface as Torrio agrees to share profits with the Irish on his Chicago booze business in return for an end to the killing between gangs. Torrio and Capone are not ready for a war yet. Torrio plans to slyly bleed his rivals of profits rather than gunfights.

1921

Warren G. Harding is inaugurated as the 29th President of the United States of America.

Iowa is the first state to impose a cigarette tax.

West Virginia imposes a sales tax.

A national quota is set in the US for immigration.

Jack Dempsey defends his title in boxing's first million-dollar gate, knocking out Georges Carpentier of France in the fourth round.

Babe Ruth sets a record of 137 career home runs and continues in this form through the season.

A Chicago jury acquit 8 White Sox players of involvement in the Black Sox scandal, but they are still banned from organised baseball.

J. Edgar Hoover is appointed Assistant Director of the Federal Bureau of Investigation (FBI).

"The Sheik", starring Rudolph Valentino, premieres in Los Angeles.

The Willis Campbell Act forbids doctors prescribing beer or liquor.

CHAPTER 12
Illinois

The only indicator of the dog's progress is the waving of the tall grass as it chases mice, rabbits or butterflies in the field below the rise, shaking pollen loose that runs with the evening breeze, all golden in the late sun. Down in the lower land, the farmhouse and outbuildings are visible, wooden structures built by his parents with the help of neighbours, nothing fancy, just practicable. The farmhouse has no more rooms than necessary. One big barn for storage, in better condition than the homestead, built by extra borrowing from the bank to take the increased production the war called for. One old, falling down barn, too much trouble and cost to repair, being slowly reclaimed by nature. A modest stable for the two plough horses.

Most of the land he can see from here is his – technically the bank's until the mortgage is paid off. Just one of the many small farms in Illinois, big enough to be managed by a family with a few hired hands and a couple of work animals.

Up on the ridge, Jesse Hakerman turns away, taking a last draw of his cigarette before dropping it to the ground and grinding it out with his heel. His startling green eyes sparkle with moisture, whether from tobacco smoke or an emotion, who can tell. A silent pause before a headstone then a touch of his lips with two fingers and a transfer of his kiss to the grave marker.

93

Emily Hakerman - beloved wife and mother – 1873 – 1918

Joshuah Hakerman – faithful husband and father – 1870 – 1919

Two years after the death of his father, it is the cheapest stone, pricewise only just up from wood, and Jesse vows to replace it with granite as soon as he can, before the weather erodes the lettering to an unreadable state. He'd have to find the extra dollars for the inscriptions, but is not satisfied with a simple names and dates; anyone who comes across the graves should have to know these are people who were, who are, much loved. His father had buried his wife while Jesse was away on the Western Front. She'd caught pneumonia and didn't survive. Jesse got home only for a brief time with his father before he had to bury him alongside her.

As the sun starts to cast long shadows over the landscape, black fingers reaching outwards to merge into one darkness, he walks down to the farm road and his pick-up truck, whistling for his dog to join him. The grasses part and a mongrel mix of hunting dog and some others runs out with a bark, before running round the truck and jumping on the tail board. An owl hoots, now free to hunt in the grass.

The last ritual of the working day has been completed. No matter how tired, it is never missed. This is the lonely time, the time when no work occupies his mind and he will sit in the house until sleep overcomes him. Making his way back to the simple building Jesse muses on his life. Before 1917 and conscription, he knew he would help his pa on the farm and eventually take it over. That is the way of life in rural Illinois. He has imagined coming in from the fields, seeing the old man on the porch smoking his pipe, ma in the kitchen cooking pork and greens singing some gospel song. Now the house seems empty. He still sleeps in his old room and his parents' bedroom is never used.

Cursing a war and the unnecessary risk he has been forced to take, which meant he hadn't made it back from Europe before his mother passed and he mourned with his father until the old guy had a heart attack and joined her in the ground. Not only was a wife and mother lost, one of the hardest working people on the farm had gone. The one who helped with the home-brewing, looked after the chickens, cooked and cleaned, the first one up in the morning so the men had a hearty breakfast before setting out to work in the fields. When she fell ill, the medical bills took their meagre savings then more, delaying the repayment of the mortgage and loans. No money for hiring help, Joshuah worked harder and harder until his heart gave way, a man broken by adversity.

As an only child, Jesse now manages the farm, works with the negro farmhands. It isn't his dream anymore, it is an obligation; an obligation that lays heavy on him. During the war, farms had experienced a demand for food – to feed the thousands of troops. It was a period of assumed prosperity but it was short-lived. His father had borrowed more money, believing the profits from increased food production to feed the army would mean he'd soon be free of debt. Farmers had worked harder than ever before, with patriotic fervour. Jesse recalls a county fair pre-war, where his father was entranced with a display by the Emerson-Brantingham Implement Company of Rockford of their new medium weight petrol-propelled tractor. If they could have afforded that, maybe his pa would still be alive, not having to work as hard as he did. With the war over in under two years and all the doughboys home, farming became an existence for those working the land and not a living. The modern age is seeing parity of population between city and country for the first time. The post-war economy backs industry. The Federal government does not come to the aid of struggling farming communities with grants and the weakest go to the wall. Men want to be seen in suits, as businessmen, not in dungarees as toilers of the soil. Factories have sprung up, offering regular work at higher salaries. This is modern America. Farmers have to manage for themselves.

Driving down from the hilltop graves, Jesse notes that Moses, his overseer, has already stabled the plough horses, two beasts that have seen better days. The pick-up, bought used, had been funded by some of the mortgage and the rest by Jesse's Army pay that he had sent home. Whatever the harvest and whatever the demand for their crops, it still takes money to pay wages, feed the animals, run a vehicle. Money goes like a river in torrent and returns like a summer brook. Jesse can see, on the approach to the yard, where a couple or four shingles need reattaching and where fresh paint would not go amiss on the house.

Parking the pick-up at the side of the house, Jesse looks back at the ridge. From below and at the distance, the graves are not visible, but the copse of trees stand like guardians over the resting place. Some way away, the lonely cry of a freight train on its way to or from Chicago. A mournful sound that has frequently punctuated Jesse's life.

"Goodnight, mom. Goodnight, dad."

Holding the door ajar to let the dog in first, Jesse can smell grits, the fried corn dish, and knows that Molly, the wife of Moses, has been in and left him some of their dinner. It has been a while since he has been able to pay their wages but Moses never grumbles, tends to the work around the farm, grows vegetables on his own plot and lives with his wife in the shanty that is part of the farm but out of sight of the Hakerman home. The other hands live off-farm in shanties and come in for seasonal work when required, something that happens less and less. There are these little communities of transient labour that survive by sharing and caring for each other.

The grits are still warm – Molly knows his habits and timed it perfectly as usual to bring over a dish wrapped in a cloth to leave on the kitchen table. Grinding some beans then putting a pot of coffee on the stove to heat up, Jesse sits to eat at a well-worn table that he had once helped his father to make, using the wood from a fallen tree. That had been an afternoon of unspoken communion, while they sawed then planed and ma made lemonade, which they all sat around on the porch and drank before resuming work.

As he sits, his eyes scan the shelves of books, an eclectic collection started by the enthusiasm of his English teacher, Mrs Buckley, wife of the town sheriff, and mother of his best friend, Tom Jr. Reading has taken Jesse beyond the confines of the farm and the midwest town. Under his bed are still the pulp westerns he devoured as a child but the bookshelves have Charles Dickens, H.G. Wells, Jules Verne, Mark Twain and Edgar Allan Poe among others, many a gift from the Buckleys. He and his friend, Tom Buckley Jr, had played as children, first cowboys then adventurers and explorers influenced by the stories. The book of Walt Whitman's poems had been a school prize for writing a short story about life on a farm. Life on a farm. How idyllic it had seemed when he put pen to paper as a boy. Now, it is hardship and loneliness. Dependent on the weather for healthy crops. At the mercy of the bank for the money they have borrowed. Hard work and luck will not be enough. Jesse needs a plan on how to escape the uncertain future that he sees spread out before him. He does what he always does when thinking hard. He takes down from its brackets and strips and cleans the rifle he has brought back from France, the automatic skill occupying his hands freeing his brain to concentrate elsewhere.

It is the Conan Doyle books that make his mind up and the recollection of the famous Holmes quote:

"Once you eliminate the impossible, whatever remains, no matter how improbable, must be the truth."

Jesse can see no other option than one.

Tomorrow he will visit Sheriff Tom "Buck" Buckley.

CHAPTER 13

"There is no security in life, only opportunity"
Mark Twain

Buck looks every inch the western lawman of myth and legend- six feet two in stockinged feet, lean, rangy, piercing blue eyes. It is true – he has come from the wild west, the cattle towns, learned his trade as a young deputy over the last decades of the nineteenth century.

The Wild West 1890

Pete, the drunk cowpoke is mouthing off. He is loud and coarse. Coming straight from a cattle drive like many, goes to the saloons to booze then look for feminine company, usually a saloon girl provided by the business. Pete gets it wrong when he goes outside to accost two refined ladies on the boardwalk outside the saloon

"Well, ladies. Which one of you is going to lift your skirts and give Pete a treat?"

The Minister, who has approached from the other direction, tries to intervene.

"Why don't you go back inside the saloon and have another drink and let these two ladies go on their way?"

The cowpoke is too drunk to take advice and drunk enough to be stupidly angry.

"Who the fuck are you to tell me what to do?"

It is little effort to pull his Colt .45 and fire at the Minister's feet, making him dance to avoid losing a toe or two.

A 6-foot, slim blur knocks the gun from the drunkard's hand and a right hook puts him on his back.

"Jail time for you."

From the sidewalk, a 16-year-old skinny lad, who has been watching, cries out "Look out, Marshal" and throws himself at Pete's friend, a second drunk cowhand who has just exited the saloon at the noise of gunfire, and is pulling a gun on the lawman who has downed Pete. They roll on the floor, an uneven battle, the kid eventually falling loose. The cowhand still has his gun and aims at the youngster with the intention of shooting. The kid is looking down the barrel and thinking his end has come, when there is a loud bang from behind him and a crimson hole opens up in the cowhand's chest. The guy just keels over and lays dead in the dirt, blood spilling red into the dust of the street.

"You alright, kid?"

"Yes, Marshal," in a shaky voice, mesmerised by the dead man next to him.

"I'm sorry I had to kill him. Always try to end a conflict without gunplay, but if you have to use a gun, don't hesitate. It's not the fastest to the draw but the steadiest hand that wins and make the first shot count."

"I understand."

"That was a brave thing you did. What's your name?"

"Thomas Buckley, sir. But people call me Buck."

"Well, Buck. Grow up a bit more then come and see me if you'd like to be my deputy."

"Yes, sir, Marshall Earp."

Tom Buckley has been the Sheriff for as long as the town can recall. Never any competition for the post. There are adults who remember being caught shoplifting and, instead of any legal process or a visit to their parents, Buck has sat them down and given them a lecture on economics. How what they took is not free, how the shopowner has had to pay for it in order to sell it on, how it is as bad as taking cash from their wallet. You are depriving them of their livelihood. You might have thought taking a few cents worth of sweets is no big deal, but if more kids do it every week, and over the year, it is as much as your daddy worked for in a week. Then the kid is taken inside to apologise and usually volunteers to sweep the storefront pavement every weekend and run errands.

Today, Buck has opened the office on Main Street early. The main public space is a simple room, one desk and chairs, Wanted posters on the wall the only indicator this is a Law Office. Buck had made the conscious decision when he became sheriff, to move the gun cabinet to a back room and put some easy furniture in. Buck thought of himself as a Peace Officer, even though he always has a gun at his hip. He'd once tried going about without it, but years of hard lawkeeping made him feel underdressed, plus the citizens here telling him they feel safer when he is armed. They are also impressed by the fact that a young Thomas Buckley had once been a deputy for Wyatt Earp, a fact confirmed by a photo of the two hung on the wall behind Buck's desk.

In this small midwestern town, he projects trust and a willingness to listen and, for that, people re-elect him without question. Buck would be firm but fair, never heavy handed and has been known to give drunks a lift home rather put them in the jail for the night. Many problems never make it to court; Buck would arbitrate and his decision accepted. The town only has one lawyer, and his work is mainly legal deeds and contracts.

In the first heat of the summer day, Buck is putting a bowl of water on the sidewalk for passing dogs when Jesse pulls up in his truck.

"Howdy, Jesse."

"Sheriff."

Jesse climbs out of the cab and Buck's honed lawman's instincts are that this is not a social visit; Jesse's demeanour is reserved and his brow furrowed, as if he has a lot on his mind. Plus, he has formally addressed Buck by rank and not the usual polite "sir". But, to give time for Jesse to work out how to say what he has come to say, Buck does the usual.

"Jesse. Mrs Buckley would be pleased to see you. Why not come over on Sunday for dinner?"

There is a strong bond between Jesse and the Buckleys. As well as best friends growing up, their only son had gone to the Great War with Jesse. Buck knew that, badly wounded, under enemy fire while on a mission, Jesse had carried his son's body back to American lines at great risk instead of leaving him to be lost in No Man's Land. Awarded a medal for bravery, Jesse had put it in the grave of his friend in France before leaving; the consolation of a grave for Tom Jr at his home is denied his parents. Buck would never say it, but Jesse is their surrogate son now, even more since Jesse's parents have passed.

"I'll try, sir. Bit busy on the farm. Been a tough year."

Jesse fusses with his belt buckle. A familiar sign to Buck that Jesse is unsettled.

"Got time for coffee? Got a pot brewing," Buck says, with a nod to the open door.

The two men go into the office, where Buck continues into the back where a pot of his famously strong coffee makes bubbling noises on the stove. Taking two mugs, blowing the dust out of one (which he will use and give Jesse his, cleaner, mug), Buck pours then takes the coffee into the office. Jesse is stood looking at, but not seeing, the Wanted Posters displayed on one wall.

Buck indicates they should both sit and when both have settled into

104

the easy chairs, taken their first sips of the coffee, breaks the silence.

"OK, Jesse. I can see there is something on your mind. What do you want to say?"

Jesse shuffles in his seat. He has practised a speech during the drive into town but nerves make him forget his spiel and he just blurts:

"Well, sir, I need your advice. Permission rather. I have a proposal and I need to know your feelings before I start. If you say 'No', then that's good enough for me, I won't do it."

Buck is wise enough not to interrupt, his task is to listen then consider. The same technique has gotten criminals to open up, people speak to fill the silence. Life is too short to hurry, is his western wisdom.

Jesse fidgets again in his seat. He thinks of Buck as the father of his friend, an uncle figure, while considering the approach but here, in the Sheriff's office, and Buck looking official, he grips his cup hard. He feels his confidence waning.

"The farm has been struggling. I can't pay the hands, they're working for almost free, just their accommodation and whatever food we grow. The mortgage that Dad took out is killing us. He thought he was investing for a better future. We all know how that has turned out. I reckon I could lose the farm within a year at best.......I've an idea that can solve all that; I've run figures and I could turn a profit within a year. We've always brewed our own beer and cider – it's popular around here – but I am thinking of making whiskey, gin, whatever I

105

can using my crops. There's a demand for booze that isn't going to go away, despite the new law. People will be running out of any stored supplies and looking for new means to restock."

Jesse pauses to see how this is being taken by Buck but the only sign is a slight furrowing of Buck's brow as he stares into his coffee cup, avoiding eye contact. Buck is only too aware that passing an Act of Prohibition is not the same as it working. Married to a schoolteacher, he knows his history, the Whiskey Rebellion of 1791 and the Lager Beer Riots of Chicago in 1855. People are not happy to give up alcohol and would fight for the right to drink. Decades may have passed since public disorder but people do not change that quickly.

Jesse continues, wanting hastily to assure the Sheriff of his good intentions: "But, obviously, it's not legal. I don't want to put you in the position of having to, well, you know. I'm thinking, people will get their booze wherever they can. That could mean bad stuff; I've heard terrible stories of bathtub gin making people blind. My stuff would be good and just for the locals."

Jesse sits forward in his chair, gaining a bit more confidence. "I've worked out what it would cost and what I could charge. Enough to eventually pay off the mortgage, keep the farm, pay the hands. That's all I want for me. Whatever I get over that, gets spent in the community – books for the school, mending the church roof, emergency fund for people who are struggling, whatever comes up. But I can't put you in the position of condoning what is basically an illegal act. So, if you say 'No', I'll have to try something else... It would only be until we're back on our feet."

"Jesse. If it's money you need, Mrs Buckley and I have some savings. We'd gladly lend it to you." Offering their life savings and an unneeded college fund.

Jesse knows he can't borrow; that just means more debt.

"Thank you, sir, but I can't take your money. This is an all or nothing gamble. I succeed or I lose the farm. I can move to the city and get a job in a factory. Moses and Molly will have to hope another farmer takes them on." Jesse stares at the photo of himself and Tom Jr in Army uniform, taken the day they arrived for training, on the sheriff's desk, before continuing. "If we hadn't gone to war, maybe things would be different. Pa borrowed heavily so he could increase production for the war effort but the war ended before he saw a return on his efforts. Then the medical bills...."

Buck knows that Jesse's mother's illness had cost dear yet still she died. He and Agnes had attended her funeral and seen a broken man in Joshuah. Buck thought, maybe, when Jesse returned things would be different. Obviously it hadn't turned out that way. He has to make a decision and prays it's the right one.

There is a beat of silence – both men looking into each other's eyes. Finally, Buck speaks

"Do you want some more coffee?"

That is his answer.

It isn't 'No'.

CHAPTER 14

SEC. 25. It shall be unlawful to have or possess any liquor or property designed for the manufacture of liquor intended for use in violating this title or which has been so used, and no property rights shall exist in any such liquor or property.... No search warrant shall issue to search any private dwelling occupied as such unless it is being used for the unlawful sale of intoxicating liquor, or unless it is in part used for some business purposes such as a store, shop, saloon, restaurant, hotel, or boarding house....

Volstead Act 1920

Greatly relieved, Jesse takes his farewell and drives further down Main Street, past Sid's Diner where, on another day, he might have called in for breakfast, to the General Store. He realises that Buck could not say Yes outright, but he has indicated he will remain blind and deaf for the time being.

Getting out of the pickup, Jesse speaks to the kid sweeping the pavement in front. "Welcome to the gang", but the kid doesn't understand.

The General Store is exactly that. An emporium of almost everything. It is one of the largest commercial premises in town and is a family business. Shelves of food and shelves of dry goods line round the

109

walls. Racks of working attire at the back. Locals say "if you can't find it at McGregors' then you probably don't need it." Counters on all sides except the window, which is clear to allow a view in and observation out. A new red poster for Curtiss Baby Ruth candy hangs behind the till, replacing the old familiar one for Kandy Kake, since the Chicago based company renamed its candy bar with the rising fame of a baseball player.

The McGregors, husband and wife, are putting out stock and both look up when Jesse enters

"Hi, Jesse. Been a while."

Both McGregors, as the name suggests, are of Scottish descent, one first generation American (Mr) and the other, second. Neither are tall and both are a more than a little overweight, giving the impressions of human bookends; it is said they eat anything they can't sell rather than let it go to waste. Both attend church on Sundays and are never heard to swear or known to drink. Jesse has wondered how his enterprise will be taken by them once they know.

Their daughter, Maggie, is not in the store. A pretty fair-haired, blue-eyed lass, she was a third musketeer with Tom Jr and Jesse and the McGregors had once hoped for a proposal from Jesse, the leader, but the young man who went off to war came back a different person; one who has seen something of the world, beyond this little town and is following a sense of duty but who would probably leave at some point in the future if he could.

Jesse shrugs. "Lot to do on the farm. Not so many hands anymore."

Both McGregors nod. The same story being told by a lot of their customers. As times toughened for the farming community, the McGregors reduced their profit margins so that people could afford the things they needed. They'd both understood and agreed, it is better to sell things cheaply than have unsold stock. It is a mix of their Christian beliefs, economic sense and community loyalty.

Jesse continues, "Need a few things.... need some of it on credit."

The McGregors are known for allowing a tab to be run, but that usually is for a week or less, until payday. Jesse needs a longer timeframe. He finds himself holding his breath as he faces a potential obstacle.

Mr McGregor speaks without hesitation. "Seeing as it's you, Jesse, not a problem."

More than just Jesse's potential as a son-in-law, the family Hakermans have been good, honest citizens, putting into the community, giving handouts to those in need, and fellow churchgoers. "Cut from the same cloth" as the shopkeeper might have said.

Jesse explains what he needs. If the McGregors are surprised or curious, they say nothing but gather the stock together and help Jesse load his truck.

Not until Jesse has driven away does Mrs McGregor speak. "Well, that's interesting."

One non-military thing he has learned in France, while convalescing on a farm, is how to build a still to distil alcohol, added to which he has Moses' knowledge of brewing, which follows a long farming tradition of making alcoholic drinks for the family and hired hands. Time to put that knowledge into use. The plan is to convert some of the cider he already has in barrels into brandy if he can, by filtering and increasing the alcohol content. Normally, all the cider would be gone for refreshing the farmhands during harvest but with the downturn of labour, he has a lot in stock. The other spirit will be gin, which is basically flavoured alcohol. Good whiskey would require ageing in casks and he doesn't have time for that in a short-term plan, but has ideas for a simple version by steeping oakchips in base alcohol before bottling to see if that works. Something else he has learned in France – the importance of flavour delivered by wooden barrels.

But first, he will need his mash. That requires mixing the yeast and sugar with the farm's pure spring water and leaving several days to ferment, which will provide enough time to build his stills. Farms are mostly mechanically self-reliant and Jesse has the knowledge and the tools to do the work. He'd purchased copper piping on credit, as the one thing he is deficient in, and will set to work making his first spiral for the condensing process.

Arriving back at the farm, Jesse enlists Moses' help to unload the truck and set up in the barn. Moses, the foreman, is around 6' 4" and about as wide. Hands that could crush a watermelon to pulp. He makes light work of unloading the truck. The grandson of slaves, Moses is proud of his ancestors who had escaped the harsh life of the plantations, travelled on the Underground Railway, and found a new life in the North. Illinois had no slavery and was an attractive destination for those escaping the harsh realities of the southern plantations. Granddaddy Elijah had fought with the bluecoats and even met General Ulysses S. Grant and Abraham Lincoln, both Illinoisans. He'd married a girl who had fled the South with him and they had one child, a boy, whom they named Freeman and who grew up, married and was the father of Moses.

Moses' wife, Molly, is as thin as a stick but harder than teak. She has a heart of gold but will not be ordered around by any man. Some people make the mistake of thinking Moses is henpecked but the truth is a perfect marriage of a gentle giant and a sharp-minded lady very much in love with each other.

They live in a shack at the edge of the farm. It has one bedroom, a kitchen and a sitting room. Jesse's father had helped Moses build it when he first came to the farm, three decades ago. Outside Moses and Molly have a porch where they can sit in the evening, quite happy to hear the evensong of birds and watch the sun set over the valley. Moses would smoke a pipe and Molly would often knit or sew.

Moses and Molly met in another part of the state. Moses, 17, had spotted Molly, 14, at a County Fair and fell for her immediately. Molly was amazed at her luck to attract the big strong lad and the bond was immediate. After a couple of dates, Moses noticed Molly was not her usual cheerful self.

"What's troublin' you, girl?" he asked.

"I'm worried about my pa. He's started lookin' at me strange and last night he walked in while I wuz in the bath."

"That ain't right. He shouldn't be doin' that."

"I's afraid, Moses. He drinks too much and he gives me creepy looks."

Moses had a solution. It was an idea that had been nurturing in his brain already. "Why don't you and I go away together? I'll treat you right. No one will ever hurt you, long as you's with me."

They concocted a plan for Molly to leave her home and meet Moses at the crossroads in town. Moses had enough money to pay for train fares away then he was certain he would find work to rent a room somewhere. They agreed to put the plan into operation the following day.

Molly packed a small bag with some personal possessions and a change of clothes. She was sneaking out of the house but hadn't realised her father was on the porch having a cigarette.

He startled her. "Where yuh goin', girl? Sneakin' aroun' like that."

"Nowhere, pa. Just to see some friends."

"Whatcha gets in the bag?"

"Nuttin'. Just a few things to show them."

"Let me see."

Molly clutched the bag tighter and her father got up and ripped it from her hands before tipping the contents on the floor.

"You thinkin' of running away. You goin' off with that big nigger I've seen you with?"

"No, pa. Just goin' out."

"Liar!" and her father fetched her a slap across the face that set Molly sprawling. "Get back in the house, you little whore. I'll deal with you later."

Moses was getting anxious. He decided to call on the house to find out why Molly had not turned up. Molly's father answered the door.

"Mr Hancock. Can I see Molly, please?"

"You got no business aroun' here, boy. Now you clear away and stay away," breathing alcohol fumes over Moses.

Beyond Hancock, Moses could see Molly step into the hall. He noticed her swollen eye and red cheek. "Did you hit Molly, Mr Hancock?"

"It ain't no business of yours how I control my kid..." but he never finished his sentence as Moses delivered a roundhouse punch that sent him crashing into the porch furniture.

"Molly. You get whatcha need and you come with me. Hurry."

They caught a train out of town an hour later.

Several days by, having walked from farm to farm offering to work, they came across Joshuah Hakerman in trouble. Josh's cart had slipped off the track and now a wheel was stuck in a ditch and the one horse could not pull it free. Josh was contemplating whether to unload the cart and try again or to take a long walk to his farm and come back with his second horse, both options unpopular as the light is fading fast as the afternoon came to an end. Moses came up to Joshuah.

"You in trouble, sir?"

"You guess?" Josh replied.

Moses took charge. "Molly will take the horse, sir, and get it to pull when I say. I'll push from the back with your help."

Joshuah did not think it would work but he had nothing to lose from trying. Moses got round by the sunken wheel, ready to lift and push, and Joshuah took the other rear corner.

"OK, girl, NOW!"

Molly slapped the horse on its rear and encouraged it with "Pull, you beautiful horse."

Joshuah pushed his side but felt nothing happening until he realised the young black man has actually lifted the cart clear so that the wheel was not caught, then he made an extra effort himself to get the cart rolling on to the track fully.

"My god, boy. That is something? How can I thank you?"

"That's alright, sir. Glad to help. You don't know anyone hiring, do you? Molly and me are looking for work."

"Why don't you both get up on the cart and come and have some supper with my wife and me? You both look like you need a good meal."

Joshuah talked it over with Emily and they offered Moses and Molly jobs to help on the farm. Proving invaluable and trustworthy, Josh taught Moses how to use all the tools around the farm and Emily helped with reading and writing and arithmetic, areas he had missed out on as his parents could not let him attend school too often, needing his help to earn money.

Over time, they grew vegetables and have some chickens for a daily supply of eggs and occasionally one for the pot. In addition to his own little domain, Moses is a fair trapper of rabbits, the meat nourishes them and the fur could be made into garments, some of which Molly sells. He is also a crack shot with his double-barrelled shotgun and the occasional wildfowl grace their table as a result.

No children blessed their union but they have seen Jesse come into the world and grow up into a fine young man. He may be their employer since his parents passed but he has respect for them and treats them as equals. They are willing to share the hard times with him.

Jesse had walked over to the shack and met with both Moses and Molly and explained his plan to them before he drove into town to see the sheriff. Neither had an objection – it is an extension of their cider brewing and a chance to save the farm and their livelihood. In truth, both are relieved Jesse is making plans, having feared he would give up and move on. They would do whatever Jesse asks of them. There is a bond that binds them together.

CHAPTER 15

"I'll ne'er be drunk whilst I live again, but in honest, civil, godly company, for this trick. If I be drunk, I'll be drunk with those that have the fear of God, and not with drunken knaves."

Slender in The Merry Wives of Windsor

by William Shakespeare

After Jesse's visit and proposal, Sheriff Tom Buckley does a tour of the town in his Ford coupe along Main Street and back along the sidestreets. It is his usual routine before heading home but this time it's different. He finds himself considering the changes ahead. Looking at storefronts – family businesses – and going over the possible consequences of his agreement with Jesse. He knows all the storeowners and the local community. Who drinks, who is Temperance. Two bars in town have closed officially and he is aware of backdoor trade over the first year of Prohibition, but that has been dying as stocks run out. Sid's Diner added a range of soft drinks for those who want refreshment but not necessarily to eat as well.

Buck is proud to be Sheriff of this town. It might not be big, in fact a bit of a backwater. If it hadn't been for the railway in 1856 running through and putting in a freightyard for the farm produce to get to Chicago in one direction and Springfield in the other, it would have remained a village. At that time, it grew quickly to 100 families and 58 businesses, not counting the rural dwellers on farms and dispersed outside the town limits. By 1906 they had a telephone service and by 1914 an electric service. The town has a civic hall, a hotel, a creamery, bakers, small hospital behind the doctor's surgery, a millinery store, a general store, a pharmacy, a diner, a solicitor's office, a bank and a school. Individual tradesmen either work from their homes or have premises off Main Street. In the fringes can be found carpenters, two blacksmiths, saddlers and a cartwright. On the road into town from the Chicago end is a Filling Station to supply the owners of automobiles with fuel.

Buck disagrees with Prohibition – feels it is a knee-jerk reaction led by Bible thumpers. They had premised alcohol as the source of all crime and with the Volstead Act expected the closure of prisons and the laying off of the police. In this Utopia of temperance, everybody would behave and life would be perfect. As a lawman from way back, Buck knows there are types who don't need to be drunk to beat their wives, or to pick a fight. But it is now law and he is a lawman. He might have a bumpy road ahead and there could be consequences he'd rather not think about. Having served his apprenticeship as a young law officer in western towns, he appreciates the quiet life he has now. He'd witnessed first-hand gunfights, knifefights, gambling, prostitution, claim-jumping, rustling and lynchings. As a Sheriff of a cowtown further west, he courted a young schoolteacher who had arrived to teach the town's children. When she received an offer to return to her home town and run a school, Buck married her and they both went. It has been idyllic, having a son, seeing him grow into a fine young man, until war is declared and he goes to France never to return.

Mrs Buckley – Agnes – hears Tom's coupe pull on to the drive. An elegant woman, still fine looking, who adores the tall peace officer she has married. Pushing a wisp of loose hair behind an ear, she puts a pot of freshly ground coffee on the stove and checks the pork chops in the oven. Tom will smoke one cigarette on the porch before coming in, so she knows how much time she has. Dinner will be on the table exactly at the moment Tom enters, hangs up his hat, washes and comes through to the kitchen.

Buck considers a second cigarette – wanting the time to think about possible problems and how to handle them. As he pulls out the makings, he mentally notes he's about three quarters of the way through his Bull Durham, leaving him possibly 10 more smokes and should buy a new pack. He remained a "smoke veteran" and filter cigarettes had not converted him. His hand is stilled when, through a half open window, he hears cutlery chink as it is laid on the table so he knows it is time to go indoors. He might take a smoke after.

The dinner is more silent than usual. Plates are emptied of food, gravy wiped off the plate with fresh, homebaked bread. Apple pie and cheese sit waiting. Buck's fingers drum on his vest pocket where he keeps his makings.

Delaying on removing the dishes, Agnes speaks first. "I can see something is on your mind. What happened today?"

Buck takes a deep breath before relating Jesse's visit; plain and simple. Then he explains his dilemma – a possible conflict of interest.

"Jesse's right. This Volstead Act won't stop people drinking. But where will they get their alcohol from? Jesse's solution is to make and provide locally. Keep the city slickers away. I've heard how things are in Chicago and spreading to the suburbs. We're free of it at the moment, but that may not last. Yet if I turn a blind eye to Jesse's plan and if it all goes wrong, I may have to arrest him. If I stop him now, he'll lose the farm and Moses and Molly will be evicted too. That's more than bad luck coming so soon after losing his parents. I feel a bit damned if I do, damned if I don't."

Agnes reaches across the table and takes Bucky's hand. "You trust Jesse, don't you?"

It is a statement, not a question.

CHAPTER 16
Illinois

After the firefight that had fatally wounded Tom Jr and injured Jesse, Jesse had been sent to convalesce on a French farm. As the war ended before he could resume duties and while waiting to be repatriated home, Jesse contributed to the work on the farm, which was greatly needed as France had lost many young men in the conflict. The farmer knew enough English and Jesse a little French for the farmer to teach Jesse about distilling the lavender crop to make perfume and how to build and maintain stills. There was always one still among the lavender ones that was kept for the farmer to distil alcohol for the home. Jesse now shares that knowledge with Moses and Molly. When creating gin, it all starts with a great mash. The base spirit only requires what they are growing on the farm – corn, barley and wheat, wheat being the best for gin.

Molly makes up a mix and adds to the pure spring water readily available, which has been preheated to 165°F in a metal tub. It is a tiring job to continuously stir a thick soup by hand but she is hardened to farmwork and sticks with it for several minutes before checking the temperature. The job is stir/test temp, repeat, until the mix has cooled to 152°F when she stirs in distiller's malt. Molly made a commitment to make a success of the new venture; she knows how much rides on it. Again, a cycle of stir/test temp, but with longer pauses, waiting for the temperature to drop to 70°F, which is a slow process due to the natural ambient heat of the day. Molly tries fanning to cool to speed things up, thinking about methods to improve the process they could try. Eventually the desired temperature is reached and the mix needs aerating by transfer back and forth between containers for several minutes more. Only then is it ready for the fermentation process.

As Jesse and Moses are building stills and cleaning barrels for storing the alcohol, Molly has the time to watch over the fermentation, which takes nearly two weeks. Her technique is to test samples of the mix with iodine (from the medicine cabinet) and, if it turns blue, leave the mash to continue fermenting. When the test sample remains clear, Molly knows it is time to filter the mash through cheesecloth so they only obtain the liquid and none of the solids.

The process is not over. For gin, the alcohol needs flavouring, by what is known as botanicals, otherwise all they have is moonshine. Molly has collected citrus peel to add to the juniper berries supplied by the McGregors. With her herb garden, she is able to supply angelica and orris root, which she adds in small amounts.

Finally, the time comes to test a still. The excitement is palpable. Jesse has so far only tested for sturdiness and leaks. Now comes the time to make gin. The men look at Molly, who takes charge. "The flavourings are wrapped in the cheesecloth. Moses. You put it in the still and mind you be careful."

124

Moses and Jesse hide their grins. Jesse is ready to siphon the alcohol over the cloth in the still, a precaution to keep the liquid as pure as possible. Molly gives him a nod when she is ready. Jesse might have explained the process but Moses's wife now takes ownership.

The purpose of the still is not simply to make alcohol but to create a quality product. As the base alcohol heats and is infused with the botanicals, the vapour rises through a pipe which goes through a vat of cold water, condensing it back to liquid. With an eagle eye, Molly watches as the first liquids begin to drip from the condensing tube. These are to be discarded as unfit for drinking, the process creating methanol then acetone. Knowing when the good stuff is coming out is chiefly a matter of smell, supported by a finger dip and a touch to the tongue. The two men are unconsciously holding their breath as Molly performs, taking some on her finger, smelling, frowning, wiping, waiting. Until a smile forms as she touches the wet finger to her tongue.

"We got gin."

Jesse and Moses perform an incongruous jig, a ridiculous sight considering the differences in height and size. Molly is not going to be distracted. With her experience of cooking and home-brewing she will decide how to dilute the strong alcohol down to a safe level of proof for drinking.

At first, they are overcautious but experience teaches them a safe level until the day Fred White at the Pharmacy, a good customer of their gin, hands over a hydrometer and advice on how to use and do the calculations, with which they can more accurately and consistently assess the proof. Fred had been involved once with the manufacture of pharmaceutical alcohol and is a helpful mentor. They are on their way to manufacturing good quality tasting and safe to drink gin. It will be their main product.

They are now in the booze business. All they need are customers.

CHAPTER 17

Chicago

Terrible Tommy O'Connor

Like Sean O'Leary, Tommy O'Connor is another Limerick man, who emigrated to the States as a child with his parents and siblings, part of the green diaspora fleeing poverty and British oppression. The family settled in an area known as Bloody Maxwell, a tough neighbourhood, but a level for the lowest, poorest immigrants to collect.

As adults, Tommy, and brother "Darling Dave", ran a taxi service, which provided a cover for their burglary outings and safe-cracking with nitro-glycerine. Sean associated with them as taxis are also useful for taking trade to the brothels and gambling dens, picking up out-of-towners looking for "a good time", but he keeps his distance on the more criminal activities. The risks and rewards not worth the effort, while booze, girls and gambling were "businesses" with no shortage of customers.

A cold November night in 1919, a cop, Dennis Tierney, was moonlighting as a night watchman at the Illinois Central Station. Before the rich bribes of Prohibition, many cops held second jobs to make ends meet. He was doing his usual round, checking doors and windows secure. Maybe when that was done, he could go for a nap in a cubby hole he'd long sorted out for such relief. Finding a door opened, he went closer and saw that it had been damaged, an obvious break-in. He thought maybe a vagrant seeking somewhere warm and it was his mistake to call out. Before he realised his error, he was shot and fatally wounded. His last vision was two men running past him to get away. It was Tierney's unfortunate fate to be shot and killed and not survive for more lucrative times. On this occasion, as it was one of their own, the police did work to find the culprits and quickly captured one of the gang, a guy named Harry Emerson, a small-time player. Emerson had been recognised running away from the station and was picked up and vigorously questioned in the cells. Emerson didn't want the murder rap, which would lead to the gallows, so he had no hesitation in fingering Tommy as the killer in a deal for a lighter sentence. O'Connor was well known to the police, who swooped in and arrested him.

He played the same game as Emerson, squealing and pointing the finger, he reciprocated by naming his criminal associate as the gunman, in an effort to avoid the noose. Unfortunately for him, the States Prosecutor turned him down, believing Emerson, who had informed first.

Tommy came up with a solution - put out a contract on Emerson, so he wouldn't be able to give testimony at his trial. He figured that eliminating the prosecution's best witness, he could again claim Emerson was the shooter and the jury would acquit him of murder. He thought he knew who would be the best hitman for the job – Big Joe

Moran - but needed a middle man to approach and seal the deal on his behalf. His timing was lousy. He picked the wrong guy to handle negotiations with a killer on his behalf - Jimmy "The Peacock" Chjerin, a minor underworld figure, was making an effort to go straight, get out of the business. He wasn't a true criminal, rather he just consorted with bad guys against his family's wishes. As an old childhood associate of O'Connor's he listened to Tommy's proposal, pretending to accept it rather than refuse face to face but it got back to Tommy that Chjerin wouldn't carry out mission. It was a dilemma for Tommy. If Chjerin blabbed about the contract, that would knock down his planned defence in court. He had to act, and without delay before anything was revealed.

The Peacock got a shock when Tommy O'Connor and an associate, Louie Miller pulled up alongside him in a car as he was walking. He hadn't heard O'Connor was out on bail and he hadn't done anything about setting up the hit on Emerson.

Hey! Jimmy!" shouted O'Connor. "Well, what do you know? We was just talking about you. I was telling Louie here what a great guy you are." Then, noticing the fear on Chjerin's face, "Hey, forget about the contract on Emerson. I was hasty. Things are gonna work out."

A weight fell from Chjerin's shoulders. He'd felt trapped by a sense of obligation as childhood pals but Jimmy had promised his father he would go straight. After all, he had a wife and a new baby now. "That's great, Tommy," letting out a big sigh of relief.

129

Tommy pointed to the spare seat in the auto. "Come on, get in. Let's go for a drink."

Unsuspecting, Chjerin sat in the back of a stolen Model T, driven by Miller, alongside Tommy, and the three men shared a joke. Miller was a stooge for O'Connor, who hadn't told him his real intention. It was easier to settle his victim that way. As soon as Tommy realised they were in a quiet neighbourhood, using the gun he had been holding out of sight down his side, he put three bullets in Chjerin. The look of surprise on the Peacock's face faded as his life passed away. The noise of the gunshots in the confined space temporarily deafened Tommy and Miller, so Tommy slapped the other man on the shoulder to indicate "get a move on", showing the gun to the surprised Miller. They drove to Stickney, south of Chicago, and dropped the body in a ditch, making little effort to hide it. After driving back to the city, they dumped the stolen car with its bloodstained seat and walk away, deed done.

It wasn't long before the body was discovered; O'Connor and Miller's laziness, or arrogance, would be their undoing. When police came to report the death of the Peacock to his family, they immediately knew what had gone down.

"That bastard is going to pay for this." Jimmy's father, Dominick, was incensed. His boy was not really bad, just hung around with the wrong people and that had got him murdered. Dominick was a municipal court bailiff and the family were respected generally.

130

"We gonna do him, papa?"

"Nah. That would just bring reprisals down on us. There's another way." The family were looking to distance Jimmy from crime; ironically it was what got his son killed.

The family had contacts and tracked down Tommy's driver, Louie Miller, handing him to the police, who enthusiastically beat a confession out of him that Tommy had murdered the Peacock. The family gave the cops their backing to go after Tommy. Chjerin senior planned that, if the State execute O'Connor, they'll be no comeback on the family.

O'Connor was not hiding; he thought he was in the clear so it was a total surprise when the police scooped him up for Chjerin's murder. His solution was to post a $45000 bail, the largest ever seen in Chicago, and he disappeared for a while, keeping low at the home of his brother-in-law, William Foley, at 6425 Ishtenaw Avenue. But he now lacked any influence where it counted and was still being charged for the murder of a cop, Tommy was tracked to that address, after the law got a tip-off.

Detective Sergeant Patrick O'Neill picked five men to go with him to arrest Tommy, to claim him as a bail-jumper, seeing as how he failed to notify the court of an address and not keeping contact.

"Let's get this mad fucker back behind bars where he belongs. No way can he escape sentence for two deaths."

They pulled up in front of the house, overconfident by numbers and firepower. Spilling out of the car, they spread in a small formation on the drive.

O'Neill, at the front, called for Tommy: "This is the police! Come out quietly, O'Connor."

However, the six cops underestimated Tommy's desire for freedom and he came out with guns blazing, having seen the car and six men alight. The cops had guns drawn and retaliated. Bullets flew, chipping the door and walls but missing O'Connor. During the mad firefight, O'Neill, nearest to O'Connor, was gunned down. In the confusion, the officers were shaken, thinking one or more of their bullets had taken him down in a crossfire. O'Neill was on the ground, seriously wounded but still alive although in agony, and the priority became to get an ambulance rather than chase O'Connor down. During their inaction of grief and guilt and the urgency to get medical aid he seized the chance to escape by leaping a garden fence. One street away, he commandeered a car by gunpoint and drove to Stickney, an old hunting ground and where one of his contacts ran a saloon.

O'Neill died later that evening and the blame put on Tommy O'Connor. With a second cop death at his door, and a cop who was respected and admired, he became the focus of one of the largest manhunts in Chicago history. At a raid at the Crystal Palace dance hall he was nearly captured but in the crowd of dancers, he slipped away. Finding Chicago and its districts too hot for him, Tommy moved fast and went away to Minnesota. He had to fund himself so, with a local hoodlum called Jimmy Gallagher, he tried to rob a train but was captured by a rail employee armed with, of all things, a hammer. Word reached Chicago that O'Connor was in custody and they lost no time in sending a squad of their toughest to bring him back.

O'Connor told the cops, "It isn't my revolver that killed him. He was shot by his own pals" and repeated the statement in court. Despite that, on 24 September, he was found guilty of first-degree murder and the sentence decreed he should "hang by the neck until dead."

The execution was set for 15 December but Tommy's family want him out of jail. The obvious man to go to is Sean "Lucky" O'Leary, a fellow Limerick man. An approach is made by Darling Dave.

CHAPTER 18

Chicago
Terrible Tommy O'Connor

Sean is in his office at the Ace of Clubs. Inside a building with an insignificant exterior and protected from raids by payouts to crooked cops and politicians, the Ace of Clubs is a gambling den on the first floor, a Speakeasy on the second, and a brothel on the third. The logo is an Ace of Clubs, except instead of the familiar trefoil black ace, it is a green shamrock and behind the bar it is illuminated. No one is in doubt this is Irish territory.

Darling Dave stands in front of Sean's desk, holding a battered old leather valise.

"Sean. Tommy is set to hang next week. The family are offering a reward if he's not around then for the big drop."

Sean rubs his chin. "It can be done but the money will have to be enough for the trouble and risk. I'll have to pay off a warder or two, organise a safe run out of the state and hand Tommy enough cash to retire and not get into trouble again. If he is recaught, it would be back in the slammer, under heavy guard and a rope around his neck for sure. Why not try the Cardinelli trick?"

Darling Dave knows the story of Sam Cardinelli, who reputedly lost weight prior to his hanging to escape a broken neck, opting to die by strangulation and then his friends tried to resuscitate him.

134

"Not a certain outcome, Lucky." He hands over the valise for Sean to open. It is stuffed with dollar bills. "And you can have our taxi business. I won't be able to run it without Tommy."

"Dave. Leave it to me." Sean raises a glass of whiskey as a salute.

After Dave leaves, Sean calls in two of his heavies and explains what is going to happen. These are big guys, dressed in smart suits, guns in shoulder holsters, brass knuckles in pockets, small leather cosh in back pocket. They are enforcers but also street savvy.

"Do we know anyone in the jail we can put pressure on or buy?"

"I think we have a guy. He comes to the Ace to gamble and is in for a fair bit of money. He's due a visit if he don't pay up this week."

"Find him and bring him to me."

It doesn't take long before a scared warder is in front of Sean. A small-framed, weaselly looking guy with worsening body odour as he stands before the seated boss with the two heavies hovering behind him. They'd picked him up on the street, one each side, lifting him and bundling him into their car. He is sufficiently frightened already and now the big boss is looking him up and down.

Sean speaks first. "I got some notes here for your debts. You owe me quite a lot for a man on your wages."

The warder starts to sweat even more and he urgently feels the need to defend his economic position, only too aware of what the two heavies behind him are capable of.

135

"I do favours for the prisoners. The families pay me to take in a few luxuries and carry messages. That's usually enough, but I've had a bad streak at the tables. I can pay you if you give me a little more time."

He wipes his hands dry down his pants' legs. He starts to think his bladder is going to give up on him.

Sean pauses for effect before continuing. "Maybe I could do you a favour.... if you do one for me." He lights up a cigar, casual, as if he isn't about to ask for anything big.

The warder grabs the lifeline. "Sure. Anything. I'd do anything for you, Mr O'Leary."

Sean holds the lit end of the cigar to the IOUs and drops them in a metal waste bin by his desk, to burn away to ash. Both parties know a commitment has been made, although Sean doesn't need paper to enforce payment of debts. It is a symbolic act to show the warder what is possible.

"If you do what I ask, there's five Cs coming your way."

The warder is now extremely interested. His weaselly face lights up.

"I want you to smuggle a gun to Tommy O'Connor. Is that going to be a problem?"

The wrong answer would be a body dump into Lake Michigan as no one must hear of the proposal. The warder is no fool. Walk away debt free, five hundred coming to him.

"No, sir. Not a problem."

Sean smiles and nods. "OK, guys. Take him upstairs and let him have the pick of the girls. When he's finished, give him a gun." To the warder, "Do it right and when you next visit there'll be five hundred on the Blackjack table. You can cash it as winnings or play it."

Sean is calculating whether the warder might have to disappear after the escape but for now, the promise of the cash will keep him silent.

CHAPTER 19

TOMMY O'CONNOR FLEES JAIL
Condemned to die Thursday
He slugs guards and gets free

Chicago Tribune, Dec 12, 1921

O'Connor has a cell mate, James La Porte, a minor criminal, whom he has to let in on his plan. It also makes sense not to only make a two-man break – the more escapees the cops have to chase down, the better his chances at getting clean away. They invite a couple of others to go with them. Tommy and La Porte check the instructions that have been smuggled in from Sean. It is a simple plan and Tommy now has a pistol to make the guards obey them. He'd sent a message to Sean, via the crooked warder who has brought him the weapon, about the best time of day. If they don't succeed today, they do it tomorrow. It all depends on the routine of the block warder on duty not changing.

As always, the warder – David Strauss – is on time. A man of set routine and conscientiousness, although his mind might partly be outside the jail and thinking about a card game he would attend tonight with pals.

La Porte is standing at the bars watching. From the corner of his mouth, he speaks.

"He's coming."

Quickly, Tommy lays on the floor clutching his stomach and starts to moan. La Porte calls out. "Hey, Strauss. Tommy's ill."

With the execution only days away, it would be a serious matter if O'Connor is too ill to get on the scaffold. Thrown from his reverie, Strauss approaches the bars to get a better look. Concentrating on the groaning Tommy, he takes his attention off La Porte, a bad error. La Porte is ready, angles himself and reaches through the bars and grabs the warder, holding him in a chokehold.

"I've got him, Tommy."

Tommy is on his feet in seconds, reaching through for the keys on Strauss' belt and unlocks the cell. His grin frightens Strauss, well aware of Tommy's reputation. Pointing the gun at the subdued warder, the two cons come out the cell. Strauss fears that this is where he dies. It's almost a relief to hear: "OK, Strauss. Get in there."

The warder dejectedly walks into the cell, totally compliant. Following behind, Tommy clubs him with the pistol, dropping him to the ground, unconscious.

"Let's go."

They lock the cell door in case Strauss recovers too soon. Tying him up would be time-consuming and risk another warder entering the block. The adrenaline is pumping through Tommy now the escape is under way. Down the corridor they must take to the yard, there are other prisoners out of cells on their way to exercise and Tommy calls out to the nearest, Sponagel and Darrow.

"You coming along? We're getting out of here."

The two cannot believe their luck and La Porte pulls another guy out of the line to make the escapees a group of five. Tommy waves his pistol about to dissuade anyone else from intervening. Five is the maximum for what they are going to do. Any more and they could get in each other's way and Tommy and La Porte had calculated for recruiting the numbers to make the escape feasible.

The door to the yard is already unlocked, expecting the prisoners coming to exercise. As soon as outside the block, Tommy directs the group to make a human ladder where the wall is butted against the building; another reason why Tommy needed extra hands. Without too much difficulty they scale the twenty-foot wall by hoisting two up to straddle the top and reach back to pull the others up, taking advantage of the rugged walls with footholds from poor building work and lack of maintenance. The guards, who are sheltering from the rain that is falling instead of patrolling, don't notice a thing.

On the outside face of the wall, all they can do is hang by their hands then drop fifteen feet to the sidewalk. They all make it except Sponagel, who lands badly, a big man, overweight.

"Fuck. I think I broke my leg."

Looking up and down the empty street, Tommy is more concerned that there is no sign of Sean with a car as planned. "Where the fuck is Lucky?"

No need to be together and not informed of Tommy's plans,

140

Sponagel and Darrow decide to make it away on foot, Darrow half carrying the injured Sponagel. That's not a problem for Tommy, who doesn't need their help anymore and actually likes the split, to make it more complex for the police to track everyone down once the alarm is raised, which he fears might be any second.

La Porte looks at Tommy with a "what do we do now" expression. The plan is all Tommy's doing and dependent on the outside help. La Porte wonders whether he should just run off too. Any minute the alarm will be raised and the area around the jail swarming with cops.

John Jensen did not expect his day to take such a turn. He'd been running some errands and was now heading home. As his car turns the corner into the side street of the jail, through his rain drizzled windscreen he sees three men on the sidewalk. They all dressed alike and it sinks in that they are wearing prison uniforms, confirmed when one of them steps out into the street and points a gun at him. Still a distance away, Jensen panics, brakes hard and stalls the car, then tries to get as low as possible on the seat, unable to restart without getting out and turning the handle. La Porte, who has been looking in the opposite directions, points and calls out. "There's a car, Tommy!"

Like Jenson, Carl Busch, curious about three guys in the road, slows down and stops in the middle of the street. Tommy runs up on the driver's side and points the pistol. "Drive or I'll drill ya."

The three convicts jump into the car and force Busch to drive them.

141

Their bad luck isn't over. In the wet conditions, the scared Busch, never a good driver, with a gun to his head and the insistence of Tommy that he drive like the devil, clips a kerbstone on the corner of Chicago Avenue and Sedgwick Street and puts his car out of commission.

Nearby, another civilian, Paul Sorci, is backing his car out of a garage when he hears the car crash. He looks around to see what has happened and gasps when a gun is pointed close up at his face, held by a demented Tommy, who is both angry and frustrated. Tommy and his two fellow escapees transfer to Sorci's car. Still the bad luck persists. Terrified of Tommy, whom he recognises from newspapers, Sorci is a terrible driver in an old flivver of a car, which he had never driven faster than twenty-five miles per hour. Forced to drive faster than he has the skill for, he skids on the wet cobbles, mounts the pavement and crashes the car into a storefront. Tommy is angry enough to aim his gun at Sorci, intending to kill him, when he hears a car horn. At last, Lucky has arrived in his Paige Glenbrook, chosen because of its reputation for acceleration, 5 – 25mph in 9 seconds, in case he has to take off chased by police in their lesser vehicles. By fortune, the convicts are escaping along the route Sean and his driver are approaching the jail from.

Sean is surprised to find three men in the street and a wrecked car and explains the delay. "We had a puncture. Get in."

Truth was, he had hung back enough not to get caught up in any failed escape and gun battles. Not hearing sirens or gunshots, he deemed it safe enough to approach the jail at the agreed time.

The three escapees could not get in the rear seat fast enough – their liberator has finally arrived.

"So you made it, Tommy. Who are these guys?"

"This is Jimmy, my cellmate. Hey, who the fuck are you?"

Tommy realises he doesn't know the guy La Porte has pulled out the exercise line.

The con is shaking. Here he is in a car with Terrible Tommy O'Connor and he recognises Lucky O'Leary. These are big timers. He'd only robbed a grocery store and been caught by an off-duty policemen who was shopping there at the time. "Hank. I'm Hank."

As soon as far enough away from the jail, Lucky drops off the two associates of Tommy's to make their own way, throwing a couple of handfuls of dollar bills at them.

"Make yourselves scarce. And if you ever tell anyone about this, I'll hunt you down and skin you alive."

The advice is not necessary. After three aborted carjacks and aware that the heat would be on Tommy, they intend to find a hole to hide out in. A quick handshake and they are gone, off in opposite directions.

Sean and Tommy drive on, to a solitary house on the edge of town, in a quiet district with no immediate neighbours. Tommy finally relaxes, exhausted by the aftermath of the adrenaline rush, as Sean explains the next part of the plan.

"You rest here until nightfall then a car will come to take you out of Chicago. You'll need to lie low. Maybe you'd like to go to New York. Or Mexico where you can't be touched. I'll send money and fresh clothes to see you on your way with the driver."

They walk into the house together, Sean with a friendly hand on Tommy's shoulder. Suspecting nothing, Tommy is laughing at his escape when Sean snatches the nickel-plated revolver from his belt and pushes him into a room.

Three guys stand up. "Hi Tommy. Remember us?"

Tommy looks at Sean. "What's going on here?"

Sean ignores him. "See you guys. He's all yours now."

The Irish cops take care of Terrible Tommy O'Connor as retribution for their partner; letting the state execute him is not personal enough. They each empty their pistols into him. They'd been blamed for the fiasco of the failed arrest and want vengeance.

"This is for Pat, you bastard."

Sean goes straight back to his club. There is already a rumour circulating about a break from the jail but names are not mentioned. He walks through the gambling area, watches a couple of games of craps at a table before going to his office. He rests back in his chair, enjoys a cigar and a whisky before calling upstairs. Everything went to plan and now he wants to enjoy the moment.

"Mary. Are you free to join me? I'm in the mood to celebrate."

144

Mary O'Shea says she will come. She enjoys her time with Sean and likes to keep him to herself, ever since he first turned up at her boarding house. She tells the girls to carry on as she may be some time. Sean never asks for any of the girls and, on the rare occasion Mary is not available, he is patient until she is. She checks her appearance in the full-length mirror. Keeping her shape. A bit of dye helps retain her tresses. Dabs some perfume on her neck before going down. The working girls smile secretly until she has departed then gossip until fresh customers are sent up.

O'Connor's body is never found and the legend is allowed to grow that Tommy O'Connor has escaped the hangman and is making a new life somewhere, far away to avoid recapture. Possibly even returned to Ireland. His family never suspect otherwise. Sean had made a few phone calls after his arrangement with the warder and, consequently, now has some pull with the precinct plus a share in a taxi business, as well as a valise full of money. He is safe from any comeback from the cops over aiding the escape and has increased his reputation with the community. Sean does not have to worry about questions on Tommy's whereabouts – the newspapers continue to print stories about Tommy and crimes he is supposed to have committed since his escape. The private execution is a well-kept secret, to avoid reprisals from the family and friends. A heavily weighted down corpse lies at the bottom of Lake Michigan.

1922

No 1 in the US charts – "April Showers" by Al Jolson.

Under the Capper-Volstead Act, farmers are allowed to buy and sell as co-operatives, no longer liable to prosecution under anti-trust laws.

Radio emerges as the new medium. Stations erupt all over the States.

Dealing in oil sees a scandal of corruption known as "The Teapot Dome" scandal, when reserves there are leased to Sinclair Oil by Albert Fall, Interior Secretary.

Breaking 100 clay tablets consecutively is a new women's record for sharpshooting, set by Annie Oakley.

Charlie Robertson of Chicago White Sox pitches a perfect game in the defeat of Detroit Tigers April 30), then, two days later, pitches a perfect, no-run game.

George Halas, owner, renames the Charter NFL club the Chicago Bears.

The Cable Act means that an American woman would not lose her citizenship if she marries an alien.

"Don't bother with wine. We have a history of home-produced wine. Anyone who wants wine can either order blocks of dried grape juice, add water then store in a warm dark place for the mix to ferment. Or buy from the back door of churches and synagogues from those priests and rabbis who sell the excess communion wine that isn't banned. The big money is in beer and spirits."

Anon

In 1900, Illinois had been the fourth largest wine producing state in the United States, not counting the domestic wine-making on the numerous farms that didn't have vineyards. When the Volstead Act was passed, sacramental wine was excused prohibition so that churches and synagogues could give communion. Vineyards in the state turned to providing that and table grapes as well as grape juice. A number of vineyards have been uprooted and ploughed over to grow corn and soybean.

"O thou invisible spirit of wine, if thou has no name to be known by, let us call thee devil."

William Shakespeare, Cassio in Othello

CHAPTER 20

Illinois

Jesse draws on his cigarette. He is sitting cross-legged on the ridge by the graves, with their new granite headstones. Looking down at the farmyard, he can see Moses and Molly going in and out of the barn, monitoring the stills. He thinks back on the past year, since he had gone to Buck, got permission to make liquor, and where he is now. Wort (a liquid which only needed yeast to become beer) is legally obtained and he has a reasonable beer production. Beer now retails at three times the pre-Volstead act and nor does he have any taxes to pay on it. He distils alcohol without dangerous additives such as industrial alcohol has, deliberately tainted by the authorities and often the cause of death or blindness in bathtub gin. Hakerman gin, branded as Illinois Water, is known for the purity and quality of the product by his customers. Molly has turned out to be a genius at the distilling and blending, experimenting with various botanicals and creating different classes of gin. The McGregors have added more exotic ingredients to their stock to supply the new demand. To offset variance of quality, due to the differences of ingredients, age, purity, storage effects, Molly blends and makes a more consistent gin for general consumption, while keeping some aside for higher retail due their particular flavour and demand by discerning customers.

The farm has picked up since he is able to pay for hands, providing work for those who stood by him and extra labour from those willing to work but who found it tough to get employment in hard times. He is earning better than before from the legitimate farming, from investment in improved methods and not having to find the mortgage repayments from that income. At the beginning, the Bank eased on pressure for the mortgage (due to the manager being a good customer and wise enough to know that a paid mortgage is better than a bankrupt farm) and he is now making regular payments and clearing the debt is in sight. Taking care not to quickly have a big balance in his account, Jesse buys with cash whenever he can and is stacking money, securely hidden in the farmhouse, for emergencies.

He'd paid the McGregors pretty quickly for his equipment and bought more with cash to increase production. As promised to the sheriff, his benevolence extended to the town. The wooden tower of the church has been repaired after a lightning strike and the school has some new readers. Early in the summer, he'd paid for the community picnic outright. Buying locally as much as possible increases the prosperity of the town and its folks. It also makes it less likely someone will inform the state authorities and have the golden goose served for dinner. All in all, the money just circulates around locally, everyone benefiting.

With increased production, making more than is needed locally, he is supplying liquor to a few neighbouring towns, with a careful eye on which towns are more strictly policed and which turn a blind eye to a domestic service. It is a direct to customer service with no middleman, although some customers do sell on, unknown to Jesse. The range is limited and Jesse gives consideration to starting a co-operative with other farmers, each to specialise, having already outsourced some beer production.

Farmers had already been in home brewing – it dates back to the early colonists and is a long tradition. Jesse is just able to offer to rent them better equipment for bigger production, another form of income, and trains them to produce high quality goods. The concern is losing control, as it is still his intention to wind up once economic conditions improve. The idea of a Farmers Co-operative is appealing – sharing equipment that is too expensive for one farm to buy, investing in improvements to larger, healthier crops, breeding of cattle. Where once people came together for barnraising, they could come together for the whole business of farming. He remembers his father's desire to own a mechanical tractor but which he couldn't afford. Many such farmers exist, trapped by their lack of prosperity into a hard life of grind.

What Jesse is not aware of, other eyes are looking at his town.

A company clerk in the state capital has noticed an unusual increase in certain goods being bought into the town. Top of the list are glass bottles. Other items that catch his attention are sugar and imported fruits. He makes a note and passes it to his superior who then passes it on to the state government offices. The information slowly passes through an apathetic bureaucracy.

Other eyes belong to an Irish gangster in Chicago called Sean O'Leary.

CHAPTER 21

Jerry Osborne is a travelling sales representative for a pharmaceutical company, sometimes referred to as a drummer – someone who drums up trade - from the old days of selling off the back of a wagon and a drummer beating the skin to get attention.

He loves his job. Setting out from the big city, travelling round the midwest. The job provides a car, true it is a Model T and not something grander, but he wouldn't have been able to afford an auto any other way.

Unmarried, he has no ties. As long as he makes sales, he is a free man to do what he wants. In some of the towns, he has girlfriends, each unknown to others and each hoping for a ring on the third finger. His method is not to go for "lookers", girls who can pick and choose boyfriends, but the plainer type, grateful for the attention of a smooth talker who brings them gifts and woos them. It saves him hotel bills, although he would still submit expenses, and it often provides sex sooner or later. Jerry is not conventionally handsome but he dresses smartly, uses cologne and is a charmer.

As a successful drummer, his method is to befriend the customer. Sometimes that would be a toy for a child, brought from Chicago. Sometimes telling risqué stories. Sometimes, since Prohibition, pulling a bottle of whiskey from his valise and going into the back room with the store owner.

Today, he is dealing with the Pharmacy store owner in Buck's town. Fred White is a "whiskey" client – one who has a glass or two with Jerry as they do business. In the backroom, Jerry pulls out a bottle of bootleg import from Chicago, expecting a bigger response than usual but Fred surprises him. With the world's biggest grin, Fred pulls his own bottle out. "Try this."

Jerry does try it and is impressed. The gin is drinkable neat and has a clean palate with a light herby, citrusy fragrance. Molly has long since mastered gin-making.

"Where DID you get this, Fred? This is the best I've ever drunk."

Fred preened. "I've got contacts."

"Any chance of buying some?" Jerry is keen to get a supply. He knows a big profit margin when he sees one.

"Not supposed to sell on, Jerry. I'll let you have a bottle to take away for yourself."

"Fred. I think we can do a deal. How about an extra case of ladies' products on the next delivery, not invoiced? Tell me how much you'd want for six bottles?"

Fred White is a businessman and likes to do deals.

*   *   *

Back in Chicago, Jerry stops by the office to drop off the orders.

He'd had less than usual trade on his tour of customers and his commission would be way low this month. The usual adjustment will be to add a few extras to his expenses claim but it won't be enough for his current needs. He is therefore a very frightened man when he walks back to his car to see Ape leaning on it.

"Hi, Jerry. Need a word."

Ape, real name Mickey O'Donnell, gets his nickname for obvious reasons, other than he is a gorilla for the Irish mob. He been monikered Ape immediately he'd walked into a saloon owned by Sean O'Leary. When muscle and not brains is needed - "Send for the ape," shortened after a while to "Send for Ape."

Ape is only about five six tall but wide. His arms are longer than average, giving him a long swinging motion as he walks. Added to which, he is hairy. Not overgrown hair, mind, just lots of it. Sticking out of his shirt collar, front and back. Hirsute forearms when his sleeves are rolled up, not something that anyone wants to see if they owe money, because it signals a precursor to a beating.

Jerry owes money.

"You owe a couple of Cs. Boss says, you ain't got it, I can break a leg."

"Hey, Ape, I mean Mickey. I'm a bit short right now. Give me a week or two and I'll have it all."

"Right or left?"

"What?"

"Which leg? Right or left?"

"No, Mickey, hang on. Let's not be hasty. Look, I've got a case of gin in the trunk, six bottles of good stuff. Take it to Lucky. Knock it off the bill and give me some time to raise the dough for whatever is left."

Jerry is almost crying at this stage. He'd had a losing streak and borrowed to bet further, believing his luck would change. It doesn't, and the interest on the loan has rocketed up.

A car pulls up alongside and Ape's partner calls over.

"What's taking so long? Get the cash or break his leg. I've got a girl waiting at Mary's place."

"Says he hasn't got the money but he's giving up a case of gin for now."

Fortunately, Ape's partner has some brains; it helps to have some level of IQ to back up Ape from making mistakes.

"OK. Put it in the trunk. We'll drop it off with the boss then I'm away for my good night."

Ape smiles at Jerry. "Looks like you bought yourself some time."

Jerry collapses against the side of his auto in relief while Ape takes the case of gin from the trunk. He's lost his booze but he's saved his leg. At the same time, he hopes Lucky would be generous on the debt reduction for the value of six good bottles. He'll buy more on his next trip. Maybe he can phone an order to Fred White for twelve bottles to be ready when he comes. The idea cheers him up a bit.

155

Ape and partner drive off. One disappointed to be denied his bit of violence, the other keen to get some action. But they get their priorities right and make certain Lucky gets the gin and will know they brought it in.

CHAPTER 22

Southside Fizz
1 oz lime juice
2 oz dry gin
1 oz simple syrup
8 mint leaves
club soda

Lucky O'Leary meets regularly with his accountant, Harold Harvey, plays a game or two of chess and looks at the figures. He'd learned to play in a British prison and took to the boardgame for its ruthlessness and finesse. At the moment, he is two pawns and a bishop up. The game does not interrupt business and Harvey breaks some disturbing news.

"Our booze sales are going down. We're not maintaining the right stock levels and some of the stuff coming in is bad. Bad enough to lose customers. That affects the gambling and the girls in the bars as customer flow is falling."

"I've been hijacked a bit too often. I think someone is snitching to the other gangs."

"What so you plan to do? Check."

"Knight takes rook. I'll have the boys look into it."

"Knight takes knight. I do have some interesting news."

"Queen takes knight, Check. What's that?"

"Mate in three, I think. The game is yours. Ape is doing collections and this drummer handed over a case of six bottles of gin as a deposit against his debts."

"So? You should have castled earlier."

"I've got the bottles here. We should try some."

Harvey fetches a bottle of Illinois Water and two glasses. Pouring a measure into each glass, they both hold the glasses up to the light and can see the clarity. Next, they sniff the bouquet. Sean's eyebrows rise. It only takes couple of sniffs to realise this is a quality product. Sean speaks with a gleam in his eyes. "Where do these come from?"

"That's what you have to find out. If we can get a regular supply of this quality, we can get the business running at its old levels."

Sean knows who to choose for the task.

Paddy and Spud work best as a team. Like an old married couple they each know what the other is thinking and can even finish one another's sentences. They met at a Dublin police station where they were attending for birching, the verdict of the court for burglary (Paddy) and affray (Spud) as they were minors and not liable for prison. They had taken their turns on the birching table while a burly sergeant vigorously applied the birch rods then they had gone off to steal some beer and swap stories.

Patrick "Paddy" Callaghan and Donal "Spud" Murphy love America. Since stepping off the ship in New York with the hundreds of other immigrants, they set out to make money by any means. Not for them the hard labour often taken up by the majority of new arrivals. When New York got a bit too hot for them – they'd robbed the wrong guy – they moved west to Chicago. Burglaries and muggings are their trade, which got them noticed by the Irish mob boss, Sean "Lucky" O'Leary. Instead of having them beaten up as a warning, he recognised a ruthlessness in them that he could use. They are soon picking up Protection money from the small businesses of the neighbourhood, bodyguarding the bookies, and collecting debts or dishing out "spankings" to slow payers.

Sean is in a meeting with Alderman McAvoy. The fat politician is comfortably occupying an easy chair, his waistcoat buttons struggling over his stomach. One of the girls from upstairs is perched on the arm of his chair and caresses his neck, while he absent-mindedly strokes her thigh with the hand that isn't holding a crystal glass of genuine single malt Scotch.

"Mac. I backed your campaign to be Alderman and keep you in post but I'm not seeing a lot coming back to me from the deal." Sean wants the politician to know he isn't happy.

"Now, Sean, that's not true. There's a lot hidden from public scrutiny that I do for you. I have to be a lot cleverer at the moment. It's not like it is, when I could ride around in your car like when Padraig passed. You're still getting your permits and advance notice of raids." He squeezes the girl's thigh and doesn't notice or doesn't car she winces, knowing there'll be bruises by morning.

"I'm being squeezed, Mac. My shipments are getting hijacked. The Italians don't seem to be suffering in the same way. Why aren't you hitting their speakeasies?" Narrows his eyes.

"It's not that simple, Lucky. They pay for "service" too. They have other aldermen in their pocket and police captains too. I have to tread softly or we'll have a civil war. Now let me do my job and I'll sort things out. Meantime, you remember my son, Mikey. He's been home out of the army for a while now and needs a job. If you can find something for him to do, I'd be grateful. Put him on the payroll. When he's a bit older, I'll get him into politics and he'll be a useful friend to have. Mikey, step forward and say hi to Mr O'Leary."

A younger, equally as chubby, version of the Alderman had been standing back until now, waiting for this moment. "Mr O'Leary. A pleasure to meet you."

"OK, kid." Just then Paddy and Spud arrive, stepping into the room without knocking, in response to a summons delivered care of Dougal. "Come in, boys. You know the Alderman."

Paddy and Spud nod to the politician. "And this is Mikey, the Alderman's son. He's working for me now. I'll expect you to show him around and then follow his instructions about business. Meanwhile, there's a job for you, out of town."

If Sean notices the look between Paddy and Spud over the news that they are to have a new boss, a rookie, because of his father's political clout and Sean's need to have support in City Hall, he doesn't say anything.

Sean continues with a briefing about an unknown supplier in the countryside that he needs them to investigate. "Ape brought me some gin that he took off a drummer. It's good stuff, very good. I need to know the source and whether I can tap it. Go and see him for details of who this guy is and where he gets his supply. Follow it up but be careful. If it's another gang's supply I can't afford to upset anyone at the moment. If it's a new line, I don't want anyone else getting there first."

Paddy and Spud nod in synchronised harmony. "Got it. By the way, we've found who's selling us out on the truck runs."

"Oh, yeah. Let Razor deal with him as a lesson to anyone else thinking they can cheat on me."

Razor Nicolae is a Romanian immigrant who works for Sean. His speciality is to take people out with a cutthroat razor – silent, deadly, lots of blood. It sends a specific message. The driver of the smuggling trucks that have been hijacked was careless enough to sell the route and dates to one of the Italian gangs. They'd stop him in the countryside, beat up his co-driver and smack him just enough to look convincing that it is a legit hijack. Unfortunately, greed is too much for him and his truck runs stand out as the one hit more often than not. Harold Harvey has pointed out the statistical incongruity to Sean, who earlier sent Paddy and Spud to investigate. They'd followed the driver and seen him talking to a guy from the Genna brothers' gang. Now he will pay the ultimate price of a traitor.

Leaving a bar, the evening Sean has given the word for a hit, the driver is stopped by a voice in a doorway. "Hey, buddy. Got a light?"

That turns him enough to expose his neck to a sweep of Razor's blade. It is done so neatly and fast that he has no time to react. A spray of blood from the carotid artery shoots up and out over the street and he falls to ground, dying in seconds, long enough to see his killer and understand why. Razor pats down his pockets and relieves him of his cash, discarding a watch as too cheap to be worth anything. He leaves the body as a warning of what happens to those who cheat Sean O'Leary and walks away whistling.

Paddy and Spud drive over to Ape's lodgings in a more ethnically mixed suburb. The Polish landlady lets them in and they wait for Ape to finish his shower. His room surprises them by its neatness and a collection of framed butterflies pinned to a card. Ape breaks their perusal when he walks into the room, naked, water glistening on the hair of his body so that Spud makes a gagging gesture of finger in

162

throat behind his back and Paddy has to suppress a smile. As he dries on an old discoloured towel, the enforcer fills Paddy and Spud in on the details of Jerry.

"Yeah. The guy is rep for the Jew firm in west side. Goes on the road around the state taking orders. We waited for him to come back to town so we could get him to pay his markers. He'll be there today because we warned him not to leave town without Lucky's answer."

Ape gives them the address and directions he'd written down in expectation of their visit. Glad to leave and not witness any more of Ape's nudity, they drive over to the wholesale company and park up in the street where they can see who comes and goes.

Spud offers Paddy some chewing-gum. "Did you hear about Joey One-Ear?"

"No. What's he been up to now?"

"He found out the guy who services his wife's car has been servicing her."

"There's a queue round the block for a piece of that ass. Anyway, what happened?"

"Joey went to the guy's workshop, stuck a gun in his face and made him get naked. Then he puts the guy's pecker in a vice, tightens it up and throws away the key. The guy's shittin' himself. Joey only goes and gets a hacksaw from the guy's bench."

"Fuck me. What'd he do?" Paddy's imagination is filling in the prospects.

"The guy's saying 'Oh my God. Oh my God. You're not going to cut it off, are you?' Joey hands him the hacksaw and says, "Nah, you're going to cut it off. I'm going to set fire to the shop.""

"Does he?"

"Nah. The guy gets the message. Be careful where you put your dick."

Laughing loudly, Paddy notices a car turn into the street. "This could be him."

They wait and watch as the car pulls into the kerb and the driver gets out.

"That looks like our guy. Pretty much as Ape described him."

Paddy is quickly out of their car and walking down the street, calling out when within twenty feet. "Hey! Jerry?"

The drummer turns, not recognising who calls him by name. "Yeah. What do you want?"

Paying more attention, Jerry realises pretty soon what type of person Paddy is and his likely role in the next few minutes. Spud has seen the exchange and pulls up alongside in the car.

"Get in. We'd like a private word with you."

Jerry gets into the back seat and Paddy sits next to him. Surely they aren't going to kill him over a debt. This is how it happens. Get a man in the car, shoot from close range, drive and dump the body somewhere.

"Relax, Jerry. Lucky sent us. He likes your gin. He wants to know where you get it, that's all."

Jerry breathes a sigh of relief. He names the town and how he sells to the Pharmacist there.

"His name is Fred White. He let me have the gin for a deal on stock. I don't know where he gets it from, honestly."

"A pharmacist. Could he be making it?"

"Guys, honestly, I don't know. You'd have to ask him."

"We will. Keep your mouth shut. If we find out you tipped him off that we're coming, you'll be taking a swim in the bay."

"No. No, I won't say a word."

Paddy opens the door of the car, getting out and pulling Jerry behind him, leaving him on the sidewalk before getting into the front seat. Spud starts to pull away then stops.

Paddy looks back at Jerry. "By the way. You still owe Lucky two Cs. The gin just bought you time to pay."

Jerry realises he has had an accident and needs to change his trousers.

Back behind the Ace of Clubs, Paddy and Spud load their car to set out the following morning early. The route will also take them past some of the businesses that are due to pay protection plus a couple of bookies have takings to collect. They can do that and arrive in the town at lunchtime. Sean comes out to see them off.

"Ready? I need you to swing by Slick Harry's in particular and pick up the takings from today's action. He's had a good day and I don't want the money sitting there for too long. Don't stir things up in that town. Find out whether any other mob is on the scene. I haven't heard anything but it might be early days. If you learn the source, check it out and contact me. This could be the answer to the hijackings of our Canada route. Now, get out of here."

Paddy and Spud twin nod, climb in the car and drive away to get an early night before starting off in the morning

Under his breath, Sean speaks, "Don't let me down, boys."

As he turns away to re-enter the club, through the open yard gates Sean sees a black auto slow down and the driver and passenger take a long look in. "Fucking wops. You bastards!"

The driver gives Sean a middle finger salute and laughs before driving off.

Paddy and Spud make an early start the following day as planned. Following Sean's instructions, on the way they stop at Slick Harry's, a bookmaking operation above a cobbler's in the suburbs, a popular place with the workforce at the Hawthorn factory who like a flutter on the horses.

Slick Harry is waiting. "Hi, guys. Lucky phoned to say you'd be collecting. I'll be glad to get this out of here," handing over a fat valise full of cash. "Favourite failed and we cleaned up."

Paddy throws the valise into the trunk alongside the tommy-gun he'd packed just in case.

"Tell Lucky we've collected and will phone him later."

Slick Harry shakes hands with Paddy and nods to Spud in the driving seat. "OK. Have a safe journey wherever you're going."

Getting in the auto, Paddy tips his hat down over his face, lays back in his seat to catch a nap while Spud drives the two-hour trip. A trip out into the countryside will be a nice change.

CHAPTER 23
Illinois

Buck goes over to have his lunch at Sid's Diner. Sid keeps a clean establishment, big open windows to let light in. He'd tried little cafeteria curtains to add a bit of class (on the advice of his wife) but found the patrons don't like them, preferring to be able to gaze out at the street and keep an eye on the comings and goings. Since the war, he'd remodelled the layout as more families visited to eat. Tables are spaced at the front and booths down the side, in an L-shaped customer area. The counter faces the door, a bottle of lollipops on it for children who eat all their dinner, and a bottle of tobacco plugs purely for a couple of longstanding customers who like to chew tobacco post-dining. Customers can get quick and easy food, or a bowl of chilli from the pot that is always bubbling.

Today there are only two other customers in the Diner as lunchtime trade is nearly over. A couple of old men, Charlie and Bert, play checkers while they eat apple pie sitting at a table by the window. Sid never hassles them for their small orders or the inordinate amount of time they take to eat. They provide atmosphere and encourage customers who might not like to enter an empty establishment. Charlie looks up as Buck comes in. "Hey, Buck. Tell Bert about Wyatt and the kid."

"That old tale. You must have heard it a hundred times."

"Yeah. But it gets better with each telling."

While Sid prepares his lunch, Buck accommodates the old-timers.

"I was a young deputy and a kid comes into town, all dressed fancy, fast-draw rig. Wyatt has a 'no guns in town' policy so I have to ask him for his. The kid stands square, I was hardly older than him, and says 'no one's taking my guns' and he pulls to show how fast he is then twirls it round his finger. Wyatt has come up behind him and speaks gently. 'Hey, kid. Mighty impressive. But you need to file down the hammer so it doesn't catch. Same with the foresight – file it real smooth. Then dip the gun in plenty of hog-grease so it's nice and slick'. The kid answers back. 'Will that make it a faster draw?' 'No,' said Wyatt, 'but it won't hurt so much when I take it off you and shove it up your ass'. The kid sees the look in Wyatt's eyes and unbuckles his belt and hands it over."

Leaving Charlie and Bert chuckling, Buck takes his meal to his favourite booth at the back. He always sits in a booth at the back, for peace and quiet; he doesn't like to be disturbed while he eats, which is a serious business for which chitchat is not encouraged. He could also sit behind the newspaper and catch up on events.

The clack of counters the only noise until the door chime rings as it is opened, announcing fresh customers to Sid, who looks up from his paper and the sports results.

169

"Howdy, gents. What can I get you?"

Paddy answers for both of them. "We'll take coffee and blueberry pancakes."

"Coming right up".

The checker players look the newcomers over – strangers in town, a couple of youths but with a swagger. They don't look like the usual passers-through. A bit too sharply dressed for drummers, and overdressed for tourists, not that tourism is a thing here but occasionally some come into town, on the way for somewhere else. The game is more important and they concentrate back on the board; this is a long-standing rivalry and the game is taken very seriously.

Having looked over the checkers players, Spud and Paddy sit at the counter and have a pretend conversation in louder than usual voices. "It'd be nice to have a real drink. Guy gets a thirst on the road in this weather." "I'd give anything for a long cold beer and a whiskey chaser."

Sid's hand shakes as he pours their coffee, spilling some on the counter.

"You OK, buddy?" asks Spud. "You wouldn't have some good stuff under the counter, would you?"

"No sir. We've coffee and we've sodas. I can get you a bottle from the ice bucket."

Paddy gives him the long stare and puts twenty dollars on the counter.

"No, sir. We'd like big boy drinks, if you catch my drift."

Sid stiffens up. "This is a dry town, gentlemen. It's been a while since we had any liquor in town."

Spud stands stiffly tall to speak. "That ain't what we hear. We hear this is a town to come to if you want the hard stuff."

Sid swallows, his Adam's apple bobs in his scrawny neck. "I'm afraid you've been misled. Wish I could help but, as I said, coffee and soda. Same everywhere."

Paddy now stands, his height domineering the shorter Sid. "I don't believe you're telling us the truth. Do you need some help remembering?"

A voice from the back of the room. Unnoticed until now, Buck has stood and taken a stance.

"Sid's telling you true. Looks like a wasted journey. Why not finish your coffee, have your pancakes to go, and go?"

Paddy hesitates. Buck might be an older man, but he stands tall, the badge on his shirt shines, and his hands rest on his belt, the right not far from the gun on his hip. Trouble with the Law is the last thing they needed. Lucky has said softly-softly until they know more.

"Sorry. No offence. Guy just gets a hankering and we thought we might be lucky, between friends so to speak," then to Sid, "Keep the twenty. Don't worry about the pancakes."

The two mobsters leave the Diner, walk down the road to a shiny auto. Buck watches from the window, alongside Sid.

Sid draws a breath. "This ain't good."

"Sid. You never spoke a truer word." Buck's eyes have narrowed as he watches the two Irishmen drive off.

*   *   *

Paddy and Spud drive out of town and park up to wait until evening. They had tried the Diner as more accessible to their cover as travelling through town on the way to somewhere else, but the interference from the local law had scuppered that. Now they plan to return and wait for Fred White to close the Pharmacy then kidnap him. Overstepping a bit but they make the decision they can't go back to Lucky without a result. Following up on the initial contact when he first proffered up the gin, Jerry has told them everything he knew. The Pharmacist is the one true link to the source of the gin.

Before they left Chicago, Lucky had given them their instructions.

"Walk carefully. We don't know who's behind this. My ears on the ground have heard nothing so we don't know if it's a new gang or the Italians working a secret supply. We can't afford a war but if we can get our hands on a more local supply of good stuff, we won't suffer the hijacks and payoffs."

Their criminal senses have not detected any sign of competition from other mobs and they grow confident that the move on the Pharmacist lacks risk of retaliation. Knowing Lucky can't protect them if a contract goes out for interfering with a rival operation, they had taken

172

a look around the town. Any sign of other mobsters would have flashed danger signs. The current market, with huge expenses and dropping profits, means Lucky can't hire the guns to defend his territory against the increasingly more powerful Italians. He would have to find allies among the Irish gangs but he would have to cut them in on his businesses and some of them might prefer a total takeover. All they have seen is a frightened Diner owner and one lawman.

Spud tries to catch some sleep while they wait but Paddy is in one of his talkative moods.

"Did you know Wyatt Earp was born in Illinois?"

Spud pushes his hat up from where he had covered his eyes to block out the light.

"I thought he was from Tombstone."

"Nah. That was the OK corral gunfight. Wyatt and his brother Virgil and Doc Holliday went up against the Clanton gang and gunned them down. Wyatt Earp was never wounded in all the gunfights he had. He lives in California now. I gotta go out there and see him."

"So you keep saying. Maybe when we've made enough money, we can both go."

They let the time pass in silence.

As the sun sinks to the horizon, Paddy checks his watch. "Time to go. We'll pick him up as he leaves. Let him lock up first."

A slow drive into town. Their new Packard would stand out among the Fords and horsedrawn vehicles if anyone is about but they are fortunate in that most of the businesses have already closed and Tom Buckley has done his tour and is on his way home, the other side of town.

A casual drive down Main Street and past the Pharmacy sees Fred White drawing down the blinds. The Irishmen pull in along the street and wait. Unaware of his immediate future, Fred is on routine – putting the cash register tray in the safe, checking that the back door is locked, pulling down the blinds. Eventually, Fred and his female assistant come out, Fred carefully locking his doors, saying goodbye and the two go in opposite directions, a stroke of fortune for Paddy and Spud, who thought they might have to abort when two came out the shop. Spud has earlier stepped out of the car and is waiting on the pavement. Had Fred White walked in the opposite direction, Paddy was ready.

Spud acts the innocent bystander as Fred approaches. "Hey, mister! Got a light?"

Fred slows, reaching into a pocket as an automatic reflex to a harmless common request. Paddy, having driven carefully down and pulled up, now reaches through the open door on the Packard, grabbing Fred and Spud assists by pushing the pharmacist inside. Before he can call out, Spud has a Colt 1911 in his face and, to Fred, the barrel looks as big as the Civil War cannon outside the Town Hall.

Paddy does not drive off in a rush. He pulls out as a normal driver would, smoothly and without drama, heading off to the outskirts. The

174

freight yards, businesses closed, previously scouted, provide the quiet spot they need. The yards are a system of railtracks and storage facilities, unstaffed at night. Railcars are parked up, able to be loaded with grain or cattle from the farms and for the through train to stop only long enough to couple up and continue its journey. Situated at the end of a road from the town, they'd be no through traffic that might disturb them.

Since burgling the house of an American businessman in Ireland and finding his son's Wild West Weekly comics and some western dime novels by Zane Grey, Paddy has become obsessed with cowboys and Jim Bowie in particular. After landing in America, as soon as he could he'd bought a large hunting knife to be like one of his heroes. Bowie had become famous as a knife fighter after what was called The Sandbar Fight. Paddy has read a fictionalised account in a dime novel, although the truth does not need much rewriting. Bowie was wounded several times, including a pistol broken over his head, gunshot wound and stabbing by the swordstick of Sheriff Norris Wright. Despite all his injuries, Bowie managed to disembowel Wright with his knife and would recover, only to die years later at The Alamo.

The Packard pulls into a yard, behind a shed for cover just in case anyone is about. The two mobsters pull a confused Fred White out of the car. He'd assumed he was to be robbed but could not understand the drive here and what might happen next. Pushed up against a wall, he faces questioning.

"You are supplying gin. Where'd you get it?"

Fred gets an inkling of what is behind the kidnapping but he stalls for time. "What? I don't know what you mean?"

Paddy doubles the older man over with a punch to the stomach, causing Fred to fall to his knees gasping for breath and with the pain.

"Don't mess with us. We know you gave six bottles of gin to Jerry Osborne. Just tell us where you get it?"

Fred is no coward. He takes a beating from Spud, but it is when Paddy threatens with his huge hunting knife – not that big is good but people do respond with fear to it- and starts on a finger amputation that he tells them.

CHAPTER 24

"It looks like a good opening for a lot of smart young men."

Al Capone on the Prohibition Law

The town is prospering. As much as possible, Jesse buys locally and sells locally. Money goes round in a circle but stays with the people of the town and surrounding area.

The McGregors, as sole suppliers of bottles and casks, are making more money than ever before. They even offer to buy used bottles, which they clean and reuse. He might, once, have asked Maggie, their daughter, to be his wife and join him on the farm but now he realises it is right that he has not. She deserves better, someone who will really love her and not someone following an expected path but lacking true passion for what marriage and starting a family should be. Jesse thinks he knows he has yet to find a true partner.

Better weather has made farming more productive and the demand for certain crops plus the franchised booze production has mortgages clearing and the bank taking more deposits and opening savings accounts. Jesse has mechanised to some degree and the equipment is rented out to other farmers as a working co-operative.

Jesse is unaware of the economics of his bootlegging that made his profitable despite lower than Chicago prices. The truth is simple maths. A good still in Chicago can generate $100 000 of monthly revenue after costs of equipment and consumables but, unlike Jesse, the mob pays half of that in bribes. Jesse can keep all his profit as he does not have to pay anyone to look the other way. Buck is clean, only employing Nelson's blind eye. Jesse's equivalent of the bribes is the largesse to the town's funds. One big expenditure is a total renovation to the church, following on from earlier repairs to the steeple. Work is underway and local trades are benefitting.

Meanwhile, no one is thinking how standing out from "the common herd" is attracting attention at State level. Conversations at business dinners in the Capital - "this bank is bucking the trend", "I'm sending 40% of my product to one district", "I'd never heard of this place two years ago" - and the whispered "I'm keeping my cocktail cabinet stocked with good stuff and much cheaper that I can get around here."

Jesse's plan to stay local has been eroded by contact with the wider territory. His booze is sold on by his customers who see they can make a profit as wholesalers, especially as they can double the price paid to Jesse without problems of demand. Jesse has not awoken to the fact that his production is so big and indicates a bigger market than the town and local countryside. Not keeping books, he hasn't realised how much the outsourced production is providing and selling. Molly is selling on casks of neat alcohol, which others can dilute to drinkable standards, and overlooked telling Jesse of the change in their own production.

There are also the Temperance supporters. While not willing to make a public stand, they do write letters to church ministers who, in turn, write to politicians. While many in public office in the cities are taking backhanders and campaigns are being payrolled by the criminals, there are some straight men and women who are concerned.

Buck is thinking it is maybe time to talk to Jesse and ask him whether he could now switch off the production. He's wise enough to know that as the business has grown, it will eventually be impossible to keep a lid on things. Plus he doesn't like the two Irishmen in town asking questions.... and he's yet to hear about Fred White's misadventure.

CHAPTER 25

"When anger rises, think of the consequences."

Confucius

Moses is driving back to the farm, having finished a round of drop-offs late. The number of customers is growing and taking longer and longer to deliver. The business has grown larger and faster than anyone thought it might and times are good. He is looking forward to supper with Molly and a few games of cards after. A pitcher of beer should wash the dust out of his throat. He whistles a popular tune he has heard on the radio, not particularly accurately or tunefully. The darkness is not absolute; it's a clear sky, the sun not long set and stars coming out to join the moon.

Picking a route near the stockyards for a quiet way home, his headlamps illuminate a bundle on the road, first thought an animal run down but which he soon recognises as a human being as he gets closer. Moses quickly pulls over, thinking there has been a motoring accident. He jumps from the cab and hurries over to the body, hearing groans. He is surprised to find Fred White in a bad way, eyes swollen, face blackened with bruises, lip cut and blood down his shirt.

"Mr White. What happened to you?"

But Fred is in no condition to talk and Moses gently lifts him into the cab of his truck and drives as fast as he dares to the town's hospital.

180

Each bump in the road extracting a groan from the pharmacist with broken ribs. The hospital looms in sight at last. It is a small affair; the usual business is maternity and occasional farm accidents that require surgery. Fortunately, the doctor lives in the house next to it and is quick to respond to Moses sounding his horn. He pulls back his curtains and sees the truck, with Moses at the open door helping somebody in a bad way. Without grabbing a coat but picking up his keyring, he rushes outside, calling to his wife to follow.

"My God, Moses. What has happened?"

"It's Mr White. I found him like this on the road from the stockyards."

"A hit and run? Help me get him inside. Come on, Fred, let's get you sorted out. Easy fella." He goes ahead, unlocking the door and switching on lights.

Fred is taken in gently, carried like a babe by Moses. The doctor has been joined by his wife, a trained midwife but who today helps undress Fred so his condition can be checked and wounds cleaned, which she does with the gentle hands that first welcome babies into the world. The doctor has made his examination, tutting and sucking teeth at each new discovery.

"Superficial but nasty. Cuts and broken ribs. Multiple bruises. What happened, Moses?"

"I found him on the road. Couldn't see anyone else. I thought he might have crashed his car but no sign."

"This is not a car crash. Someone did this to him. I'll phone the sheriff."

A moth that has come in through the open door, flits against the overhead light. Its futile dance unnoticed.

Buck is enjoying an evening smoke on his porch, watching fireflies matching the glowing end of his cigarette when Agnes calls him in.

"There's a phone call for you. Fred White has been hurt and is in the hospital."

"Tell them I'm on my way." His brain is computing what might have happened but he is not ready to give space to his thoughts until he knows more. Pausing only to put on a coat and attach his holster and gun, Buck drives to the hospital to see what has happened. On his arrival, he recognises Moses' truck and pulls up alongside. Nothing indicates what he is going to find when he goes inside the hospital. Bucks enters the treatment room, passing Moses waiting and watching anxiously through the doorway, to find the doctor administering painkillers to his patient.

Moses tells the sheriff all he knows. "I was driving near the stockyards. I'd finished a run and was heading home when I saw Mr White in the road. There was no car about and I hadn't passed one for some time."

Buck is incensed at the obvious conclusion Fred White has taken a beating. The only signs of his anger are a tightened jaw and he fidgets with his gun, tugging on it then reseating in its holster, an unconscious movement. He moves closer to the bed to look at Fred. Not a pretty sight, broken nose, eyes just slits in the puffiness of his face and bruises galore, the sort of injuries last seen as a lawman in a cattle town when a cowboy got stomped by a steer. But Fred is determined to speak, pain eased somewhat by the medications.

"Two of them, in a Packard. They had Irish accents."

"Know them, Fred. They were in Sid's Diner earlier in the day."

"They wanted to know who is making the gin, Buck. I had to give Jesse up. They were going to cut my fingers off." Tears roll down Fred's cheeks.

"It's OK, Fred. Take it easy. I'm going to get them." Fists clenched.

The doctor steps forward firmly.

"He needs to rest, Buck. I'm going to give him a sedative and some more pain relief."

"Thanks, Doc. Take care of him. I have work to do."

It is an angry Buck who leaves the hospital. But angry at the mobsters... or angry at himself?

Moses slips away to tell Jesse the news. His instincts tell him a storm is coming.

CHAPTER 26

One has only to fear the things that have the power of hurting others

~ Dante, Inferno

In setting up on the hill at first light, Jesse calls on his training at the Sniping Observation and Scouting school as well as his war experience. He takes great care to have nothing that could reflect sunlight and reveal his position as well as camouflaging his location, which gives him a good view of the farm and the tracks around. Knowing he might be there for some time, he chooses shade under the guardian trees and has some provisions. A little water poured out on the ground in front of the rifle will prevent pop up dust from the wind disturbance from the passage of the bullet as it leaves the barrel. His faithful dog is safely with Moses. The rifle is sighted in for the long distance to the house. He craves a cigarette but knows to light up would be a mistake. Jesse is in his sniper mindset and has switched off all other thoughts. Whether he'll be there minutes or hours is not an issue for him. A bird lands only feet away to grab a worm, oblivious to his presence, not sensing a threat.

Early morning, he watches a dustcloud rising from the ground in the distance, the dry weather laying its power on the dirt road to be stirred up when a vehicle is taking the route from town. A pause in the cloud's movement indicates that the driver has stopped at the side road leading to the farm before it resumes in a direct line to the farm buildings, stopping and settling before the vehicle comes into sight. Whoever the visitors are, they are not driving right up to the house. The Ross telescope that he received at the SOS school and had been used by Tom comes into use. He scans the road and the fields to the side, familiar territory so he is looking for activity. Eventually, he can see two figures furtively approaching his home. He expects two but remains cautious that there may be a third, previously unrevealed, man. Switching to the rifle, Jesse follows their progress with his scope sight, the crosshairs sharing two potential targets.

Paddy and Spud have no idea they are observed. They thought by stopping far enough back and walking the rest of the way they could approach unnoticed. Not rating some hick farmer as a particular danger, except he may have a shotgun for vermin control. Spud has his handgun, a Colt 1911, and Paddy carries a Thompson sub-machine gun, which he only expects to handle as a threat to impress. His pride and joy, massively produced but too late for the Great War, adopted by the gangs for their fearsome fire power, holding either 30 rounds of .45 calibre in a box magazine or 100 in a drum, rounds with the ability to punch through steel plate. Costing half the price of a new Ford automobile, they are also a sign of prestige. Paddy bought his out of the backdoor of a police station, part of a confiscated arsenal which the cops sold back to whoever could afford. Truth is, gangsters are terrible shots and unless up close and personal, rarely make fatal woundings, hence the number of assassinations inside a vehicle with the gun barrel pressed against the victim. Paddy has seen the potential of a weapon that would spray more than a shotgun. Weighing only at most when fully loaded with the drum, a little over 20 lbs it is a weapon that requires a two-handed operation but has a huge psychological advantage over a pistol that the intended target would not stand and draw to return fire but dive for cover. It makes him confident.

The two Irishmen walk cautiously up to the farmhouse; they want the element of surprise. The closed curtains lead them to believe the occupant or occupants are not awake yet. As city boys, they are unaware that farmers rise at dawn to get a day's work in. Paddy stands back a little, for a wider arc of fire if necessary and in case anyone comes from either side. He's not so dumb as to fail to anticipate farmhands. Spud starts to approach the door on tip toe. The plan is to overpower the farmer then persuade him to supply the Ace of Clubs. Impress Lucky with their work. They want the kudos now they feel downgraded by the recruitment of MacAvoy.

As a right-hander, Jesse has set up his quick double shot to be a span of right to left, assuming the gangsters are not too far apart. The crosshairs centre on Spud's back. Jesse knows the distance. No wind.

No heat of day to compensate for as it is still early. Just make the allowance for the drop and distance. Heart rate low. Total focus. Release breath and hold. Gently squeeze the trigger.

Spud falls forward, dead before he hits the ground, hit centre of his back, through the spine.

Jesse swiftly reloads and pivots the rifle before the bullet has reached Spud and has Paddy in the sights. Pulls the trigger and watches Paddy go down. Both men on the ground, neither moving, Jesse decides he doesn't need a second shot into either body. Unlike France, he will have to see the men he shot close up. He knows he'll have to bury the bodies on the farm. The pickup had been parked on the far side of the hill, so as not to be visible and he runs to it now. A fast and bumpy drive down to the farmhouse, dry mouthed and his pulse pumping hard. His first civilian kills and a gap of years from combat. Training is all well and good for the discipline but not the emotions.

In front of the farmhouse there is only one body – Spud's – and a Thompson sub-machine gun with a bullet in the wooden butt. Paddy had turned on hearing the first shot, raising his weapon to fire and it stopped the second bullet. He has not got off scot-free though. The bullet has been blocked by the butt but the force has driven the gun into his ribs and he suspects he may have cracked one. He was lucky enough not to have moved while Jesse was watching, alerting the latter that his target had survived. While Jesse was running to his truck then driving down, he'd recovered enough to crawl off. Having moved into shelter he sees Jesse arrive in the pickup and notes he gets out, leaving his rifle in the cab, and has no gun in hand or belt. Paddy will mourn Spud later. This is life and death now and he has to eliminate the threat.

Jesse is dismayed by only seeing one body and that slows his initial reaction as Paddy bursts from cover, holding his big hunting knife. Paddy slashes the air, forcing Jesse back to the pickup. Then, to Paddy's surprise, Jesse jumps forward and with a leg sweep puts him on the ground; the ju-jitsu training from the Brits at the SOS school has not been wasted. But Paddy is not beaten. Despite the pain from his rib, he knows his survival depends on getting up. He throws a handful of dirt and dust at Jesse and, while Jesse protects his eyes and pauses, Paddy is able to regain his feet. Jesse immediately grips the wrist of the knifehand with his left hand, while his opponent grasps his right, preventing him punching. It becomes a battle of strength which Paddy looks likes winning, using his height and weight advantage. Jesse might be hardened by farm work but Paddy keeps his fitness in the boxing gyms. High School and College wrestling is nothing like fighting for one's life, especially when there are no rules and the opponent is an experienced streetfighter and very angry. The blade is getting nearer Jesse's throat, the honed edge could cut the carotid artery without resistance. There is no time to regret not taking the confirming second shot; it wasn't something he was taught to do in France. The men are locked hand-to-hand and the Bowie style knife adds inches to Paddy's reach. Sunlight flashes off the blade, increasing its sense of menace. Sweat is stinging Jesse's eyes and the Irishman gets the hint of smile as feels he is gaining the upper hand, Suddenly, a furry blur runs in and sinks its teeth into his leg. A ferocious bite and the dog grips and pulls. As Paddy loses his balance from this new attack, Jesse is able to turn the knifehand and the blade away from himself. Paddy had already lost his footing at the unexpected intervention and falls with Jesse on top of him, pushing the knife into his chest and piercing his heart.

"Mister Jesse. Are you OK?" Moses has returned with the dog and his shotgun in time to see the last act. Moses has the composure while Jesse is in shock. "We need to move these two. I'll use the pickup and bury them below the creek in the rough ground. I'll use some of the lye we have. That will speed up the decomposition."

Jesse nods. The adrenaline is coursing through his veins and he slows his breathing down to get back control. "Thanks, Moses." He regains control of himself. "Let me search them first. There may be something to tell us who they are."

Moses has part of the answer. "Sheriff Buckley told me of two Irish guys in town. Look like these two here."

Pockets only reveal a fat billfold, cigarettes, and a lighter. There is nothing to identify them, give them names or say where they are from. Jesse is unhappy at the mystery, although if he has to guess, he reckons

Chicago.

"I'll go back down the track and find their car. Moses, can you manage here?"

Moses is already lifting the bodies on to the pickup and grins. Jesse lifts the Thompson. Apart from the bullet in the butt, it seems OK. He'll take it with him in case someone is waiting at the car. Moses sticks Spud's Colt 1911 in his waistband, having examined it and decided it is too good a gun to waste.

* * *

Jesse crosses the field rather than approach the car by the track. He hunkers down in the crops to check out the ground ahead, more of his sniper training at play, back in control of himself. Look and listen. Remain invisible yourself. No unusual sounds come to his ears. Downwind from the auto, no smells – body or cigarette coming at him on the wind. No smoke rising from a smoked cigarette. No signal from the local wildlife of human presence. Moses has only mentioned two guys in town, but always the chance of a third.

He waits a full ten minutes before approaching the car cautiously. It would be hard for a person to stay silent and still unless they know to hide. Had the two gunshots alerted them, they would have considered them to be their two companions firing. Finally satisfied it has only been the two gunmen, Jesse starts the Packard and drives it down the

190

track to the farmhouse. Moses has already left in the pickup and the only sign of disturbance is some blood in the dirt, which Jesse kicks about and hides.

While he waits for Moses to return, he examines the auto thoroughly. Under the seats he finds compartments that he, rightly, assumes are for smuggling purposes. In the trunk, is a bag of money and receipts. He wouldn't be aware, but Paddy and Spud had made a collection of bookmaking cash before heading out of Chicago and had not had time to bank it with the accountant. There is a lot of money there. Adding to his new arsenal, Jesse finds two drums and two stick magazines of ammunition for the Thompson and an unopened box of cartridges for the Colt.

Jesse realises he has to hide the Packard; it is far too noticeable and would tie him to the gunmen if seen. One of the farm outbuildings has ceased to be of use and is waiting repairs. It will be ideal for the purpose. For the moment, parking as far in as it will go, Jesse plans to return with Moses and cover it with a tarpaulin then hay. Walking back to the house, he checks for tyre tracks and is satisfied that, on the dry ground, he'd left none that wouldn't be soon gone in a breeze. Broken stems of grass are not that noticeable and flattened grasses and weeds would soon stand again. It will serve for the moment, while he ponders what to do and what might happen when the two mobsters do not return to Chicago. Things have now taken a turn for the worse and Jesse has never expected this problem.

As soon as Moses returns, the two of them do cover the Packard in the old, derelict barn. Having cancelled the workers for the day, he wants no signs of trouble or visitors when they return tomorrow. Now walking back to the farmhouse, Jesse can hear a car coming down the track and not yet in view. He signals Moses to take the Thompson and hide himself in a good shooting position, while he takes the Colt 1911 and sticks it in his belt at his back. Heck, what if the mobsters have back-up and they are now rolling in, assuming the takeover has gone down successfully. It is with great relief when he identifies Buck's coupe, then a hint of panic as to why the sheriff is coming.

Buck pulls up in front of the farmhouse. He isn't quite sure about Jesse standing in the middle of the track, expecting, well, he doesn't know what he expects.

"Sir. What brings you out here?"

Buck looks around as he answers, querying with his eyes. "Did Moses tell you about Fred White?"

Jesse shuffles straight, as a schoolboy might when caught misbehaving. "Yessir, he did. It's terrible."

Buck turns round slowly. His instincts are sending signals that all is not normal. Turning back to face Jesse, he asks with deliberation, "Any visitors, Jesse?"

"No, sir."

"Put some coffee on, Jesse. We need to talk."

192

CHAPTER 27

Chicago

"Wheresoever you go, go with all your heart."

Confucius

Sean O'Leary is concerned that Paddy and Spud haven't returned. One phone call late at night to Dougal to say they'd identified the source and it is not gang owned, then nothing. They are supposed to take a look then head back with the intelligence so he could decide what to do next.

"Mac," he says to the barman. "Let me know the minute Paddy or Spud turn up or phone."

The silence is not like the boys and he feels a niggling itch of worry. If the town were closer, he'd drive down himself to investigate but he needs to be on site to deal with the increasing problems. His stocks are dwindling. Smuggled shipments are being intercepted – the police, the competition – and it is knocking trade so that customers are drifting to other speakeasies. Every so often, to make headlines and look as if something is being done to defeat crime, the Chicago illegal distilleries are raided and closed down. Federal agents and police pose for the cameras, taking axes to barrels and tipping beer into the drains. At least they don't arrest the real players, locking up the smallest operators and their customers in order to look effective. It is hard to write off the losses while the profits are down. The crooked politicians and cops do not expect their payouts to stop because of glitches in trade. If people don't come to the drinking dens or brothels, they don't buy booze there or gamble, a domino effect of diminishing returns.

The Italians in their sectors seem to be doing better, having organised numerous breweries at the beginning and having connections in New York for imports. John Torrio and his lieutenant, the twenty-two-year-old Al Capone, recruited heavily from New York and have a loyal band. The makeup of the gang members is ethnically related to regions in the old country, being family either through birth or marriage or have worked with the bosses before and are proven. It is thought that the gang has twice as many gunmen as the Irish Northsiders, their neighbours. A turf war would be madness. For the moment, Torrio's arrangement across the districts for monopolies to each gang is keeping the lid on things. Torrio, the businessman, had worked fast to secure his legacy of the older Colosimo gang.

Sean needs to earn. He needs money to keep his gang together, to hire the best, to buy loyalty. Any sign of weakness and he rightfully fears the Italians will move on him. He'd considered Callaghan and Murphy to be among the best and can't think where he might recruit anyone of the same calibre. To take his mind off his worries, Mary, his ex-landlady, now his brothel manager and lover, suggests an evening of entertainment.

"There's a new boy with Joe King and the Creole Jazz Band. They say he's hot on the cornet. I think he's called Louis Armstrong."

"Book us a table. Been a while since I've taken you out, Mrs O'Shea."

"I've been thinking of changing my surname."

"Yeah? What to?"

"How does Mary O'Leary sound? I wouldn't want our child to be born illegitimate."

Sean is lost for words at first.

"What? You mean?"

"Yes, Mr O'Leary. I'm expecting our child. Will you make an honest woman of me?"

"How do you know/"

"Really, Sean?"

"Sorry. I'm a bit thrown. This is a surprise."

"Me too. I waited until I was sure. I've missed two periods and can feel   the   changes."

"And I'm the father?"

"Don't make me mad? You know I've always been exclusive for you. Since you came to stay at my boarding house. Just 'cause you brought me here to run your girls doesn't mean I do tricks as well."

"Sorry. Still in shock. A lot on my mind."

"Well. Let's go and see the band tonight and talk about the future tomorrow."

"You book a table. I'll book the church. We'll get this done quickly."

195

"Oh, Sean. I love you."

"I hope so, Mrs soon-to-be O'Leary."

The Creole Jazz Band with their new cornet player are every bit as good as promised but Sean's mind is engaged elsewhere. To be a father. He hadn't expected that. He hadn't planned that. He'd assumed that Mary had taken care of the contraception. He hadn't even considered he had an exclusive arrangement with her, even though they had first been intimate when he was her lodger and never been with another woman since. Mary is a strong character – what is that saying? Ploughs her own field? And what can he offer at the moment? His business is starting to fail. Over several years since allying himself to Padraig Hennessey and taking over after his mentor's death, he'd increased the businesses until constrained by range of territory indicated by proximity of other gangs and their rising successes. For a while, profits, while still considerable, were down and only going in one direction as his supplies of booze are cut. Shipments of smuggled alcohol are being blocked by successful law enforcement or intercepted by rivals. Local production cannot match the quality of professionally made spirits until the new source had been discovered. The Italians have the market in beer production and charge for it. Torrio, for example, sad increased the numbers of brothels and that takes clientele from Sean, one of the few Irish gangs in vice. Gambling needs no special premises and can be conducted anywhere, only table games requiring a place and not being a high earner by themselves. The silence from Paddy and Spud is unsettling. Two of his best men, plus thousands of dollars disappearing into the night. He has doubts about whether he would see them again. He pretends to Mary he enjoyed the evening but he really didn't pay attention.

CHAPTER 28

April 1, 1992. The Illinois General Assembly create the Illinois State Police.

It has been a couple of weeks since Paddy and Spud visited the farm and been disposed of. Jesse is starting to think they've dodged trouble. After attending the Easter Service at the recently renovated town church, Jesse catches up with Buck and Agnes as the congregation leaves.

Agnes allows her delight to show at seeing Jesse. "Nice to see you back in church, Jesse. It's been a while."

"Yes, ma'am. Long overdue."

Buck can't resist a joke. "Good sermon on Resurrection, eh, Jesse?"

It is a second or two before Jesse realised that the sheriff is ribbing him. He grins. "Yessir. Makes one think."

At that moment, the McGregors, with Maggie, have said their goodbyes to the Minister and Agnes notices. "Well, here's someone you might rather be talking to. Do come over for dinner soon, Jesse."

"Yes, ma'am. Thank you, I will."

Buck and Agnes nod to the McGregors and walk over to their car, to drive home. Buck is looking forward to a siesta while Agnes prepares Sunday dinner.

Maggie says something to her parents and walks over to Jesse. "Haven't seen much of you, Jesse. Moses has been giving me news when he calls in for stock."

Jesse smiles apologetically. "Been hectic. Finding time to ease up a little now."

Maggie had noticed the look from Agnes. "Do the Sheriff and Mrs Buckley think we are an item?"

"Could be."

"My parents have hopes."

"Maggie...."

"Oh. It's alright, Jesse. Don't get nervous. I'm not the girl for you."

Jesse feels uncomfortable. He'd known Maggie and Tom Jr were attracted to each other and he'd stood back, putting his interest in Maggie aside.

"I'm sorry I didn't bring Tommy back for you."

"I was angry with you for a while. But it isn't your fault. I realised that eventually."

"I haven't realised that. I feel it every day. If I'd done things differently...."

"We're not masters of our own destinies, Jesse, even if we think we are.... Don't go yet. Come home with me and have some lemonade."

Jesse is tempted. To do something normal. The pressure of work is getting to him. But he feels an obligation to get back and help Moses and Molly.

"No, sorry. Better get back to the farm. Another time."

Maggie stands on tiptoe and kisses Jesse on the cheek.

"Make sure you do."

The McGregors watched Maggie walk off with the boys. When Jesse was in town, he'd call for Tom Jr and the two of them would then drop by for Maggie. From the back, as they walked away, three figures in denim, only Maggie's long hair revealed one of the three is a girl. Sometimes she is holding Jesse's hand, sometimes Tom's, sometimes in the middle holding both boy's hands. Mr McGregor would occasionally slip a couple of dollars to Maggie and the trio would go to the Diner for sodas. Nothing changed when they became teenagers – inseparable friends. People wondered, as small-town people do, which boy would marry Maggie; the more confident Jesse or the shyer Tom.

*   *   *

Jesse drives into the farmyard to find a disturbing scene; a Republic truck parked in the farmyard and two men standing guard over Moses and Molly, who hold hands to comfort each other.

Getting out of his pick-up, Jesse asks, "What's going on here?" wishing he'd taken a gun with him today, but he hadn't, it being a Sunday and Church.

200

A coupe is parked to the side of the yard, positioned for the occupants to observe activities. Its passenger door opens and a man climbs out.

"Well, well. If it isn't my old comrade in arms, Jesse Hakerman."

Jesse feels sick to the stomach to see the man responsible for sending Tommy to his death. If he'd had a pistol, he would have used it there and then. Instead, he has a gun pointed at him by the driver of the coupe who had also got out.

"Yeah, I'm not your captain anymore but I'm here to give you orders. Two of our guys have disappeared after phoning me about you. What do you know about that?"

Jesse keeps a stone face and still says nothing, but his insides are boiling, keeping the madness within that wants to punch McAvoy into the grave.

"I'm going to have a look around. You stay here." McAvoy indicates to the gunmen to cover the men while he checks.

With two guns pointed at them, Jesse and Moses aren't going to go anywhere. McAvoy walks over to the main barn and pulls open a door. It could not now be denied that Jesse is in the booze business, a line of stills, barrels and sacks of corn and barley plain to see. McAvoy signals for his men to bring Jesse and Moses over.

"Quite an operation you got here," indicating unnecessarily the interior.

Jesse has been thinking hard to save their lives. "Two guys, eh? In a Packard?"

"That's right."

"Yeah, they came here. Took as much of my stuff they could fit in the car and all my cash and cleared off," making his voice sound indignant.

McAvoy is slightly knocked back but is easily convinced, knowing his own standards. Loyalty in the crime business is a commodity one buys. He'd noticed that O'Leary's placing him over the two pals did not receive their best support. And again, Paddy was always talking about going to California. Maybe the temptation has been too big for Paddy and Spud. They have gambling takings from the bookie when leaving Chicago to come here, could fit a big load of hooch in the Packard with its superior spring suspension, plus this guy's business takings. That might be enough to persuade them to strike out on their own in another city, especially if they are thinking O'Leary is losing his hold on his turf, something that is a suspicion in his own mind and he means to talk to his father about.

One of the mobsters is taking a look around but rather than walk in his expensive town shoes through the horse droppings that Moses had, with forethought, laid in front of the dilapidated barn, he disregards it. Meanwhile there is business to be done and McAvoy gives his orders.

"OK. This is what is going to happen. We'll take everything we can fit in the truck." He waves back at the truck for the driver to come down to the barn. "From now on we are your only customer."

Jesse tries a bluff.

"I have a lot of regulars. I can't commit to just one."

"Oh, I think you can," McAvoy pulls a pistol and shoots Moses through the thigh, "or I'll be back and the nigger gets one through the head. Have a truck full by next full moon. Bring it to the freightyards in the evening– we're not driving down these shitty roads again. We'll make a regular monthly pick up each full moon."

Nor would he give home ground advantage in case of a double cross.

McAvoy's bullet has passed right through Moses' thigh and Jesse has taken his shirt off to use as bandages while the mobsters load their vehicle. As soon as they go, he can take Moses into town to see the doc. His brain is working overtime. As he has a value to the mobsters, he knows his life is not at risk today but this is not how he intended his farm-saving plan to go. He could have supplied directly to Chicago at much higher profit, but Jesse has seen it as an altruistic enterprise for the locals and not a truly criminal undertaking. The realism, initiated by killing Paddy and Spud, now hits him full on.

"I'm a bootlegger...and I'm working with gangsters."

CHAPTER 29

Chicago

Sean O'Leary is back in his office at the Ace of Clubs. He'd personally oversaw the unloading of the truck. There is not enough stock to sell on and he is determined to keep it for his speakeasies, the biggest being the Ace of Clubs.

He smokes a cigar as his brain works overtime, staring out the window at the yard behind the club. McAvoy has filled him in on the desertion of Paddy and Spud. Best to put out a message that they are still away on a mission for him. At the same time, he can send out for information on their whereabouts. There is a tame journalist in Chicago who could talk to his peers in California for starters. He'd call him in for a chat later. Still, he finds it hard to accept they had deserted. An indicator, he fears, that his dominance is slipping. There are many more bigger players than he. The North Side gang, run by Dion O'Banion with two lieutenants, Hymie Weiss and George Moran have the muscle and reputation, dominating the Irish sectors and he is paying up to them for permission to operate and buying their beer. Sean's operation is pincered between them and the Italian mob of Torrio and Capone and without O'Banion's protection, he knows they would be taken over in a flash if he falls. Paddy and Spud had brains as well as brawn and left a significant hole by leaving. McAvoy's brat is someone to tolerate for the political power attached but he'll never be an adequate replacement.

He is regretting the shooting of the big black man at the farm. That wasn't a clever move by McAvoy, who told the tale as a boast of making the farmer compliant. Lucky isn't hijacking the kid's stock. He needs him as a supplier. On the next pickup, he'll pay for what McAvoy took as well as the new stock they'll be collecting. If the quality stays good, he might bring the farmboy in as a partner and invest in more stills for him to supervise. They could all get very rich with a home-grown, local production with none of the risks of smuggling in from Canada. One wrinkle on this perfect horizon is it might be necessary to eliminate the Sheriff and get his own man in post. Sean starts to feel better about himself. Pours a gin. Thinks about Mary upstairs, running the brothel; time to set up home, a refuge from the club and business he can slip away to when he wants peace and quiet. Another year, stash money away and he could walk away from all this before someone puts a bullet in him or the law puts him in prison – both outcomes to be avoided. He is smart enough to want to get out at the top. A gangster funeral with waggon loads of flowers is not for him. For fuck's sake, he'd get hayfever.

Upstairs, Mary O'Shea is adding items to a drawer, a special drawer for her future as a wife and mother. She hasn't shared the secret with anyone but the desire to tell is a constant burn. This is a new beginning for her and she is happy. Happier even than she has been in a long,

205

long time. She is still young and fit enough to have many more children with Sean. They can be a family. She touches her bump and wonders if a boy or girl. As long as it is healthy, that's all that matters.

CHAPTER 30

Full moon, Illinois

Unusual to have a Romanian in an Irish mob, but "Razor" Nicolae has impressed Sean O'Leary with his ruthlessness. Just short of six feet but packed with muscle and a fondness for his straight razor for business, Razor has a terrible reputation around Chicago. If Razor reaches for the innocent looking top pocket, it is to pull the blade, a technique least expected in a town where guns are kings. If Lucky wants a man alive, Razor can bring him in. A quick slash of his blade above the eyebrows would fill eyes with blood and a reflex to raise hands to the face, not to reach for a gun. If the result required is a fatality and done quietly, the blade would cut to the side of the throat and open the carotid artery. O'Leary only holds him back for the dirtiest jobs and this time his instructions are

"The sheriff could be a nuisance. Take care of him."

Which is why Razor is in town on the first full moon since Lucky's mobsters visited Jesse's farm, while the rest of the gang are at the freightyards waiting for Jesse to deliver. The Romanian patiently checks Main Street with an eye on the Sheriff's Office. The town is quiet, businesses locked up and little reason for people to be out and about rather than at their firesides.

Buck has lingered later than usual, reluctant to go home before he feels the town is safe. The incident with Fred White has changed his

207

routines and his concerns. Paperwork has been completed, filed away. Checks the stove is off and leftover coffee poured away. Eases his gunbelt for comfort, having sat for so long at his desk. Looks out his window as he closes the blind.

When he sees Buck coming out of the Law Office, locking the door, Razor crosses the street casually and approaches, making no threatening moves that might alert the lawman, putting a smile on his face as if a tourist about to ask for directions. Once on the same sidewalk and close enough, Razor pulls his cutthroat out in a slashing move intended to blind Buck with his own blood from a face wound then a second to the throat avoiding arterial spray on himself. As a streetlamp glints on the blade leaving his pocket there is an explosion. A gut wound for Razor, who drops the blade to hold his stomach and looks at the sheriff in total surprise and incomprehension. Holding his smoking gun, Buck kicks the gangster on the leg, toppling him to the ground. The last words the dying man hears are

"I learned from the best. Think a punk like you can take me?" Spoken with mean anger.

Buck has never got rusty despite not needing his skills in this peaceful town before. The previous evening, at dinner, he told Agnes about a phone call.

"I spoke with Wyatt the other day. He wanted to come right over when I said we were having unwanted visitors."

"How old is he now?"

"Must be in his mid-seventies. You wouldn't think it to hear him talk. Still a tough SoB."

"Some times haven't changed. What we hear from Chicago sounds like the old west. The young Wyatt would be right at home there."

"Well, he made good. Could have so easily gone down the wrong road but he took up lawing and found his vocation. If it wasn't for him, I don't know what I'd be doing."

"You're a good man, Tom Buckley. You'd have found a career in something. As it is, the town know they have a good sheriff and are pleased to have you."

"As long as you're pleased to have me."

They held hands across the table. Life would have been perfect had Tom Jr survived the war. With no son there won't be grandchildren. But maybe Jesse will marry and have kids and that would be a consolation of sorts.

Buck goes back into his office and gets a blanket from the cell. Taking it outside he covers the body. He is angry that violence has come to his town. This failed assassin stinks of Chicago mob and he now knows for certain the danger that Jesse is in. He hopes the steps he has taken will prevent a disaster. Meanwhile, he phones the Funeral Director at home and asks him to come over to collect a body.

"It's a bit messy." An understatement.

CHAPTER 31

Here you must leave all wariness behind.
All trace of cowardice must be extinguished.

~ Dante, Inferno

The Freightyard, which also takes cattle in pens, is not huge. It serves the town on the main rail road into Chicago purely so crops and the like can be shipped cheaply into the city. There are several warehouses and when a pick up is needed a phone call goes up the line so they know how much they are collecting. The rail company also "park" waggons as an overflow from the main depot and also for the ease of having them loaded so all that is needed is to hook up to the loco and little time is lost.

In an ironic twist of fate, unacknowledged by those present, this was where Paddy Callaghan and Spud Murphy had brought Fred White, the Pharmacist, to be interrogated. Now, waiting at the yard, McAvoy and two mobsters can see a truck approaching, just the one vehicle and one visible driver by the light of the evening sun coming down to hug the horizon. Cocky that Chicago muscle beats farm boys, they are relaxed about the handover, even if bored by the wait. These aren't Lucky's best, he needs them in Chicago to keep the lid on his business against the encroachment of other gangs, notably the Italians. Typical bully boys who like people to fear them, they think they are invincible and they only have a farmer to deal with, already cowed by the threat in his farmyard to his black worker. As for the sheriff, Razor is expected to take care of him then join them for the transfer and drive back to Chicago. Their minds are already on what they will do when back in Chicago. Unload the booze then go inside to gamble before ascending the stairs to the girls.

Jesse waves then does a U-turn in the yard, to make it easier to transfer the booze to their vehicle, reversing towards it. It is going perfectly in the mind of McAvoy. He has a couple of cases of cash, on Lucky's instruction, to pay for this load and the last, although he disagrees paying for what he took before. He signals the two mobsters to step up to Jesse's truck and open the rear tarp. Flicking it back, instead of casks and cases, they are met by a grinning Moses holding his double-barrelled shotgun. There is just time for surprise to register on their faces. The noise is deafening as one then the other barrel blow the men away, catching each centre mass in the chest and sending them flying back. McAvoy has stayed by their truck, smoking a cigarette. Dumbstruck at first, slow to react, he eventually draws his gun and fires wildly. Then self-preservation kicks in and he decides to leg it, the option to get in the truck and drive off denied as he sees Moses reload then aim his way. Using his vehicle for close cover, he is able to run out of sight of Moses and across to the buildings along the rail tracks, in the cold sweat of a coward, wondering how it has all gone so terribly wrong.

Like lightning, Jesse is out of the truck with a revolver and takes up the chase, determined not to let McAvoy get away. A cold anger has enveloped him. Time to get revenge for Tom Jr and payback for Moses' wounding. In the cab of Jesse's lorry, Molly rises from where she has been hiding from view and sits behind the steering wheel, ready for whatever will happen next. The scared mobster has made a head start and is darting among the buildings, firing back as he runs, not stopping to take aim. At last, he reaches the tracks and the stockcars, where he intends to hide in ambush. It becomes a game of cat and mouse between him and Jesse. Not knowing that Razor is dead, he thinks the Romanian should be here soon and will help. He curses O'Leary for only sending him with two men. "Three of you and the farmer can manage to load up our truck." Jesse cannot let one get away, that would ruin the plan. He'd expected more, which is why he had brought the tommy-gun, but seeing only three and two downed by Moses, he'd picked up the pistol instead. McAvoy has the desperation of one who wants to survive. Jesse has the passion to right a wrong and revenge Tom Jr. A cornered rat is a dangerous rat.

The sun touches the horizon, casting longer shadows. It will be gone out of sight in three minutes, leaving a fast-dying twilight. Time is not on Jesse's side; darkness will be his prey's friend. The waggons parked on the side tracks have become a maze. Debating which way to go among the stockcars, he hears an engine. At first he fears the mobster has reinforcements but, looking back, he is relieved to see Molly driving his truck and Moses hanging out of the window with his shotgun. Moses, unable to run due to his wounded leg not fully healed, can only stay by the truck. Secure that McAvoy can not now leave without coming out in front of Moses, Jesse goes round and cautiously works his way along, stooping to look under the railcars and paying particular attention to any with open doors. The full moon, which had risen earlier, now is the dominant light source in a clear sky, painting a ghostly silver light over the rail stock and yard.

McAvoy has few options. Shoot and kill Jesse and Moses, even Molly, but he is unlikely to have enough ammo. He'd started with seven in the magazine and one in the breech. He must have fired five, possibly six. Hide somewhere and hope not to be found. Run into the fields the other side of the tracks – too easily seen until darkness fell then thwarted by the moonlight. His ears intensely listening for an approaching car, meaning his support had arrived. He'd heard the truck move but now that was silent.

A hunt and kill game among the railcars ensues. Jesse using all his sniper school training to silently track down his adversary, eyes, ears and nose seeking out his prey. A whisp of breeze had brought the smell of old cigarette to him; the scent that lingers on a heavy smoker's clothes. He pauses to check ahead. The moon sets regular shadows of the waggons, blocks of rectangles, but one shadow is uneven and out of place. Jesse picks up a rock and throws it away from himself.

Hearing the noise past his hiding place, McAvoy falls for the ruse and steps out to check, thinking he'll be able to shoot Jesse in the back.

Jesse stands square, double-handling the gun for accuracy and aims his pistol at the man he hates. "This is goodbye from Tom."

McAvoy spins round to face his death but the hammer clicks on an empty chamber. Jesse hasn't counted his shots nor reloaded. The bully loses his look of fear and a smug look takes over. He only needs one bullet now and can enjoy the moment. Jesse feels a cold pit form in his stomach. He has failed. He prays that Moses can take McAvoy as he leaves.

"Well, well, Hakerman. Looks like you're fucked. I'm going to enjoy wasting you. You know, when the Colonel got back and learned your fag pal, Buckley, was dead and you were in the field hospital he tore me a new asshole."

"No more than you deserved, you yellow prick. I told you it wasn't safe to go into the copse again. Tommy would be alive 'cept for you."

"You were supposed to be shit hot, the pair of you. Colonel's favourites for knocking out Germans. Me? I got put on Admin till the war was over. No medals for Mikey. You know how my old man looks at me? Disappointed. I was supposed to come back a hero and he would get me into politics alongside him. Well, this is my compensation. Putting one right between your eyes."

McAvoy savours the moment of raising his pistol and aiming at Jesse. No need to hurry this, neither man is going anywhere until the deed is done.

They fail to notice the new arrival until he speaks. "Hey, shitbrains."

A tall, elderly man stands with a six-gun aimed at McAvoy and smiles. McAvoy freezes then two slugs tear into him, killing him instantly, knocking him back and over. He lays with a surprised expression on his face.

The stranger turns to Jesse. "I guess you're Jesse. I'm Buck's friend. You can call me Wyatt. Is that true what he said?"

Jesse is glad to be alive and he knows this is the legendary lawman, mentor of Thomas Buckley.

"Yes, sir. Tommy and me shouldn't have been in the copse that morning. We'd already overused it as a firing position and the Hun was on to us. I tried to tell him but he threatened us with disobeying orders if we didn't go. I should have stood our ground. I'm sorry."

"Is that what has been weighing you down, these past few years, son? War is a risky business. Some men come back. Some don't. No one said it is fair. What is important to Mrs Buckley and Buck is that Tommy wasn't alone. He had a friend with him." He places a friendly hand on Jesse's shoulder. "Right, work to be done. We'll get the bodies on their truck and drive it south into the next county. The Klan have been active there, hitting bootleggers, so we'll let them have the credit for this. Send your people home and I'll follow you in my car to bring you back after you ditch the truck."

Hoisting the body over his shoulder Jesse makes his way back to

Moses and Molly, calling out so he doesn't get a shotgun blast to himself.

"It's OK. I got him."

Moses limps over to take the body of McAvoy from Jesse and puts it in the back of the truck. Molly gives Jesse an eyeball inspection until she is satisfied the blood on his shirt isn't his. She then drives them back to the scene of the first gunfight at the yards and where Earp had parked Buck's coupe, which he had borrowed to get here.

Jesse drags the bodies to the lorry the gangsters came in, where Moses is able to help him lift them in, and transfers the corpse of McAvoy from their truck. Looking at the dead men and thinking about the two he has killed at the farm, Jesse wondered how many more would die before this is over. A weight sits heavy on his shoulders and he feels he has set out on a journey of no return. Meanwhile, Molly has collected the mobsters' guns and two bags of cash and put them in Jesse's cab. Jesse looks at the two people he loves and who have stood by him.

"You head back to the farm. We got this covered." He nods to his saviour who waits patiently.

CHAPTER 32

"Deep into that darkness peering,

long I stood there wondering, fearing,

Doubting, dreaming dreams no mortals

ever dared to dream before..."

Edgar Allan Poe, 'The Raven'.

In the Chicago truck, Jesse, and following in his car, Wyatt Earp, drive for a couple of hours in a southerly direction to the most remote place they can find, with a bit of a ravine where Jesse can park the mobsters' truck. Jesse's plan had been to do this, but with Molly and Moses following. This is to buy time so he can fulfil a mission later. Losing men and the danger presented to the mob boss of coming out of Chicago, Jesse hopes is enough incentive for the gangster to lay off and allow him time to achieve his objective. The tipping point for Jesse was the involvement of McAvoy and the shooting of Moses. To have that sneering bully in his life again, the ghost of Tom Jr hovering on his shoulder, and the volatility of temperament that could spell death for two people he loved dearly required drastic action.

The full moon and clear starry sky help illuminate the road better than headlamps alone. Jesse finds it comforting to see Earp in the coupe in his rear-view mirrors. He'd told Buck of the plan but had had no idea that the legendary lawman and mentor of Buck had arrived in town. If McAvoy had killed him tonight, it would have all been for nothing and, no doubt, Moses and Molly would have been killed also. He has time to reflect on his journey from farmer to bootlegger and the naivety of his plan to save the farm. He could have kept production small enough for income to pay the mortgage and, after, buy a tractor, but he'd been carried away by success. Ignoring the illegality of the enterprise, the community had welcomed the economic boost to the town and rural dwellers. He'd enjoyed the philanthropy that he was able to disperse, he admits to himself. His conscience now does not let him weigh that against being a killer, no matter how bad the men he had exterminated were, and accepts he is of their ilk now.

Arriving at a destination deemed suitable, not near any habitation, the truck with bodies is driven off the road into a small ravine. Jesse prepares to delete the evidence with fire, remembering a conversation in Paris. Choosing a ravine will diminish the glare of flames and, it is hoped, provide enough time for the job to be done and he and Earp be well on their way home before anyone investigates. Jesse thinks of asking for Earp's gun to wipe clean and throw in the truck in case bullets from the corpses can be matched to it. Then he calculates that the old lawman will head back to California and the likelihood of such action is minimal with several states dividing. The two mobsters that Moses had taken out are not an issue of ballistics, having been blasted by a shotgun. His brief acquaintance with Edmond Locard is not wasted. Jesse has checked that Moses had not left the empty cartridges at the freightyard. Any bullets lodged in rail waggons will hardly be noticed and, after a couple of days, those waggons will be dispersed across Illinois.

Taking a can of gasoline from each vehicle, Jesse thoroughly soaks the interior of the Chicago truck and bodies, avoiding getting himself splashed by the fuel. Earp has stayed back by the road to watch for any traffic. He waves an All Clear to Jesse. Seeing the signal, Jesse removes the truck's fuel cap, stuffs a rag, already soaked, into the filler pipe and lights it. Another lit rag gets thrown inside the truck and he runs clear. The truck goes up in flames with a roar, fingers of fire reaching into the heavens and he and Earp stand some distance to watch the blaze and to be certain the truck would not survive too well. With a comforting hand on Jesse's shoulder, Wyatt wryly comments, "should have brought marshmallows," before offering a swig of bourbon from his hipflask.

The fire rages fiercely, consuming the truck and its cargo of corpses and they are eventually satisfied that not much would be recognizable by the time it burns out. No one is likely to see the blaze, it being past midnight and miles from any town or farm, but Jesse is not relying on remoteness to hide the evidence. On Earp's advice, he has led them far enough into a territory where the Ku Klux Klan is known to operate. The Klan has started targeting immigrants, especially Catholics, under the pretence of enforcing Prohibition. When the truck and bodies are found and identified, it would point to the KKK hitting Irish bootleggers. That might not fool the mob boss back in Chicago but it would satisfy any law enforcement from trying too hard to investigate.

It is a tiring drive back to the farm, the adrenaline worn away, Jesse and Earp taking turns. They don't talk until the ex-lawman drops Jesse off at the farm.

"I'll go to Buck's. Stick around for a few days."

"Thank you, sir. You saved my life."

"Hell, kid. I haven't had this much fun in ages."

CHAPTER 33

"Take courage, my heart: you have been through worse than this.
Be strong, saith my heart; I am a soldier; I have seen worse sights
than this."

Homer, *The Odyssey*

Jesse crashes out with exhaustion on his bed. Before leaving them the previous evening, he'd told Moses and Molly to sleep in his parents' room despite their protestations.

"We'll stick together. Things to do in the morning."

Molly is first awake and up. She has depthless resources of energy and resolution. Finding the bacon and eggs she'd brought over previously for Jesse, she cooks breakfast for them all after brewing a pot of coffee on the stove. The smells seep into his bedroom and wake Jesse up, realising how hungry he is. The three of them sit round the old table and breakfast is eaten in silence. The enormity of last night hangs over them. None of them are eager to talk about it.

After eating and still without speaking, Jesse goes to the old barn and uncovers Paddy and Spud's Packard. He is going to need it. Moses has followed him over and sees him load it up with a selection of guns they had collected. The bag of money that Paddy and Spud had collected is still there and will be Jesse's fund for his mission. Last nights' money will stay at the farm for contingencies, considering the plans for the business he has made. In the smuggling compartments he hides some of the gin they have made. It might be currency where he plans to go, the price of admission.

Moses watches the preparation with a heavy heart. He has an inkling of Jesse's intentions and wonders how he can help. Waiting for his leg to mend makes him, he feels, a liability. It is one thing to sit in the back of the truck but he hadn't been able to chase the last man down with Jesse. Luckily, Molly had known what to do and had driven the truck to block an escape route. Even luckier, Mr Earp had appeared in time to save Jesse's life. Moses carries a guilt that he should have been there to protect Jesse.

Jesse turns to the silent giant, holds his eyes with his own.

"Moses. Take down all the equipment. Time to go back to farming. I want you and Molly to move into the house. The farm is yours; I've made the deeds over to you. See Mr Buckley, he's expecting you, and go with him to see Mr Norris at the bank. I think it will be a good idea to rename the farm in case anyone comes looking for the Hakerman place. I suggest Freeman is a good name for it. There's enough money under the loose floorboard in my bedroom to pay off the mortgage and tide you over any upsets and the money we took last night. Don't give it to the bank in one go; spread the payments out so it looks like farming revenue."

Moses is confused by the finality indicated by this plan.

"What you gonna do, Jesse?"

"I've got to put an end to all this. If they come again, looking for me, I can't be here. Nor can there be any trace of distilling. Make a good job of cleaning up the place. I'm hoping it won't be necessary but take some of the guns and hide them around the place where you can get to them in a hurry. Never be too far away from a weapon, Moses."

Molly has walked into the barn in time to hear Jesse's instructions to Moses. With tears streaming down her cheeks, she rushes to hug him as if she will never let go.

"Molly. You understand why this must be. Look after Moses. I know I am leaving the farm in good hands. What this has taught me is I have no mind to be a farmer. I was locked into a sense of duty but I realise that duty is to save the farm and look after my friends. I've achieved the first; I have to see to the second. I'll come back to visit when it's over."

Molly wipes her face raising the skirt of her apron to dry her tears.

"We'll do what you ask, Jesse, but we're only holding the farm in trust for you. You may want a place to bring a family one day and raise children."

"Maybe. But you must do exactly as I say. Get the deeds and rename but first lose every trace of distilling. We don't need the income anymore and we certainly don't need trouble. I think the sheriff will be relieved."

"Jesse," Moses speaks. "You be careful. Once my leg is mended, you need me, you call. I'll be right there."

"Moses. Molly. You're my family. You always will be. So.... time to be going. I've got a drive ahead of me and things to do."

The new owners of Hakerman farm, soon to be the Freeman farm, watch their young friend drive off down the track to the road with deep sadness in their hearts. Jesse's dog whines, sensitive to the emotions and Moses reaches down and pats his head. "I know, old fella. But he'll be alright. That boy is made of steel."

Molly dries her tears and straightens up. "Come on then, Moses. We gotta a lot of work ahead of us. You heard what Jesse said."

They walk over to the barn and pull back the doors.

"What we gonna do with all this?" Moses is concerned at the size of the task.

Molly has thought. "You start dismantling. I'm gonna drive round the neighbours and get help. If they want to take anything, they can. What is left, we'll bury. The sooner this place looks like a farm again, the better. Who knows who might come looking."

CHAPTER 34

"Our revels now are ended. These our actors,
As I foretold you, were all spirits and
Are melted into air, into thin air;
And, like the baseless fabric of this vision....
.... Leave not a rack behind."

William Shakespeare, The Tempest

Buck steps out on the sidewalk to drink his coffee. A daily routine to check up and down Main Street, say "Hi" to any passers-by, maybe a longer conversation with those not in a hurry, have his face seen by the locals. He checks that the bloodstains from the razor-wielding failed assassin have mostly washed away with a sluicing he did after the body had been collected. A quiet word in the right ears and it was recorded as death of a vagrant from natural causes. No need to alarm the townsfolk that violence had visited last night. He'd been informed by Wyatt about the freightyard shootout and disposal of the mobsters. Relief that Jesse was OK had washed over him and now he is to oversee his son's friend's instructions carried out. He approved of making the farm over to Molly and Moses and wrapping up the distilling. His county will be less attractive to those in Chicago now, he hopes.

Today, he sees two shiny black limousines coming down the street, which give him a momentary start. Surely this is too soon for mobsters to be visiting? Both vehicles pull in a little up from the Office and out of each step two men, identically dressed in dark suits, white shirts and plain ties, as alike as bowling pins. Buck knows immediately what they are.

"Sheriff Buckley?" asks one of the quadruplets.

"I am," replies Buck.

"Government Agent Richardson. My associates, Wrigley, Pugh and Henderson."

Buck nods at them. "Gentlemen."

Richardson speaks again. "You must know why we're here."

"I'm afraid I don't. Please enlighten me."

Richardson looks at his colleagues, a mix of surprise and doubt.

"It's about the bootlegging."

"What bootlegging would that be? I regret you have the advantage of me." Buck, looking the picture of innocence and bewilderment, takes a drink of coffee from his cup.

"We're following a lead that there is a source in this town, supplying the speakeasies in Chicago. We'll need to visit the General Store to ask about what they do with the large number of specific items they order."

Buck manages a realistic laugh.

"Bootlegging? You have got to be kidding. This town is drier than the Sahara desert. Isn't that right, Wyatt?"

He enjoys the look on the agents' faces as Wyatt Earp steps out of the office and stands alongside him, nursing his own cup of coffee.

"I could murder a whiskey, gentlemen. Let me know if you find any."

Awestruck the men forget their mission and agree to go inside for coffee and spend the rest of the morning listening to anecdotes of the wild west. Wyatt Earp is reluctant to retell the story of the OK Corral but is pressurised by the insistent agents, keen to hear from the legend a first-hand account. Buck appreciates his old mentor occupying their visitors, allowing more time for the clear up at the farm should it be necessary to go there, and for Jesse to get out of the county. He's not worried about the McGregors being interrogated. They had long worked out an explanation of their need for ever-increasing orders from wholesalers as demand from the farms for preserving and pickling their unsold produce. Spread over a wide area, it would take armies of agents to visit each farm and collate whether the sums added up.

Leaving the talking to Wyatt, Buck wonders how Jesse is getting on......

Finale – Part I

Jesse looks at his watch. Only another hour to Chicago and unfinished business.

> *"Not I, nor anyone else can travel that road for you.*
> *You must travel it by yourself.*
> *It is not far. It is within reach.*
> *Perhaps you have been on it since you are born and do not know.*
> *Perhaps it is everywhere – on water and land."*
>
> Walt Whitman, Leaves of Grass

> *"Let your plans be dark and impenetrable as night, and when you move, fall like a thunderbolt."*
>
> Sun Tzu (The Art of War)

> *"Trouble is bad for business."*
>
> Johnny Torrio

THE BOOTLEGGER

PART II

CHICAGO

"Before You Embark On A Journey Of Revenge, Dig Two Graves"

Confucius

PROLOGUE

"No one starts a war – or rather, no one in his senses ought to do so – without being clear in his mind what he intends to achieve by that war and how he intends to conduct it."

Carl Von Clausewitz

Jesse has to make plans.

He must cut the head off the snake.

He must not get caught.

No one must know it is him.

He must protect his friends at all costs.

Jesse stops twice on the way to Chicago. At his first stop he buys a small truck, the sort used for town deliveries. Plain, unobtrusive, not new, but not in disrepair. In that town, he also buys workman's overalls and boots, plus some tools. He kicks the clothes around to age them, adds a nick here and there with a knife and scuffs the boots. The contents of the Packard, gin, cash, weapons and ammunition are transferred to the truck before parking it safely to await his return.

At his second stop, he wipes the Packard down all over where he or Moses did or might have touched it, checking he hasn't left anything in it to be traced back to him, his town or the farm. Taking the licence plates away he walks until he can throw them in a river, watching as they leave a trail of bubbles as they sink. This town has a men's haberdashers and he purchases a good suit, a couple of shirts and ties, smart shoes, hat and a suitcase to put them in. That leaves him enough time to catch a bus back to the previous town, where he had parked the truck.

Now he is ready to hit Chicago........

CHAPTER 1

"When sorrows come, they come not single spies, but in battalions."
Claudius in, Hamlet, Act IV, Scene V.

Sean "Lucky" O'Leary is not so sure of his nickname at the moment.

No news has come back about Paddy and Spud; the newsman's contacts in California have not heard anything about two Irish guys arriving in the state but he knew it was a longshot to ask. He is loath to cast the net wider in case it draws attention that two of his top guys have either deserted or, just as bad, been taken out. Razor Nicolae had gone to kill the Sheriff in Hakerman's town and not been heard of since. Another one of his team down and going to the town to investigate too hot to risk. Nor has his truck come back from the pickup, instead found burned out, with his guys shot up inside, in the south of Illinois and the Klan accused and taking credit for seeing off booze slingers. Sending his people out of Chicago is proving costly and the Italians, led by Johnny Torrio and his top man, Alphonse Capone, are taking control of the city, bit by bit. Another blow is losing Alderman McAvoy, who blames him for the death of his son. Sean had realised the kid was a lightweight but needed to keep the politician on board and he had trusted Paddy and Spud to mentor him, keep him in line. Had taking on the politician's son pushed his top two men away?

Thoughts spin around his head and alcohol dulls the questions he can't answer. Sheer depression at not being control and events whirling away from him has sucked him into a monumental binge.

Dougal is concerned about Sean. He's never seen his boss so worried before and the empty bottles in the office need clearing out. After knocking tentatively on the door he enters to be staring down the barrel of a Colt 1911. Sean blearily focuses his eyes and realises it is Dougal and not a threat.

"Boss. Want some coffee?" Ignoring how dishevelled O'Leary looks and is relieved when the gun is put down.

Sean slumps back in his chair behind the mahogany desk, reaches for the nearest bottle, tips it up only to find it empty. There is no resistance as Dougal takes the bottle away, picks up the gun and puts it back in a drawer. He's never seen his boss this drunk before. There's a sour smell of stale booze and unclean body so he opens a window to the yard, uncertain what to do next. He's shaken when the door opens unexpectedly while he's contemplating action. Competing with the closed-up odours, a whiff of lavender reveals the newcomer.

"Where is he?"

Mary O'Shea walks in, closing the door behind her, and looks with a mixture of disgust and pity at her fiancé. "Oh, Sean."

"Hi, Mary. I've been trying to clean him up but he never leaves his office."

"Thank you, Dougal. Tell no one. Get a big pot of strong coffee, will you?"

Dougal nods and heads out, relieved to share the responsibility. Mary ignores Sean to start to put the bottles into a corner where they can be collected and taken away later. She is not showing much, wearing looser clothing to hide the bump, which she now gently rubs. They haven't shared their news with anyone yet but soon it will be impossible to cover up. At this moment, her concern is their baby will need a father, not a drunk and not a failure. What had been joy was turning into worry, a nagging fear. Mary knows what it was like to be a child in a family where the father hit the bottle as often as he hit the kids. Her reverie is interrupted when Dougal returns with the coffee as ordered. Putting down the tray with jug and mug, he steps back for Mary to administer, then thinks he should wait outside to leave the two together.

Mary walks round the desk, slaps Sean. "Come on, Sean. Wake up. Drink this."

Sean does not resist and most of the cup of coffee goes in his mouth, only some on his shirt. Two further cups and he is looking more alive. Through bloodshot eyes he acknowledges Mary.

"Hello, sweetheart".

"Sean. You have to get yourself together. This is no good. Whatever has happened has happened. You can overcome this but you need to be sober."

"I'm sorry…sorry." he slurs pitifully.

"Oh, baby. Remember the plan. Get enough money to get out of here. We haven't enough yet so you need to stick with it until we do."

Sean suddenly leans over and vomits into a waste bin by the desk, at least making an effort to contain the mess, a vile smelling liquid. He heaves until his stomach is empty, no solids as he hasn't eaten for two days. Dougal returns, having heard the noise through the door, wrinkles his nose at the new smell.

Mary thinks. "Is anyone about yet?"

"No one in but me, It's too early."

"Then get him upstairs to my room. Give me a hand."

One each side, Dougal and Mary assist Sean out of his office, through the bar and upstairs to the private rooms. At Mary's instruction they strip him and put him in the bathtub.

"I'll come down later and clean up the office."

"It's alright, Mary. I'll take care of that. No worries." Dougal volunteers.

"You're a good man, Dougal." Mary is grateful for the offer.

With Dougal gone to do his chores, Mary turns the shower on and soaps Sean down, head to toe, repeating until she is satisfied and can sluice the suds off. Turning off the shower, she lathers up his face and, taking an open razor, shaves him, a skill she learned in her childhood to earn money. She hasn't realised she is singing an Irish folksong softly, as if calming a baby. Without opening his eyes, Sean smiles. Patting her husband-to-be as dry as she can while he lays in the bath, she next covers him with towels to keep him warm and fetches a pillow for his head. She pulls up a chair so she can keep her eyes on him and Sean sleeps for several hours.

Meanwhile, Dougal has chucked the waste bin away, taken all the bottles out of the office and thrown wide open the windows that overlook the yard to let in fresh air. Noises alert him to staff arriving for work, the people coming in for setting up the bar and gambling, the usual routine. The girls arrive later to wait to entertain clients and have no duties beforehand. No one mentions Sean at this time, it not being their business to ask where the boss is. Dougal has more respect as Sean's right hand than he ever had as Padraig's barman and driver; for that, Dougal will always be loyal to Sean, whatever it takes. He is also in love with Mary, although he knows she will never leave Sean for him. Whatever she needs, he'll be there for her.

Mary has been upset by Sean's decline into drunkenness. She'd never seen him lose control before. Now she needs the old Sean, the strong Sean, back. She'd watched over him while he slept, herself napping in the chair. Sounds from the bar filtered up, creating a background hum of music and chatter. Nothing too much to disturb their rest. Occasionally, she had left Sean to make herself a cup of mint tea. She didn't eat. Looking at him, she remembers the day he had turned up at her lodging house. Big and rough was her impression but he had a manner with him and a politeness to her that set him aside from the rest. Once he had visited the barber and came in dressed in a suit, he was a different man, confident and amusing. It hadn't been long before they shared her bed. She hadn't asked questions. She'd assumed there were other women in his life. It was the norm for gang boys to sleep with the whores and also pick up hangers-on. It had been a surprise when Padraig had asked what spell she had cast over Sean, why he never looked at another female. Sean never spoke of feelings, but Mary's had grown from comfort to love. Now here they are. Her carrying their child, Sean a proud father-to-be but lapsed into drunkenness. What would this all mean?

Dougal puts off any questions about Sean, covering for his absence from the bar, while greeting customers. "Ah, you know he's a busy man." Things are a bit quiet anyway. Paddy and Spud are not around making fun and raising a ruckus. Razor is not missed – his sullen quiet presence a constant reminder of the coiled spring, tension to be released violently without notice – no, that is not missed; Dougal, and a few customers, are relieved at his absence but few know the story. What is of concern - stocks of booze getting low. Dougal has tried to maintain the smuggling as well as the home-brewing but has had to buy off other gangs to meet demand. That has cut profits. Dougal often mutters a prayer for Sean to take back control.

Upstairs, Sean opens his eyes. He is surprised to be naked in a
bathtub, covered with towels, his feet wet. Mary hadn't realised that
the tap was dripping, the sound muffled by the towels. She is seated
alongside, touching distance but he sees that her eyes are closed yet as
he moves, she stirs, opens her eyes and checks him over. Seam
manages a weak smile. "What happened?"

"You drunken bastard," she replies, but affectionately. "You went
on a bender."

"So I did...... And now?"

Dougal and I got you up here. No one else knows. Sean. You have
to get back in charge. I know things went bad but you'll find a solution."

"Ah, God, Mary. I'm so ashamed. I just took a few drinks while I
tried to figure out what to do but it just became another one and
another one. Fuck it!"

"I'll make some coffee. Can you eat anything?"

"Coffee first. Then maybe bacon and eggs. I'll get dressed," and he
pulls himself up from the bath.

Mary indicates clothes on another chair then goes into the kitchen,
grinds beans from a tin and puts a pot of coffee on the stove to heat up.
She checks whether there is bacon and eggs and bread in a cupboard
while it brews, sets out a plate and cutlery, takes the loaf, slices it and
butters a couple of pieces, the domesticity reassuring. The pot starts

to rumble as the water begins to boil. She takes two mugs from an ornate hand-carved wooden rack, a present from Dougal when she moved in above the club. Having dressed, Sean comes into the kitchen, rubbing his chin. "Did you shave me?"

"I did."

"I'm surprised you didn't slit my throat. I'm sorry, Mary."

"Stop apologising. It's done and it's over. Have something to eat then get back to work."

"I need to tell you something first." Sean hesitates.

The pause worries Mary. "What?"

"We're seeing the priest on Friday. He'll marry us and backdate so our bairn is legitimate. At least I had that organised."

CHAPTER 2

We have come now to the place where, I have told you,
you will find the people for whom there is only grief.

~ *Dante, Inferno*

Jesse draws up at the premises he has rented. Telling the leasing company he is a general-purpose handyman, they have provided a workshop with accommodation above and a yard behind a tall gate, not overlooked. It's alongside a brewery that was closed down by the Act and remains unused. He likes the look of the neighbourhood; a quiet district where he'll fit in. He's been in the suburbs of Chicago for a week now, stopping at a boarding house while he scouted around the city to find a place for his base of operations. This seemed perfect.

He backs the truck in so he can drive out forward, which also allows him to unload from the rear and into the workshop. It's not overbig but a good enough size had he genuinely intended to set up a trade. It really needs sweeping out but Jesse doesn't see the urgency. The cases of gin, which he brought for potential bargaining, he stores at the back and covers with sacking he found there. They might be needed as an intro, if he can infiltrate a gang. His personal possessions he takes to the rooms above the workshop. The living accommodation comprises a small lounge adjacent to a kitchen and bathroom, furniture left by the last occupant. There is one bedroom and he tests the springs and examines the mattress of the bed. Not happy with the latter, he plans his first nights to be on the sofa until he acquires clean bedding. He'll need to buy food and drink but that waits until he has placed his arsenal around the place where he can access it quickly if attacked here. Too tired to do more, he beds down without eating and falls immediately asleep.

It's mid-afternoon when he wakes. It takes a second or two to understand where he is, having dreamed he was back on the farm with his parents. He would like to fall back asleep and continue with the dream. Maggie and Tom Jr had turned up and they were all having a picnic on the ridge, making plans. The reality is a brutal punch in the stomach. Tom Jr lays cold in the ground in France. The man responsible for his death had been killed by Wyatt Earp and Jesse and the old lawman had burned his body along with other gangsters. Somehow that does not wipe away the regrets.

Having risen, washed and dressed, Jesse checks his pistol and tucks it in his waistband where it won't be seen. On the drive here he'd noted a Diner a couple of streets away, a working-class establishment. Ideal place to fuel himself but also pick up any gossip. Dressed in working clothes to fit in and for his new persona, he leaves the premises, checking up and down the street before he locks the door in the yard gates, placing a piece of straw wedged in, that would fall out when the door is next opened. The day is dry and mild, the air carries no particular scents, the lack of active industry and few residential dwellings leaving it almost sterile. Somewhere a dog is barking and the sound has carried. In another street, car horns. As a country boy, Jesse is alert to all sensations. He does not take long to reach the Diner which he first observes from a distance before approaching and entering; his sniper training kicking in on appraising his surroundings. A clean establishment, prices set to feed locals rather than culinary experiences. Inside, a scattering of men, some together but a number solo, are eating. All working class. A menu is propped on the counter, written in chalk. It probably never changes, except maybe seasonally, at a push. Jesse orders ham and eggs and coffee from the man behind the counter, a middle-aged, plump cheerful Chicagoan. He is happy to find a table where he can watch both the entrance and through a window. When his food is ready, a waitress, a skinny girl of about seventeen brings it to him. She lingers after putting the plate and cup down; Jesse is a change from the usual clientele. Better-looking for one thing and closer to her age. Jesse looks up with a "do you want something?" glance, which jerks her back to her duties and she goes back to the counter blushing. Jesse leans towards another customer who has put his newspaper down.

"Mind if I take a look?"

His mouth full, without talking the man pushes it across and continues to fork huge mouthfuls past his lips. Jesse lays the newspaper on his table so he can read while eating. He sticks the tip of his knife into the eggs and the yolks spill out over the ham. Not the best he's ever had but, being very hungry, the meal is consumed quickly. He waves to the waitress and points to his cup. She comes over with a pot of coffee and pours a refill.

"Do you want anything else?"

Jesse considers and stills feels a bit hungry. "What you got? Apple pie?"

"Sure. I'll fetch you some." She tries to swing her hips as she walks away slowly.

While she gets his pie, Jesse checks the newspaper for any information that could assist his quest. He pauses at news that Alderman McAvoy will be attending his son's funeral tomorrow. No mention how Mike McAvoy had really died; reporting a road accident of a war hero, while ignoring any lack of medals. But Alderman McAvoy is not his target. Jesse needs to get to the gang boss and his associates. Break the chain from Chicago to his town. The elder McAvoy might lead him to his target. He wonders how much the Alderman knows about his son and him and whether he could risk an "old comrade" approach, pretending to be a friend who served in France too. His thoughts are interrupted when the waitress returns with his pie, a large portion, probably larger than other customers got.

"You're new around here," as she puts down fresh cutlery.

"I am. Up from Springfield."

"I'm Maisie. My dad owns this place."

243

"If he needs any work doing, mostly carpentry, I'm available." Jesse is working his cover.

"I'll tell him. So I guess we'll be seeing you around a bit then?"

"Man gets hungry...."

Maisie smiles and goes off to clear tables.

Jesse passes the paper back to its owner. "Thanks." The apple pie is surprisingly good and, now fortified with food, Jesse has an idea. Maisie is only too happy to tell him the phone number, even though he'd requested it with the explanation he needed somewhere for his clients to contact him until he was connected at his workshop.

Watching the funeral of Mike McAvoy, Jesse mentally notes down who attends and who might be gang-related. He ranks the attendees by how well they dress and how much deference is shown to them. He doesn't know it, but Sean O'Leary misses it, being post-drunken binge. After eating at the Diner, he'd phoned Sheriff Tom Buckley and given him his address, saying he could leave messages for Jesse at the Diner with Maisie but using his alias, Harry Maguire. He'd avoided outright asking the waitress for a date but had indicated he might be interested. He doesn't want complications but he needs a way of Buck reaching him should anything arise. Satisfied all is quiet at home, he feels he needn't rush things and surveillance is his priority. The Press is all over the funeral and Jesse keeps his cap pulled low and his head down, avoiding being in any photograph. He realises he hasn't anything as a lead but seeing the Press attending, he has an inspiration he should visit the newspaper offices and read old editions. These Chicago mobsters like being in the papers. He could ignore the Italians, except for background, and just follow up on Irish connections. The mourners at the funeral seem to be politicians, which surprises him, having assumed the McAvoys would be in someone's pocket. All the same, he asks of a man also watching, "who are these people?" and the man obliges with names and descriptions. Jesse notes the names in his head, intending to write them down when back at the workshop. He was right about the lack of gangsters, just minor public figures attending. The clouds which have been threatening rain start to deliver. A slow sprinkle, a *plop plop* of big drops then a downpour, turning the sombre occasion into a rush for shelter by the mourners. Jesse, turning his collar up, decides he has seen enough. He feels anger at Mike McAvoy getting a better funeral than his friend, Tom Jr, and his jaw is clenched tight. He's grateful Wyatt Earp saved his life by shooting McAvoy but Jesse had always thought he would have the revenge of strangling the cowardly bastard.

Back in the workshop, he hangs his clothes across chairs near the stove to dry out. Breaking his intentions, he had retrieved one of his bottles of gin and is drinking. The funeral had brought back memories he wants to subdue. Coming back, he'd checked the street carefully and noted that the straw was still in the door. It would have been a surprise if he had been discovered already but there is also a chance of casual thievery on premises and he will not let his guard down. Pulling out a notebook and pencil, he writes down all the names he can remember and a description, both physical and what they did, according to his obliging bystander. The SOS training standing him in good stead for observation and recording. Looking up he notices steam vapour rising from his clothes and he moves the chairs further back to avoid scorching. He realises he is hungry again and takes a break to get bread and cheese from the kitchen, having stocked up on groceries on his way back from the funeral, before he returns to his plotting. He has no information on the first two gang members who visited him at the farm – there'd been no names in their clothes, or wallets- but with the arrival of McAvoy he is confident they were from Chicago and the sheriff had heard their Irish accents. The one who had tried to cut Sheriff Buckley was unknown but Jesse felt instinctively that the razor was a signature, the man not carrying a gun as one might expect. Surely, he'd be known and some gossip somewhere. There is a lot of ground to cover in the Irish districts and he will start tomorrow. He needs to overhear conversation about six men missing from a gang. For that he has to get inside a gang himself.

CHAPTER 3

"No sooner met but they looked, no sooner looked but they loved, no sooner loved but they sighed, no sooner sighed but they asked one another the reason, no sooner knew the reason but they sought the remedy; and in these degrees have they made a pair of stairs to marriage."

William Shakespeare, As You Like It.

Sean gives an admiring glance as Mary enters the room. In a new dress and hat, with carefully applied make-up, she looks years younger. Sean congratulates himself on his choice of future wife.

"Ready?" Mary asks, a hint of nervous excitement in her voice.

Sean nods and offers his arm. Since his binge, he'd been cold sober. Not a drop of the hard stuff. The Ace of Clubs is empty, this being an early start. Dougal, in his best suit, waits by the bar, ready to perform his duties as driver. Sean and Mary come down the stairs arm in arm and Dougal notes what a handsome pair they are, a bittersweet moment when he both is happy for them and sad for himself not being the groom.

Sean doesn't speak but squeezes Dougal's shoulder. He knows what Dougal has done for him, in protecting him and caring during his relapse. Mary speaks, "Let's go then. Mustn't keep the Father waiting," which makes both men laugh and Mary blushes at the word's double meaning.

"I've got the car ready," says Dougal, and the three of them go into the yard at the rear where, indeed, the automobile is parked, and gleaming from an intensive valeting by Johnny Miller, the one-legged newsboy, now a teenager since his recent birthday.

Sean helps Mary into the rear seat then gets in alongside her. Dougal takes up the driving seat, starts the engine. Nods to Johnny to open the gate. As the kid crutchhops across to do that, Sean remembers he'd thought about getting the kid an artificial leg so he could give up the crutches, reprimands himself for not having done it. He'll get on to it after the wedding. The kid, a smile splitting his face, waves as the automobile goes through the open gates, which he closes and locks after. Mary had blown him a kiss.

The streets around are empty. No suspiciously parked cars or loiterers. They'd picked a quiet neighbourhood and a priest who could be bribed. Even so, Dougal has driven round twice before drawing the car up behind the church and shutting off the engine. They want no accidental witnesses, people who may gossip about seeing Sean O'Leary and his madam attending church on a weekday. Dougal looks over his shoulder and checks with Sean, who nods, getting permission to get out of the auto and walk up to the church where he knocks on the vestry door. He rolls his shoulder to settle his suit and his nerves. After less than a minute, the door opens and an elderly priest, Father O'Riley, looks out and up and down the road. Seeing no one about other than those he had expected, he summons Sean and Mary impatiently. At his signal, they get out of the car and hasten inside, to be welcomed by smells of dust and years of incense that assail the senses. Sunlight coming through a panel of coloured glass patterns the aisle to bring some display on the party as they come together before the altar, Dougal one step back. A nervous cough from Sean and Mary touches his arm. The ceremony, if it can be called that, does not take long, a quick exchange of vows and no trimmings. Dougal is best man and gives the bride away as well as signing as witness. Oaths exchanged and no prayers offered, Sean hands the priest a fat envelope, which he pinches between finger and thumb to check the thickness before it is quickly tucked away in his vestments. The date on the marriage certificate is checked and Sean is satisfied that it is earlier than the conception; their child will not be born a bastard. The priest is keen to get them out of the church now. He knows this will not have the approval of the Archbishop. Envious of the prosperity of Catholic colleagues in Italian districts with larger donations, he agreed to do just this one thing. Why, Father Costa in New York had spoken about how Frankie Yale, the mob boss, had single-handedly saved his church, providing the funds needed. A coincidence his church is dedicated to St Rosalia? Suspicious that Yale's daughter was named Rosalia? It's easy to draw a straight line. Anyway, Father O'Riley's mind was also swayed by Sean's mentioning "Should a priest have a mistress?" Something he

249

doesn't want attention drawn to. He's relieved to get through the ceremony and decides a bottle of communion wine will be opened the instant the wedding party leaves. He can write the stock discrepancy down to "corked and thrown away" to satisfy the diocese's auditors. Happens a quite a lot, getting bad wine.

Dougal goes first through the vestry door first and checks the street, a careful perusal in both directions, watching for any suspicious loiterers. Only when satisfied does he call back, "All clear."

Sean and Mary, now Mr and Mrs O'Leary come out of the church and hasten to get in the back of the automobile. They hold hands and do not speak as Dougal drives back to the Ace of Clubs, where Johnny Miller has stood duty at the gates, ready to unlock on their return. That reminds Sean.

"Dougal," he says. "Give the kid twenty then I want you to see about where he can get an artificial leg – good quality, not a pegleg. Do that, will you?"

"Of course. I'll get straight on it." Dougal is taken by surprised but pleased at Sean's generosity.

Mary gives Dougal a kiss. "Thank you, Dougal. You're a good man."

As they had planned the timings, the bride and groom enter the club before any staff arrive and immediately go up to Sean's room.

"Let's not say anything, Sean. Let people notice my wedding band

and ask. We can say we were married a while back but kept it quiet until now."

Sean had wanted to throw a celebration but sees the sense in this. "You're right." He looks around the room. "But we need to find a home for us, away from here. You are out of the business now and must prepare to be a mother."

Mary kisses him. "And a full-time wife."

Sean needs to take care of business. "Who can look after the girls in your absence?"

Mary doesn't have to think for long. "I think Josephine can do it. She's the most sensible and the other girls look up to her."

"Give her the news and a rise. I must get back to work. You start hunting for our place. But rent. We don't want roots in Chicago that will slow us down leaving. We need to keep our plans a secret."

"I must change first. This finery is wrong for the morning."

Sean does not go immediately but watches Mary undress and assesses her bump with a smile.

"Get out of here, you big eejit," and she throws a cushion at him. And so married life begins.

Downstairs, Dougal is behind the bar stocking up, and cleaning staff have begun arriving, preparing for midday trade. In a very good mood, Sean has come down the stairs, nodding to a few of the workers before addressing his manager.

"Dougal. My office".

Dougal wonders what now and follows his boss into the office, standing as Sean sits down behind his desk. Has he done everything to Sean's satisfaction?

"Ah, sit down, man. We have to talk." Sean waits until Dougal rests his bulk in the opposite seat.   "Six years, Dougal, Six years. I've never had reason to doubt you. You're a good friend, Dougal. I think it's about time you should be my partner – fifty-fifty."

"I don't know what to say, Sean." Dougal had no inkling that Sean was thinking of this. He'd stopped skimming the minute Padraig Hennessey had died and Sean took over. Instinctively, he knew the big man would be more savvy. But his mind had whirled over any possible slip-up that might have upset Lucky. The relief is palpable.

"You'll earn it. I need you to take more control here. I need to get out to find new sources and I'll also be taking care of Mary. I know I can trust you, Dougal."

"You can. Never doubt it."

Sean reaches over the desk and both men shake hands. Sean has set the wheels in motion for a future retirement, a secret he keeps from his number two.

Back in the Club's entertainment area, Dougal feels ten feet tall. From Hennessy's barman and driver to joint owner of a business combining entertainment, gambling and prostitution. He hands out tasks to the staff and once the full team is in, delegates work to those he can rely on to take responsibility. He has other obligations to perform before the evening trade arrives. Sean says he has no need of the auto so Dougal takes off to find someone to make and fit an artificial leg for Johnny Miller. The kid has done well for them over the past two years, with looking out and reporting gossip of interest. His mother is a diligent worker of the laundry and causes no problems. Dougal would have liked a family and feels protective of the kid, who is cheerful despite his injury and has a cheeky sense of humour that never fails to raise a smile. The Club treats him like a mascot. Dougal finds himself enjoying this task. He tracks down a company that makes artificial limbs for ex-servicemen, a business that grew post-war, by asking some amputee WW1 veterans for recommendations. He drives over immediately, keen to get the task started so he can get back to the Ace.

It's a business situated off a busy road, in an area with a few artisans set up. As he walks into the yard, the smell of wood-shavings is dominant and the sound of mechanical saws through an open double door. Walking inside he is hailed by a small man in carpenter's apron as to his business, the man seeing Dougal has both his legs.

"I want a leg for a kid. Lost his above the knee." Dougal can see racks of wood ready for conversion, amazed how much business the company must do, even nearly 4 years after the Armistice.

The carpenter, who is the manager, shakes his head. "We've nothing in stock for kids. All our customers are adults."

253

Dougal reins in his urge to grab the guy by the lapels. "You can make one then. Fit him up with a good one. I'll be appropriately grateful."

"Hey, aren't you the guy at the Ace of Clubs?" Recognition has dawned. "No problem. Tell Mr O'Leary it will be a pleasure."

Dougal feels slighted but subdues his ire. "I'll send him in to be measured. It had better be a good leg, not a stump."

"Of course. My carpenters can shape it to resemble a natural leg so that trousers fit over it. It will only be obvious when walking. We can't do anything about that. And it will be comfortable, I promise, no chafing."

Dougal nods. "Send your bill to the Ace when done."

Rather than go immediately back to the Club, Dougal decides to make one more call. Rosie Miller, Johnny's ma, is hanging out sheets to dry when he draws up in the auto.

"Hiya, Rosie."

"Dougal. Is everything alright?" Rosie's first thought is that something has happened to Johnny.

"Yeah, no problem. Some good news."

"Well, come on in. The kettle's on the stove."

Dougal turns the engine off and follows Rosie indoors. He looks at her differently than he has ever before. The morning's wedding and Mary's commitment to Sean has shut a door for Dougal. Rosie is not in Mary's league but has pleasant features, a little flushed at the moment from the heat of laundering and exertions. A wisp of dark hair has escaped her headscarf and twists down to just above an eyebrow. Dougal has followed her closely so that when she stops, he walks into her. She turns, laughing, and without thinking Dougal kisses her.

"Dougal! What are you doing?"

"Oh my God! I'm so sorry, Rosie." Confused by what he has just done on instinct.

Rosie reaches up, places a hand behind his head and pulls him down to kiss him passionately.

CHAPTER 4

"We are merely the stars' tennis-balls, struck and bandied which way please them."

John Webster

Dougal reports back to Sean that he has arranged for Johnny Miller to be fitted with a false leg. Sean is deep into his accounts and just nods so he then goes in the yard to smoke a cigarette and reflect on what happened earlier.

He looks up at the ceiling. Patterns run across, light through the curtains, competing with cracks and some mould, unavoidable with the constant washing of laundry in the building. Rosie's head is on his naked stomach, his arm across her naked back. It had been quick, an urgency from both of them but in the aftermath, he struggles to come to terms with the passion from nowhere. He had seen Rosie on many occasions over the past two years, since she was given the laundry from the Ace and not once had he felt any emotion akin to affection let alone sexual interest. He acknowledges to himself, while not a classic beauty, there is an attractiveness to Rosie and her figure is not over-weight and her breasts are firm with small pert nipples. Dougal usually took his needs upstairs at the Ace, one of the perks, and had never considered a relationship elsewhere. Did he want this to go anywhere?

Mary stirs, and looks up at him with a sleepy smile. "Oh. Dougal. I needed that."

Dougal cannot find words and makes an attempt at a nod.

"Oh, don't worry, big man. We scratched an itch, that was all. I've not had a man since Johnny's father died. It was long overdue, so thank you."

Dougal had initially felt relief at Rosie's comments but on the drive back to the Ace, he had conflicting emotions. Perhaps he should look for a permanent arrangement. He is fond of Johnny and Rosie is still capable of child-bearing to give him his own children. Then again, his lifestyle and the violence waiting every day do not make him a good prospect as a father. Sean had waited until there wasn't a choice and did the honourable thing. But Sean had always been faithful to Mary since the day he met her, despite all the temptations of free sex upstairs. This is a new world for Dougal.

In the meantime, Sean has been on the telephone, making confident contact with suppliers and concealing his business worries. Alderman McAvoy was avoiding him but Sean's agents have reported he hasn't tied himself to anyone else. Sean feels the politician will return to the fold when he needs money. Dougal had organised a big floral tribute to the funeral and made apologies that Sean felt he should step back from openly attending, a ruse to hide his incapacitation. Another debt

Sean owes Dougal, another reason why he made him a partner. Looking to a desired future, Sean is planning to get away from Chicago with Mary and their child, build a new life, maybe in California, once he has enough money to see to all their needs. Dougal can have the whole business then.

Alderman McAvoy, now the funeral and a suitable mourning period had passed, is back to considering his options. He'd banked on Michael to be his future, letting him slip into semi-retirement while still taking a share of the payouts from O'Leary and others. The clubowner thought he had exclusive rights over the politician but the canny rogue had not let his left hand know what his right hand was doing. As long as he had clout and influence, there would be mobsters willing to fill his coffers. He'd suspected he hadn't been getting enough from O'Leary and a secondary purpose to getting his son inside the organisation was to report to him about how much money the Club was making. The red-haired gangboss should have taken care of his son. Where were those two thugs he'd met in O'Leary's office? They were supposed to be look after his kid. Maybe it's time to ditch one source and put his weight behind one of the bigger players. He'd worked his way through the girls of the Ace and is fancying new flesh anyway. The other Irish gangs were less keen on the vice trade but the Italians had plenty of brothels. Torrio and that young sidekick, Capone, were the up-and-coming men in town. They'd pay for information about the

Ace and the other businesses in that district. Meanwhile, he ought to ask his wife if she has any nephews who would like to work with him. Keep it in the family.

CHAPTER 5

Jesse has been visiting districts across the Irish neighbourhoods. Seemingly an odd-job-man looking for work and fitting in. He picks up small, one-time jobs, such as delivering in his truck, and chats to his temporary co-workers, collecting gossip but nothing substantial. Visiting various cafes, a few drinking dens, have revealed little clues as to the man he is tracking down. A day spent in the Library and a few hours at a newspaper office, have given him a lot of background on the mobsters in Chicago, the various gangs, who owns what and where the boundaries are. He'd bought a city streetmap and has marked off the territories. It now hangs on a wall in the workshop and Jesse has several notebooks with his findings. He's beginning to get a feel for which people to ignore – the big players wouldn't have tried his small distilling operation and if they had, and lost men, they'd have hit the town big time in reprisal. Nor need he check out the Italian, Jewish and Black neighbourhoods. He's now confident he's looking for an Irish middle-ranking mob boss, one who lacks the manpower to replace quickly the team that Jesse and the others had taken out. Some-one who would not want to broadcast his failures and show weakness and vulnerability.

Maisie has proved useful. After several visits and leading her on, Jesse had eventually taken her to the movies. Maisie is a chatterbox and gossips about the customers and who is a player in town and who is small fry. Although he is discounting the big players, Jesse decides he should check on Dion O'Banion, fast becoming the top Irish mobster in Chicago.

The Flower Shop stands at 736 North State Street. Jesse thinks he has been fooled into believing a top mobster operates as a florist, but as he is here, he might as well go in. Arranging flowers is an ordinary looking guy about 30. Plump round face, jovial appearance.

"Hello. What can I do for you, fella?" checking Jesse over, an unknown face in the neighbourhood.

"I'd like some flowers for my girl. Treating her nice," answers Jesse, while sizing up the man and the place.

"Special occasion, or just to surprise her?" The florist considers whether he has roses enough.

"Just a treat. Nothing expensive." Jesse doesn't want to overdo the effect on Maisie, nor suggest he is flush with money.

"We can do that. Let me put together a bouquet."

"I notice your cabinet is a bit in need of attention. Looks like it's ready to fall apart anytime soon. I have my tools in the truck. I could fix that in a jiffy."

"Well, why don't you do that while I make up the bouquet?"

Jesse thinks he may be wasting his time here but flowers for Maisie will keep her sweet while he needs her assistance in taking messages should Buck phone. He carries a tool box into the shop. The flower-seller keeps a keen eye on him and his hand near a pistol under the counter. A tool box could conceal a weapon. Jesse is aware of some tension in the room and moves slowly and careful, taking out the tools he needs to fix the cabinet. A bit of trimming then screwing back for strength and stability. "That ought to do it. How much do I owe you for the flowers?"

"On me. Nice to meet ya, swell fellow. I'm Dion O'Banion."

Jesse is slightly staggered but recovers quickly and shakes the proffered hand. "Harry Maguire."

"You look after that girl of yours. Come back when you decide to marry her and I'll give you a discount on the flowers."

"Thanks. Say. I'm new in town. Looking for work. Anything really but I can do decent carpentry."

"Come back tomorrow and I'll see if anything is going. That's a neat job on the cabinet." O'Banion rubs his chin in thought as Jesse leaves with the bouquet.

On his way back to the workshop Jesse stops by the Diner to give Maisie her flowers and check if any messages for him. There are none but Maisie is delighted with the gift, the first time ever anyone has brought her flowers, not counting the sidewalk weeds a kid had given her in kindergarten. She starts to think this young man is serious. So far, he's been the perfect gentleman. They'd been to the movies and taken walks round the park and he hadn't tried anything on, even though she is willing. Her father seems to approve, possibly relieved by the attention of the fresh-faced youth on his only daughter over the local males.

The next morning, Jesse is back at O'Banion's, nervously excited that his quest may be moving along. Two other guys are present at the flower shop. One is a slim, early twenties guy with a hint of east European accent. The other is big man, powerful presence, dimpled chin, scary until he smiles then his face lights up and he is "hail fellow, well met".

O'Banion makes the introductions. "Fellas, this is Harry Maguire. How'd your girl like the flowers, Harry?"

"Well pleased. I think I impressed her ma with my good intentions," for something to say, although he recalls that Maisie's mother is not alive and he should have said 'pa'.

O'Banion laughs. He indicates the slim guy first. "Harry, this is Hymie. The big bastard is George, but everyone knows him as Bugs. Why don't you go on out back? I need some shelving put up. Do a good job and I'll put you on a retainer."

Jesse recognises, from his newspaper research, that he has just met Earl "Hymie" Weiss and George "Bugs" Moran, the right hands of O'Banion. Weiss, really Henryk Wojciechowksi, a Polish immigrant in his early twenties, had been a minor criminal but was now one of the trio forming the North Side Gang. The other, George Moran, born Adelard Leo Cunin in Minnesota and of French descent, is in his mid-

263

twenties. All three are contemporaries of Jesse by age, which comes as a surprise to him. None of these are the man he is looking for but he hopes for a lead from them. Having collected tools from his truck, he re-enters the shop and goes into the back area. He can see that the shelves are make-shift, unstable. He'll need wood and goes back into the shop to tell O'Banion, interrupting the three men in a huddle. O'Banion stops the conversation to reply to Jesse.

"That's alright. Here's twenty. Get what you need." As soon as Jesse has driven off to get wood, he turns to his henchmen. "What do you think?"

Weiss speaks first. "Young but confident. Might have some experience."

Moran adds, "Doesn't seem Irish. I'm thinking Dutch."

O'Banion muses. "When he's finished here, have a couple of the boys follow him, see where he goes."

Jesse's skills in observation were already good but honed to an almost supernatural level by the Brits at Linghem. He realises that a car had pulled out behind his truck when he left the flower shop later, having returned with the wood and making a start on the shelves and is keeping to his speed and staying back the same distance. Several turns later, it is still on his tail. He doesn't want to lead them to the workshop or even to Maisie's diner. Jesse spots a Mechanic shop, sees an opportunity to check for certainty and pulls in under an advertising sign for

Sunoco Motor Oil. *"Give up the expensive habit of asking for just oil. Drain your crankcase regularly, select a high-quality oil of the proper type..."*. A mechanic, wiping his hands on a rag comes up to the truck as Jesse steps down. Pointing at the sign, Jesse says, "Can you do an oil change and pump up the tyres? I'll be back for it in the morning."

"Sure thing. Leave it there and I'll get on it once I finish on the engine of that car."

With that agreed, Jesse walks away, taking a direction opposite to one he had arrived from. Using reflections in a store window he sees the trail car pull up to the Mechanic's place and one man get out, walk over and talk to the mechanic. Jesse can see him reporting the conversation to the driver before he begins to follow Jesse on foot. As soon as possible, Jesse takes to alleys, acting nonchalant so as not to reveal he knows about his follower. At the opportune moment, he ducks into a doorway, where he is completely hidden from view unless the man takes the same route and Jesse is prepared to pretend he'd stopped to relieve his bladder should that happen. The follower comes round the corner and is faced with a choice of alleys to take and can't see Jesse in any of them. Not knowing where to go, he turns and rushes back to his companion with the car, parked at the garage. Seeing him go, Jesse takes a different route back to the same place, arriving in time to see the two men conferring before driving off. He figures they believe they can return tomorrow and pick up his trail when he collects his truck. Walking up to the mechanic, Jesse speaks. "Hey, sorry. I need the truck after all. Here's a couple of bucks for your trouble. I'll come back when I have more time."

"No problem. Hey, you just missed a pal of yours. He recognised your truck. I told him you'd be back in the morning if he wanted to leave a phone number but he said not to worry, he'd catch you up at work."

"That's fine. He probably wanted me in the card game tonight but I'm too tired. See you in the morning." Jesse gets in his truck and drives carefully to the workshop, constantly checking his mirrors and taking a couple of turns around blocks before he is satisfied he is not tagged.

The next day, Jesse returns to the Flower Shop. Nothing is mentioned. O'Banion has asked around and nothing about "Harry Maguire" is known, he hasn't rattled any cages in Chicago and is a jovial enough fellow.

"Harry. Don't worry about the shelves right now. I need a delivery taken to a friend at the Ace of Clubs. George will give you directions. You don't have a problem with this, do ya?"

Jesse shakes his head. "No, sir. I'll get right over there." This is the break he wants, to be inside an organisation where he can learn more about the action among the gangs. and his truck is loaded with cases of beer.

Moran has provided an address and a hand-drawn map as Jesse confesses that he is not familiar with the streets, being from Springfield, setting detail to his assumed identity. Setting off, he checks his mirror and notes he is being followed again. This is a test and he needs to be cautious until he is more trusted. However, he doesn't notice the Italians trailing his followers and nor do they, being keenly watching Jesse's truck so he doesn't lose them again.

After they see Jesse pull into the yard at the Ace, O'Banion's guys drive on, job done and with some relief nothing has gone wrong, but the Italians pause to see who the new guy is and why he had protection during the drive from the Flower Shop. They see Jesse talking to Dougal, a handshake and a friendly conversation while cases of beer are unloaded from the truck.

They wait down the street for Jesse to leave and follow him back to North State Street. Satisfied this is a routine between the Irish centres, they go off to report to their boss.

"O'Banion and O'Leary have a new guy working for them. We've never seen him before."

Their boss is interested. "What's he look like? He might be a replacement for the mick's missing guys."

"Five nine, five ten maybe. Early twenties. Could be Irish but we never got close enough to hear him speak."

Later, when he sees his own boss, Al Capone, at the Four Deuces in

Wabash Street, he reports the news and a description. Capone likes to know everything and casually mentions it to Torrio, having heard rumours that familiar faces from the Ace hadn't been seen for a while and Alderman McAvoy having offered his services to them.

Torrio says, "Let's pay attention. There's something not right with O'Leary's operation and we can never trust O'Banion."

Attention to detail is what helps the Torrio-Capone gang grow its business and keep it.

CHAPTER 6

"The trouble is not in dying for a friend,
but in finding a friend worth dying for".

Mark Twain

His work done and the day drawing to a close, the evening arriving with the dimming light struggling into the concrete canyons of Chicago, Jesse turns into the street to park at his lock-up. He feels he is making progress but wishes it to be speedier so that he can protect his friends back home. The longer he takes to find and eliminate his enemy the more chance of discovery and action against him and his. Jesse wants it all to be over, to shed this existence that he never sought.

His thoughts are scattered when his senses prickle as sees a coupe across the street from his doors. A curl of cigarette smoke from an open window on the driver's side, indicates an occupant and potential risk. Has he been discovered? What reason could there be for a car to park up here? Instinctively, he takes his Colt from under his seat, pulls the slide to load a round and lays it on the passenger seat where he can easily reach it. Thinking "They've sussed me out," he prepares to draw level and fire through the windows to take out the suspected hit man first. Slamming on his brakes as the two vehicles line up, he raises the weapon and is squeezing the trigger when he recognises the driver in time to prevent a shot. The occupant is startled to looking down the barrel of a gun.

"Jesse!"

"Sheriff Buckley! What are you doing in Chicago?"

"Can we go inside? I need coffee and a glass."

"Of course." Relief flows over Jesse in a cold rush.

As Jesse opens the doors to the yard to park his truck inside, Buck locks and leaves his car in the street, drops the stub of his cigarette and grinds it out with his boot. The sheriff looks drawn and tired. As Jesse parks up against the building, he closes the gate and walks over.

Jesse is curious, but will wait to hear the reason for the sheriff's arrival without notice, all the same, rather pleased at a familiar face. "This way," indicating they should go in the workshop and up the stairs. The sheriff notes the layout automatically, his natural response to entering new premises, looking for where a threat might come from and avenues of escape. Wyatt Earp taught him that habit and after a few decades it is still ingrained. Once in the living accommodation, handing Buck a bottle of good whiskey that he had obtained during one of his outings by swapping a couple of bottles of gin, Jesse gets the pre-ground beans out and brews coffee. Buck pours a generous measure into the mug provided and downs it quickly, Jesse notes to himself.

There is no conversation until sitting down, facing each other across a table, Buck speaks first.

"It's Maggie....She came to Chicago to work in a department store.

At first, she kept in touch with her parents but they haven't heard anything for a couple of weeks. Obviously, they are worried. That isn't like Maggie so I thought I'd drive here; check she is okay and double up to see how you are. I went to her lodgings but they say she left with a man, took all her belongings. They didn't know who, but said he looked Italian."

"Maggie! I never knew she was in town." Jesse is surprised at the news.

"I never told her I knew how to contact you. I figured your life was too dangerous to have Maggie turn up on your doorstep. I'm concerned about her disappearance, and with a stranger."

"Yeah, me too. This doesn't sound good." Jesse rubs his hand over his head, thinking, worried.

"How's your quest? Can you put it aside to help me?" Buck knows he can't search by himself but Jesse has a mission to complete for the safety of those back home.

"Look. It's too late to do anything tonight. Bunk here and we'll go back to the lodgings first thing in the morning then to the store. Do you know which it is?"

"Yes."

"OK. Let's get something to eat, get some sleep and set off first thing in the morning." Jesse reprioritises. He's here to save friends and one is more in need right now.

Buck is snoring gently, tired from his drive and relaxed by a good dose of whiskey. Jesse, on the other hand, can't sleep. A feeling of guilt and responsibility over Maggie nagging his brain and refusing to shut down. This is more important than his mission and whatever it takes to find Maggie and get her back safely.

Morning eventually comes round and Jesse is first up and brews coffee. While drinking, Jesse consults his streetmap and works out a route. They decide to go in the sheriff's car as more non-descript than the truck and less chance of unwanted attention to Jesse.

The lodging house does not provide much of a clue to Maggie's actions except to confirm she was picked up by a man in a Packard and that he looked and sounded Italian, swarthy skin, slick black hair. He'd come back alone for her belongings, paid her rent up-to-date but hadn't provided a forwarding address. The landlord didn't seem concerned; he'd got his money and could soon find another tenant. "Kids these days! Too much time at the movies."

They are more successful at the department store. Jesse lets Buck approach the manager while he chats with the shopgirls. The manager is angry that she just stopped attending without notice but the serving girls are able to provide a better description of the man who had repeatedly come in the store and spent time talking to Maggie. They figure, with some envy, that she had eloped, each with their own dream of romance.

Outside, Buck speaks first. "That's not like Maggie. She wouldn't cease contact with her parents. I'm fearing the worst."

"This is not a good town for a country girl. Why did she come?"

"I guess home was too small for her and....."

"Go on."

"Perhaps she was looking for you."

That lays on Jesse's conscience and his even more determined to find her and get her home.

"Buck. Sir. Whatever it takes. We're getting her back."

"Yes, Jesse. Whatever it takes. I'm not going home without her."

Yet, neither know what to do next.

CHAPTER 7

"In a storm the Willow bent and survived
but the Oak could not and was felled."

Aesop

Guiseppe looks in on Maggie. She'd shown more spirit that he'd expected. Breaking her in is going to be hard work. Slapping her and raping her is not turning her into a whore quickly enough. He'd been taken by her beauty and intelligence and figured he could pimp her for big bucks. But no matter how much he hit her and fucked her, she lay like a dead fish until he finished then spat at him. He wondered whether it had been worth the effort and maybe he should cut his losses. Kill her and dump her body in the river. Go back to picking up new arrivals at the station for the racket the gang runs.

When Guiseppe had walked into the department store he had immediately noticed the new girl, country fresh, not a city pallor. He might be a pimp and hustler, but he dressed in a smart but understated fashion. Sold the look of honest young man with a good job. One small gold ring on the little finger, no necklaces or bracelets. Sports jacket and slacks. Always with a good word and compliment for the shop girls. Decided he should buy some handkerchiefs, which was the counter Maggie was staffing.

"Hello. New here? I haven't seen you before."

Maggie was charm and politeness. This was a potential customer and not a bad-looking one at that. "Well, yes. I started yesterday. Is there something you'd like help with? We have some linen handkerchiefs in boxes of three, or silk individually for a few dollars more."

"Show me the silk. Something blue to match your eyes."

Guiseppe bought two handkerchiefs on that visit. He would come back every couple of days, applying his charm, sometimes making further purchases ("a scarf for my grandmother"/ "a hankie for my sister") before inviting Maggie to the movies. A Harold Lloyd film was showing – "Safety Last" – and Maggie was easily persuaded, after all, this was a man who was thoughtful of his feminine relatives.

He picked Maggie up from her lodgings in his automobile, an older model Packard but well-maintained. "We're early for the show. Let's have a coffee first."

Maggie thought this might be a good idea. Get to know each other better before going into a darkened moviehouse for a couple of hours and not talking. There was still time to call the date off. The coffeeshop was clean, cloths on each table, some posies in vases, waitresses in aprons. Quite respectable.

Guiseppe asked what she wanted and ordered for them both. "Black coffee and a soda, please."

Maggie thought he had excellent manners. She'd never met an Italian before and found him quite exotic. She wasn't looking for a relationship, just a friend in the city, although if things developed, she imagined it could be exciting. Coming to Chicago was meant to be an adventure. Any future she'd once imagined was dust. Tom Jr was no more. Jesse had changed and moved away. Although she did hope he was in Chicago and she might come across him. She'd asked Sheriff Buckley if he knew where Jesse had gone and he'd said "Jesse has decided to take the heat away from here. He'll be in touch when he feels it's okay to do so." Maggie only had a slight idea of what had been going on. She knew about the distilling – it was an open secret in town and her parents were involved with the logistics. She was less clear about Fred White, the pharmacist; people who might know had become tight-lipped. Sheriff Buckley had gunned down a stranger who had tried to kill him, that was only known to a few. Moses and Maggie were running the farm, now called the Freeman Farm. And the booze business had stopped, except for the few home-brewing. They'd been a bit of excitement when Wyatt Earp paid a visit to the Buckleys but then it was back to a quiet town, nothing happening and Maggie needed a change.

"I'll just go in the ladies' room to freshen up," and Maggie had taken directions from a waitress to go out the back.

Guiseppe decided this was the opportunity he was waiting for. The original plan was to watch the movie then overcome Maggie after. He slipped a powder into her soda and swirled it to dissolve.

Maggie returned a few minutes later. "Should we go? We don't want to miss it."

"Nah, it's alright. There's always something first. Finish your drink." Which Maggie did.

They made it back to the automobile before Maggie started to feel faint and swayed against her date.

"Here, take it easy. Get in the car." Guiseppe was the concerned gentleman in case anyone was watching, but the street was empty at that moment. With Maggie inside, he waited until she was fully unconscious then lowered her on the seat, out of sight. It was only a short ride to the place he rented. Guiseppe was happy to have saved the money on movie tickets and not having to keep up the pretence any longer. He had his victim and could move on to his plan. The white slave racket was profitable for him and the gang he was a member of.

Maggie had come round with a small headache and a sense of confusion. As her wits returned, she realised she was in a strange room, naked and her hands were tied to the headboard.

"Hello? Is anyone there? Where am I?" a quaver in her voice from the fear than ran through her.

The door opened and Guiseppe stood there, holding a cup of coffee, dressed in undershirt and trousers, no socks or shoes. "Well, welcome."

"Guiseppe. What's going on? Why am I here? Where are my clothes?" She put her knees tightly together and turned her legs away from him, but she couldn't cover her naked breasts.

"Let me get you some water," and Guiseppe went outside the room, on to a landing, and Maggie heard a clunk of a cup being put down, a cupboard opening and water from a tap. She surveyed the room, a shabby place. Dirty curtains pulled closed across a single window. Wallpaper peeling and cobwebs in the corners of the ceiling.

Guiseppe returned with a glass of water, sat down beside her and lifted her head. "Drink."

Maggie realised she was really thirsty and consumed all the contents of the glass. Guiseppe put the glass on the floor, took a handkerchief from his pocket and dried her lips and dabbed at some splashes on her chest. She shrunk from his touch. He laughed, "this is a great hankie you sold me."

"There'll be people looking for me. Let me go and I won't tell them about this."

"Now, baby. We both know that's not true. You're out of town. You don't have people here and haven't been here long enough to make friends. I went to your lodgings, collected your stuff and paid your rent. They've written you off. They'll be another girl in your room by tonight and the world keeps turning."

"When my parents don't hear from me, they'll send someone to find

278

me and God help you when he does."

"Yeah? You hope. This is a big city. Too many places to search. Whoever comes, if there really is a someone, won't know where to look and won't be getting any help. Cops don't care about missing girls – no money in it."

"Why are you doing this?" Maggie was close to tears but fought them back, not wanting to appear weak, although being naked and helpless was scaring her immensely.

He licked a finger and ran it across her pubic hair. "Money, girl. Although, I'm going to have my fun first." Guiseppe left Maggie with this terrifying thought.

Maggie realised, at least felt hopeful, Guiseppe was not going to kill her. She had an inkling about what he intended - she wasn't totally naïve – and wondered whether death might be preferable. Then she thought that her parents would send someone and that would likely be Sheriff Buckley. He would have contacts perhaps in Chicago PD. He certainly would know how to track her and he would be relentless in the search. Yes. And if Jesse were to learn of her predicament, she knew he would never desert her. She must survive. She found a courage she never knew she had, or had needed before. Her hands tied and a rope fixing her to a heavy bedpost meant she couldn't move far but she was able to reach a bucket in the corner to relieve herself. At least she was spared the embarrassment of urinating on herself. The house was quiet. She assumed Guiseppe had gone out. Maggie looked around the room for anything to assist an escape but the room was barren. He had picked up and removed the glass when he left. She had hoped he would forget so that she could break it and use it to cut her bonds. The curtains were drawn and out of reach to open to see into the street and maybe call out to a passer-by. No sounds from outside. Should she try shouting? What if Guiseppe hadn't left but was in the next room. What would his reaction be? She must wait for a weakness in her situation, one to exploit.

CHAPTER 8

Buck goes off early to seek out information from the Chicago Police Department, picking a station on the fringe of the Italian neighbourhoods, announcing his role as Sheriff looking for one of his town's girls. Even at this early hour, it is busy. Drunks, squabbling couples, a shopkeeper reporting a robbery creating bustle and noise. When he eventually gets to him, the sergeant at the front desk is unimpressed and a despondent Buck is a nearly out the door when his name is called.

"Sheriff Buckley?"

Buck turns and sees a beat cop, young and fresh, bright uniform still pristine from the wardrobe.

"You won't remember me, sir. My family left town when I was nine. Jimmy Wild."

Buck holds his hand out for a shake. "Jimmy Wild. You're Pete Wild's son. Good at baseball, I recall. How are your parents?"

Jimmy Wild is flattered to be remembered. "Dad's not so good. Lungs. Ma is running a boarding house."

"And you're a cop."

"Yes, sir. I overheard what you were asking the sarge. Is Maggie McGregor really missing. She was a year above me at school."

" 'Fraid so. Came to work in a department store then no word. Her parents are worried."

281

"Look. There's a restaurant round the corner – the Bakehouse. Give me half an hour and meet me there. I'll see what I can find out. Can't promise, but I liked Maggie and it would be awful if anything bad has happened to her."

"Thanks, son. It will be appreciated." Buck is relieved to have someone willing to help.

Jesse goes to the Flower Shop. He had been asked to make more local deliveries so he keeps up his pretence in order to learn more about the Irish mobs but he also sees an opportunity to discover where he might look for Maggie. While loading cases of beer, he talks to the men helping. "I haven't seen any action with girls around here."

A guy, about Jesse's age answers. "Don't let Mr O'Banion hear you asking about girls. He's very much against it. You'll find girls at the Ace if you want one."

"What about the Italians?"

"Fuck me. Stay away. You'll end up in an alley if you tread their turf."

"Nah. I'm alright. Got a regular girl. Just some pals arriving in town and they might like some action."

"Then stick with the Ace. They won't get rolled there. Lucky O'Leary runs a clean business."

"Thanks for the advice. I will," but Jesse is secretly disappointed at hitting a dead end. He hopes the sheriff is having more success.

Buck is on his second coffee with a cake, having skipped breakfast, when Jimmy Wild turns up. Buck waves to him from a corner table and then signals the waitress to bring more coffee for the cop. Jimmy drops his hat on the table and sits.

"I could only find some general information. Don't know if it will help."

"I need anything at the moment, Jimmy. Let's hear it."

"OK." Pauses to accept the coffee from a waitress. "The talk at the station is that most girls operate because they want the money. There are some independents from the clubs, you know, work with one pimp, usually a boyfriend or husband. Having a girl kidnapped and forced into prostitution doesn't happen much but there is a rumour that one of the Italian bunches do take them in if the girl is something special. We have weirdos who like to take girls who are not tame, if you understand what I mean." Jimmy blushes at talking like this.

Buck leans forward. "Where might I find such guys, Jimmy?"

The young cop takes out from his pocket a streetmap, which he pushes across the table.

"I've marked the neighbourhood under the control of the gang. Here's a name of someone who works at the Da Vinci hotel. He's the contact for out-of-towners to set up with a girl. I asked a cop who takes backhanders," embarrassed that he is admitting to corruption in the force.

"Thanks, Jimmy. That helps a lot. When I get her, I'll tell Maggie you helped. Give my regards to your parents. They raised a good kid."

Both men stand and shake hands. Leaving Jimmy to sit down again and enjoy his coffee, Buck pays and leaves. He figures that is it is too soon for Jesse to be back at the workshop so he might as well take a drive round this neighbourhood to get a feel for it. With the map provided by Jimmy Wild, it is simply a matter of counting blocks and where to turn. He may have some information from the reconnoitre when back at Jesse's and they can discuss a plan of action.

Jesse pulls into the yard behind the Ace to make his delivery for O'Banion. Two men are talking by the back door of the club. Jesse recognises Dougal from his previous visits but the big guy with him is a new face. However, his shock of red hair tells Jesse this is Sean "Lucky" O'Leary, the boss. Even in an expensive suit, the man is impressive, exuding strength. As Jesse draws up, Sean frowns and narrows his eyes at the stranger. Dougal sees this.

"It's OK, Lucky. This is O'Banion's driver. Harry, meet Sean O'Leary, the boss here. Sean, this is Harry Maguire."

"Pleased to meet you, sir."

Sean nods and looks Jesse up and down. It's an assessment. A lean youth, no Irish accent so not one of the clan. Finishes his conversation with Dougal as others help Jesse unload. Jesse notices a stack of empty bottles by the bins and recognises a number are his. Molly had stuck labels on bottles to date the production and batch. They are obviously

284

from his farm. Surreptitiously, he pays more attention to O'Leary. So this is the man he must kill. A certainty, because not enough gin was taken on the first visit to allow dispersal across bars and club, just enough to serve one establishment for maybe a month at best, depending how busy the trade. Jesse has a dry mouth.

Having returned earlier, with a feel for the lay of the land, Buck has been working out a plan while he waits for Jesse. Hearing the gate open, he looks out of the upstairs window and confirms it is Jesse returning. He makes a pot of coffee and puts it on the stove to brew. Jesse comes in, carrying a loaf, cheese and meats.

"Thought you might be hungry. I am."

"Coffee's brewing. I've had some success about finding Maggie." Anticipating Jesse's question, he continues, "No, nothing definite, just potential and the only lead I have."

Jesse puts the groceries on the table then sits opposite Buck, who fills in more detail.

"Remember Jimmy Wild. Class below you but played baseball in the juniors?"

"Yeah. He's alright. But didn't the family leave town some years back?"

"That's right. Came to Chicago. Well, Jimmy's a cop and I came across him at the precinct." Lays the streetmap on table and flattens the folds. "He gave me the info of where to start." Pointing with finger,

"Italian gang operates around here. One of the few to run girls who don't want to be in the game."

Comparing to his own map, Jesse agrees it is an Italian neighbourhood. "Be hard to ask around. We'd stick out like a sore thumb."

"Thought of that. Jimmy told me about a guy at the Da Vinci Hotel who caters for guests looking for action. Figure I should book in as a guest then make an approach."

Leaving Jesse to mull the plan over, Buck gets up to attend to the hissing pot, pours two cups of coffee and brings them to the table.

"We may only get one chance. What if they produce another girl, not Maggie?" Jesse worries.

"I'll have to be specific about my tastes." A look of distaste over Buck's face over the part he will have to play.

Jesse speaks. "It will be easier if you come across as wealthy. I have cash. Offer a premium for the right girl."

"Thanks, Jesse." Buck drinks half his cup while thinking the next move.

Jesse confesses, "I'll give everything I have for Maggie to be safe. Kinda feel this is down to me. If I hadn't started the distilling, everyone would be happier."

"Not true, Jesse. You saved your farm. Moses and Molly are doing well with it. I think Maggie would have come to the city anyway. You can't write other people's story." Buck recognises that Jesse carries a burden on his shoulders. Not something a young man should be weighed down with. He can still see the kid inside this new man, a veteran of war and crime, and is sad for a moment.

"When Maggie's safe, I have a job to do here. I have to protect the town from these people. I've found my man."

"When Maggie's safe." Buck salutes with his cup. He feels the bond.

CHAPTER 9

Jesse drops Buck off in another district, with an overnight bag, so he can take a cab to the Da Vinci and not be traced back to the workshop. All part of the image of an out-of-towner. As the Elcar taxicab of the Diamond Cab company approaches the hotel, Buck can tell this is an Italian neighbourhood. Shop signs, cooking smells coming through the open window of the cab, even the people look Italian, in their appearance and the way they dressed. These are probably first-generation immigrants.

The Da Vinci has four floors, a double door to the street under a pigeon faeces-splattered awning. Trying to look better class than it probably is. Paying off the cab driver – "keep the change" – Buck assesses the street. A few businesses, retail with stalls on the sidewalk, an alley alongside the hotel worth noting for access and egress. Buck misses his home town; this place is too crowded and no familiar faces. Mentally girding himself, he takes the few steps up from the street and enters. Behind the reception desk is a short, chubby guy with slicked hair and wearing something that might once have been a uniform. Judging by the misshape it was not made or bought for the guy wearing it. He either inherited or maybe even shared it with another employee. The desk in line with the door, he'd noticed this guest arriving in one of the better cabs to be found in Chicago and not taking change from the driver. He senses opportunities for profit.

On walking in and placing his bag on the floor in front of the desk, Buck speaks.

"I need a room for a couple of nights while in town on business."

"Yes, sir. We have a room free on the second floor, overlooking the street. Pay in advance."

"No problem." Buck's pleased to get a street-facing room without having to ask. He opens his wallet, allowing the receptionist to see how much cash he has and hands over a couple of bills. "What's your name?"

"Luigi, sir." The greed positively glitters in the man's eyes.

Buck smiles inside, he's found the man Jimmy indicated was a go-between. Must not rush it. Holding his wallet open, "Is it possible to get a bottle of whiskey, Luigi?"

Luigi looks Buck over. He's senses something about this guy. Not a youngster but tall, straight, with a commanding air, perhaps ex-military. Yet the lure of the dollar bills does its stuff. "I'll ask around."

"Appreciated," and Buck slides a ten over the counter and winks.

Buck drops his bag on the floor of his room. He may have to stay the night, a frustration but better not to act too quickly and set off alarms. The whiskey request is a test. He looks through the window at the street – Little Italy. Voices coming up are rarely in American. Ordinary people seeking a new life but not leaving the old one behind.

Bringing their culture and language with them. That's what his ancestors did and Buck respects that. The United States of America is a melting pot of the world. Many decent, hard-working people came but they were followed by the predators, those who fed on their own. Protection rackets on businesses made Buck clench his fists. That wasn't serving the community. He might not approve of gambling but it was something people wanted and he hadn't been averse to games of poker in his younger days. He'd never gone for paying girls. In fact, he was pretty inexperienced in the romance stakes before he met Agnes. But soon he would have to act the part of a lecher. He hopes he can pull it off. His only contact with Jesse will be through the girl, Maisie, at the diner after their next planned rendezvous, which is in an hour.

Jesse has left his truck in a street then walked a couple of blocks for the meeting with Buck. He is careful about checking for a tail or anyone recognising him being off his patch. He must not draw attention to Buck at this crucial moment. He sees Buck walking towards him and a tap of his pocket as if checking he had something in it, a subtle signal he has spotted Jesse. Satisfied that Buck has seen him, Jesse turns into an empty alley and walks far enough in for secrecy. Seconds later, Buck turns in but pauses inside the corner of the building. He pulls out the makings for a cigarette, rolls one and lights it. If anyone has been following him, they would have thought he is sheltering from a breeze while he makes a smoke. When satisfied he too has not been followed, Buck walks deeper in the alley. Both men are on edge.

"OK, Jesse. I'm booked in. Second floor front. If I need to speak to you, I'll hang a towel in the window to catch you on a drive-past. I'll also leave a message at the diner with Maisie. No success yet, the message will be – I don't need the doors fixing until next week. If I have hooked our fish, it will be – my mother needs cupboards putting up."

"Got it."

"We only get the one chance once we have found her. It might be messy getting rid of the bastards holding her."

"Whatever it takes."

Buck looks with renewed eyes at Jesse. The kid he once knew has gone. War, then the events recently have made a man. Buck feels the adrenalin rush of anticipated action and knowing he has someone trustworthy backing him. He wonders whether Wyatt had had the same thoughts when he was the Marshal's deputy. He hopes so. Handshake on an unspoken contract and Buck leaves the alley while Jesse counts to one hundred before doing the same.

Jesse goes back to working for O'Banion, delivering beer around a couple of speakeasies. The Ace of Clubs is a big customer for beer and the Italians who keep an eye on the goings-on have assumed he is working for O'Leary as he is most regularly there and spends time chatting with Dougal or the bar manager. Orders down from Capone, they have been working the district for more information. They have spotted Jesse's regular diner too and been using it themselves as a convenient location, fitting in as it has a multi-ethnic customer base. The paranoia among mobsters is huge. They always assume someone is after their business and a takeover is usually by gunfire. Not being paranoid can get you killed. Having themselves brought hitmen in from outside Chicago, they make a point of researching any new faces in the Irish gangs in case they have the same strategy. Outside hitmen bring in deniability, a tactic used by Torrio for the hit on Big Jim Colosimo. They relaxed a bit when Jesse seemed to be settling in and making the waitress at the diner his girl. Dining there themselves, some casual flirting of Maisie had got her talking about Jesse, which did not reveal much, but had them marking him down as labour and not a threat; a hitman would not set up in business in town and would keep a low profile. He's not been brought in as a replacement for the absent guys of O'Leary's gang.

Buck had gone back to the Da Vinci after a call in at a cafe to pass time. Luigi is not on the desk but a bottle of whiskey is in his room. He opens it and pours a third down the sink, rinses a glass with more and pours that away. Leaving that to tell a story, he goes out again for a walk. He's also noticed that his belongings have been searched but he has no concerns that his real identity or purpose will have been discovered, he had cleaned personal items out at Jesse's. He walks the nearby streets, taking in sights and sounds and learning the layout. Smells from a Ristorante make him realise he is hungry and he enters and orders spaghetti and meatballs in tomato sauce. It's a waiting game.

Jesse has made his last delivery so takes a drive past the Da Vinci. No towel in the window. He knows it is too soon but he had hoped. He drives to the diner for the dual purpose of a hot meal and to be present should Buck phone there. Maisie's face lights up when he walks in.

"Missed you, Jesse."

"Sorry, Maisie. Picked up a lot of work and been busy."

"Walk out tonight?"

"Mmm? Can we do another time? Got to get some stuff together. Big job coming up. Keep the customer happy and I'll have regular income." Leaving that as a suggestion of the future.

Maisie is disappointed but accepts the excuse. Jesse is too distracted to realise how he makes her feel.

Hunger sated, Buck returns to the Da Vinci and, this time. Luigi is back on duty.

"Hello, sir. I trust your room is satisfactory," with an emphasis on the last word.

Buck smiles back. "Sure is. I see you are a man who gets things done.

293

I wonder …."

"Sir?"

"No. Nothing. Just an idea."

"My job is to keep our customers happy. If there anything you want, anything."

"Well, I'm only in town for a few days and a fella gets lonely, has needs, if you get what I mean."

"The gentleman does not have a lady friend in the city? That is a shame….. However, I do have contacts that can fix that," leaving the proposition open.

Buck takes his wallet out in a casual manner. "You're a man of the world, Luigi. I guess I can speak freely with you."

Luigi's eyes are transfixed by the fat wallet. "Of course, sir. What would you like?"

"I don't want any girl. I have…. tastes." Buck pauses to see if Luigi is accepting his words. "I like young girls, not been round the world, if you get my drift."

"Any age you like, I know where there are …"

"Oh, Christ, no. Not kids. Just young, early twenties, before they are worn out."

"Forgive me."

"No, it's OK. I didn't make myself clear." Although Buck now yearns to pull Luigi over the counter and beat him to a pulp, he restrains himself. The emotion however, is read by Luigi as embarrassment. "And I don't like them broken. I like to tame them myself. A bit of spirit, eh." Buck is trusting his assessment of Maggie is helping him give the right description.

"That is a bit more difficult." Luigi plays a game to raise the price.

Buck opens his wallet and examines the contents. The Italian can see the thick wad of dollar bills.

"I think a few Presidents could sort out any problems. I'd prefer a nice country fresh girl and I won't be taken in by some made up townie. I know the real article."

"I'll ask round." Luigi feels lucky, because he knows where to make a request for such a girl and get a finder's fee from both ends of the transaction.

"Good man." Buck takes out a twenty and lays it on the counter. "More to come if I am satisfied."

Jesse has eaten dinner and dessert and drunk three cups of coffee as slowly as possible, praying for the phone to ring. He fears if he sticks around any longer, Maisie will demand that they walk out as he obviously has no work to do. The food sits like a lump of lead in his stomach.

"Don't want to leave you but I guess I had better get going." Pays the bill and kisses Maisie on the cheek. She thinks Jesse is being a bit cold towards her, sensing a change in his demeanour and a distant occupation of his mind.

Rather than go back to the workshop where he will have no communication with Buck, Jesse decides to drive over to the Da Vinci and check for the signal. The inaction is gnawing at his insides and giving him indigestion.

Buck has put a towel in the window but stays there, watching the street, anxious for contact with Jesse. He isn't ready to call the diner as what he has to relate is neither zero or success but he does want to talk. He's smoked three cigarettes when he spots a truck that looks like Jesse's.

Jesse drives slowly along and takes a look up to the second floor, not only a towel but he can see Buck looking out. He presses his horn at a convenient pedestrian crossing the road to attract the sheriff's attention in case he is overlooked.

With relief, Buck recognises Jesse and watches his progress along the street until he turns a corner. Grabs his coat and leaves the hotel to follow, no one on the desk to notice. Jesse has parked down a side street and is waiting in his truck. Checking over his shoulder and satisfied no one is paying attention, Buck walks up and gets inside quickly, agilely for his age.

"He's taken the bait and I hope it leads to Maggie. Can you stay around? Maybe keep an eye on the hotel and, if I leave, follow me? If you lose me, meet me here again in…two hours. If I don't turn up then, drive past every thirty minutes until I do. Got that?" Buck is breathless from anticipation.

"Can do. Be careful. You armed?"

"I have a twenty-two on me and a knife in my boot. That will have to do until we can arm up and go in, provided it is Maggie they take me to."

"I've two automatics, and a shotgun in the back."

"Good man. OK. See you later." Buck lithely leaves the truck and is off down the street. Age seems to have fallen away from the lawman as the potential for action offers. Jesse checks the street and the sidewalks and is content no one has paid attention and moves off to another street.

Luigi, back at his post, looks up as Buck enters the lobby of the Da Vinci. "Ah, sir. A gentleman will be here to pick you up at seven. I trust that is alright."

"Local? I'm a little unsure about going with someone I don't know."

"He's my cousin. No problem. No, it's a couple of streets away. You can walk it from here."

"That's good. Luigi. If I am a happy man when I return, there'll be a bonus for you."

When in his room, Buck finally breathes again. He has a couple of hours to wait. And it may not lead to Maggie. He may have to playact all over again. Even start somewhere else. It's been a while, but Buck prays, prays hard.

Jesse has parked his truck and, walking back to the same street as the Da Vinci, finds a coffeeshop where he can sit by the window and keep an eye on the hotel. He realises the fragility of their plan. He's taken one of the automatics from the back of the truck and stuck it in his waistband, under his coat where it cannot be seen. It digs into him as he fidgets but he feels reassured by its presence. His cup of coffee grows cold. No contact is possible with Buck now except when they next meet up and he must not miss the sheriff leaving the hotel.

Buck keeps checking his watch hasn't stopped. He's never known time pass so slowly. He splashes his face with cold water. He's been in gunfights as a deputy. He never broke a sweat in dealing with that guy with a razor. Yet, this is different. It isn't about him but an innocent young girl, daughter of friends, whose future, even life, is at stake. He accepts he is frightened at the thought of failure.

The guy behind the counter has been eyeing Jesse for some time. The coffee sits untouched and grown cold. The young man has been glued to the window the whole time. As if realising he is observed, Jesse rises, shrugs. "I guess she isn't coming," and the act of a young man being stood up by his date quashes the curiosity of the owner, who nods in sympathy as he takes payment.

Buck feels his chest tightening as the minute hand touches the twelve, making it seven o'clock finally. He checks his 22 once again then returns it to his pocket.

Jesse walks the street, always within sight of the Da Vinci. He'd seen a guy go in a few minutes ago and felt his pulse race. Was this a guest or a sign of something happening?

A knock on the door and Buck opens it to see Luigi.

"My cousin is downstairs ready to take you to your party."

There's an oily obsequiousness to the doorman that nauseates but Buck hides his feelings. His mouth is too dry for him to speak so he nods and follows Luigi down to the lobby where another Italian is waiting. A younger and more dapper type than the receptionist, more dangerous-looking to the lawman's instinct. Buck wonders if he might be being set up for a robbery and they take all his money and leave his body in an alley. He tempers the temptation to stick his pistol in the guy's face and make him talk. He has to go through with this in case it does lead to Maggie. He hopes Jesse is in place to have his back.

Jesse has waited by a corner, so as not to be visible, and sees two men come out of the hotel. One is the same guy who went in several minutes ago and the other is Buck. Relief that they are walking and not driving, Jesse doesn't have to run back to his truck to trail them. There are enough people out on the streets for Jesse not to stand out. He looks like a workman probably returning home after a day's graft. Buck has not seen Jesse as, coming out of the hotel, they had turned in the opposite direction. He resists a desperate urge to look around to check.

"My cousin tells me you want a fresh country girl."

Buck coughs to clear his throat. "That's right. I can't do this in my home town but I'd like to pretend that's where I am, with one of the local girls. Is that strange to you?"

"No, signor. We all have our different tastes. I think I have just the young lady for you. Fresh in to Chicago. Luigi said, you want to 'break her in', I think."

"Like breaking a wild horse. They resist until you show them who is master."

"It will not be cheap. This can only be done once. If you tame her, she is tamed forever."

"I'll pay for the privilege. But I want to see her before I agree she'll do. Sorry, but I don't want second rate or a ringer." Buck is finding the role of a lecher becoming easier with the practice.

"Genuine article, I assure you. We're nearly there." The Italian smiles expansively.

Buck feels the pistol in his pocket for reassurance. He worries this is seeming too easy.

Jesse watches the two men enter a building down a back street. Light is beginning to fade early, partly because of shadows of tall buildings and partly due to the overcast sky threatening rain. He doesn't know if Buck is aware that he is nearby. Standing in a doorway of a closed building, he checks his automatic has a round chambered. If this turns into a gunfight, he only has the one gun and Buck only has his 22. Jesse would have liked to have brought his shotgun, but it is not a weapon to carry through the streets.

Buck follows Luigi's cousin indoors. Two Italians are seating at a table, playing cards and they nod as the newcomers enter. This is the moment when it might be a hoax to take his money and kill or beat him up. Buck is ready to draw his pistol but nothing untoward happens and he is led up stairs by the cousin. They pause on the landing.

"Well, mister. If you like what you see it's forty dollars. More if you want to take it even further," and he unlocks a door and opens it.

Jesse has checked his automatic yet again. The waiting for news is making him crazy. Has Buck found Maggie? Is Buck alright? Should he go in after him?

Buck stands in the doorway. At least he now knows it's not a trap.

A girl is lying on a bed, dressed only in a shift, facing the wall. From what he can make out, it is Maggie, but he is not one hundred percent sure until he can see her face. Curled up, her size is not obvious and her hair is lank although there are some signs someone tried to wash it to make her more presentable. His hands shake as he takes out two twenty dollar bills and passes them to the pimp. "I don't want to be disturbed," and he steps inside and the door closes behind him. Cautiously and doubtfully, the girl turns over at what new abuse she is to face. Now certain, Buck holds a finger to his mouth – say nothing. He walks over to the bed and sits and Maggie puts her arms around him and cries into his coat. Buck checks around for spyholes and when satisfied there are none he whispers. "It's alright, Maggie. I've come to take you home." Nothing is said for several minutes. Buck does not know if Maggie really understands what is happening. He can see that the pimp cleaned her up for this night but the make-up does not hide the bruises. As Maggie begins to regain control of herself, Buck explains what is going to happen, keeping his mouth close to her ears in case someone is listening the other side of the door.

"Maggie. I will have to leave you in a moment but I'm coming back. Jesse is here. We'll take you somewhere safe then home. You have to be strong for a little while, an hour at the most."

Maggie is frightened to think of being left and tightens her grip. She's not sure she can take being left now that Buck has arrived. Buck takes out the pistol.

"I'm going to leave this with you. Keep it hidden but close to hand." He empties the bullets and takes Maggie through the safety catch operation, and lets her take dry shots before he reloads. He watches her put it under the pillow. Buck figures enough time has passed to convince the pimp but no longer to keep Jesse waiting. He hugs Maggie and kisses the top of her head. "If he checks in on you, you have to look as if I had….. if I had used you and you were worn down. Sorry." Maggie nods. She understands, feeling she has some control with the gun to hand.

Buck leaves the room and locks the door, not knowing the sound makes Maggie flinch, but is meant to assure the Italians. They are playing poker when he walks downstairs.

"Yeah, OK. I'd like to come back tomorrow to do it again. I don't want anyone else touching her. I'll pay fifty next time."

In the street, Jesse is coiled up inside, worse than he ever felt when sniping in France. Light spills on to the street as the door of the building opens and Buck comes out. He lets the lawman walk towards the Da Vinci and catches up with him in the next street.

"Is it Maggie?"

"It's Maggie. Give me a gun." Buck has never been angrier.

The two of them go to Jesse's truck. Buck takes an automatic and Jesse now takes the shotgun. No words. They nod to each other.

Guiseppe and his buddies are still playing poker; happy with forty dollars tonight and the expectation of fifty tomorrow. After that, the girl can go in one of the brothels. The door opens and Buck walks in.

"Sorry, guys. My wallet must have dropped out in the room. Have you got it?"

Guiseppe regrets not looking in on Maggie after but says No. "Go and check." He has a winning hand and doesn't want to leave the table.

Buck goes up to the room. Maggie hears footsteps on the stairs and grips the pistol, checks the safety is off. She hears someone stop the other side of the door and the key turn. She can't face it if it is the Italian. She can't wait to be rescued; her nerves won't take it. She points the gun at the door.

Jesse is alert for any noise coming from the house, ready to burst in if hears shouts or gunshots. The shotgun is loaded. His automatic is in his waistband for easy access. He is coiled like an overloaded spring.

Buck was going to walk right in but pauses and knocks on the door first, a sixth sense warning him that Maggie will be scared and needs reassurance.

"It's me," he whispers, mouth against the wood, before completing the unlocking and going in. He sees that Maggie had the gun pointed at the door. "Let's go. Follow me." He takes Jesse's spare automatic out of his belt, flicks the safety catch off and chambers a round.

The men are surprised when Buck walks back down, followed by Maggie.

Guiseppe speaks. "What's going on?" the last words he ever utters as Maggie empties all her bullets into him, holding the pistol two-handed. Already taken unawares, the other two card players freeze as Buck points his automatic at them. Out on the street, Jesse hears the gunshots and rushes in ready for a gunfight. He is relieved to see both Buck and Maggie unharmed but Maggie is semi-naked so he takes off his coat and places it over her shoulders.

Buck is in control now. "Leave me the shotgun and get your truck. I'll take care of these two."

Buck locks the two hoods in the cellar, checking the door is strong enough to detain them long enough for him to get away with Jesse and Maggie. Luckily for them, it is, because Buck was prepared to shoot them. He reaches the street at the same time Jesse pulls up at the kerb.

"I'll make my own way back. I have an errand at the hotel." He passes the shotgun back to Jesse and watches him and Maggie drive away. The street is empty, no one has come out to investigate the gunshots, although those dark windows could have faces behind them, watching. He walks back to the hotel. Knowing Maggie is safe, the pressure is off. One more thing to do though.

Luigi is reading a newspaper and looks up to see Buck entering.

"Hello, sir. Had a pleasant evening?" expecting a bonus if his guest has.

"It's about to get better," and all the anger comes through Buck's fists.

CHAPTER 10

"Heav'n has no Rage, like Love to Hatred turn'd,
Nor Hell a Fury, like a Woman scorn'd."
The Mourning Bride (Act III Scene 2) by William Congreve.

Maisie has been mulling over Jesse's behaviour and decides she should visit him. He's the first real boyfriend she has had. He's always been a gentleman, not like the local lads who would take her out then grope through her blouse or try to get up her skirt. She knows she's not a beauty but thinks her looks are good enough and when aided with a little make-up she can shine. His recent behaviour seems to be avoidance. Is he preparing to break up with her and is trying to find the right time to tell her? The very idea scares her. She thinks "he is the one", her father likes him.

As an excuse to visit him at his place, she takes some cakes from the diner.

Suspecting that Buck is covering their retreat, Jesse concentrates on Maggie, who is shivering, not with cold but shock. With one arm he pulls her into his side while he drives. What he saw makes him angry. He would have killed the pimp but he is worried for Maggie's mental health that she did, and especially after what she must have been put through. Maggie has gone into her shell and he must get her to his rooms where she can be warm and rest. He doesn't notice Maisie as he turns into his street and pulls up in front of the workshop yard gates. But Maisie has seen Jesse, and seen a woman in the truck's cab, up against her boyfriend and with her head on his shoulder. She watches as Jesse opens the gates, drives in, and closes them from the inside. Maisie's world has just collapsed.

Buck has been making his way across town. Stepping over the prone, unconscious and bloody Luigi, he had collected his bag from his room, taken back his dollars from a cash box under the desk then rode a cab to the rail station. He walks through, out the other side and catches another cab. He makes two more cab rides, using different cab companies, before he walks several blocks to arrive in the street where Jesse has his workshop, satisfied he has confused any trail. There is no love lost between the taxicab companies - it's not been long since there was open warfare between them – so he is confident there won't any co-operation in any investigation about their passenger. As he approaches the gates of the workshop, he notices cakes on the sidewalk and steps round them.

Jesse hears the door in the gate open and looks down to see Buck. He puts his gun back in his waistband. Buck climbs the stairs, drops his bag on the floor. Exhaustion now setting in.

"How is she?"

"I made her tea and she's sleeping in the bed. God, sir. What did they do to her?"

"Worst things you can think of." Buck runs a hand over his face. "I know Maggie. I know she is a tough girl. I figured she would not give in easily so I had to play a part I hated so they might offer her to me."

"You found her. She'll be safe now."

"I can't take her straight home, Jesse. She needs a couple of days to recover, lose the bruises. I'll phone Agnes tomorrow and let her know. She can tell Maggie's parents she's found and with me."

"We'll be safe here. I haven't told anyone my address."

"What about your mission, Jesse? Is it over?"

"Not yet, sir. It can wait until you and Maggie are away. I believe I've found the snake pit," and Jesse reveals fully all he has found out and that he will be going after Sean O'Leary. Buck tries to dissuade him but can see that Jesse is determined, a penance he feels he must pay whatever the personal cost.

In her rooms above the Diner, Maisie cries herself to sleep.

CHAPTER 11

Vincente Gabbini (Vince the gab) is angry. He'd thrown a glass of Chianti at the wall on hearing the news and now a red stain weeps down the wallpaper as if the wall was bleeding from the wound where glass cut in. One nephew is dead, another in hospital, and an asset taken from them. A minor mobster, specialising in white slavery, furious enough to act now without asking for permission up the chain of command. He wants answers. One of the poker players claims to have recognised the younger rescuer.

"I am sure he is the guy we've seen at the Ace of Clubs. I'd swear to it." Having been loaned to the Torrio-Capone gang for a surveillance task.

"Why would they want the girl?"

"To send a message?"

"Find out more about him."

"We know how to find his girlfriend." Relieved to offer something to the infuriated boss.

"Go to it. They are not getting away with this." Gabbini stares at his wall. It is uncertain to the men what the boss is seeing but in his head are two assassins, tied to chairs and him beating them to death.

If these guys are working for O'Leary, it is time to deal with the Irishman. Gabbini knows Torrio and Capone have had their eyes on the Irish and he is an easier target than O'Banion. He'll get recognition for action against the Ace gang, knowing they are not the force they once were, since those brothers-in-arms, Callaghan and Murphy, moved on and no one has heard of Razor in a while. The Capo Dei Capi understands Vendetta and may even send work his way if he shows he can handle trouble. Confirmation, as he believes it is, comes when he receives reports from his men.

"The guy who booked in the Da Vinci is from out-of-town. Hired-in gunman. Took out Guiseppe and beat up Luigi. Sending a message, boss. I reckon he let Luigi live so we'd get it."

Another reports, "went straight from the Vinci to the rail station. Probably back in New York or Philly now."

"And the kid, the back-up?"

"Got a man on it."

Maisie is working but her heart is not in it. She plays over what she saw last evening. No more tears, she cried herself out of those through the night. She's applied make-up but her red eyes and blotchy cheeks cannot be totally hidden.

Franco had been the one to check out the kid he knows as Harry Maguire and is back at the diner to find a trail to him. He pays attention to Maggie who comes to take his order. "Hey, sweetheart, everything OK with you?"

"Yeah. You want coffee?"

"Sure. Stick a cake with it." He watches her go to the counter, assessing her mood.

Maisie deals with his order and Franco checks the other occupants. It's a quiet morning, before the rush, and the place is not busy. Maisie returns with a cup and a slice of cake on a plate.

"Do you get time off? Talk a walk with me? See a movie? Oh, I forgot. You got a boyfriend."

"That jerk!" vehemently. Maisie tightens her lips in a grimace that Franco can't miss.

"Wow. What'd he do? A pretty girl like you." He rests a gentle hand on her arm.

"Two-timing rat. He's got another girl at his place."

Franco is alert at "his place".

"That sucks. What a dick. Excuse me."

Maisie smiles at this. Maybe not all is lost. This young man finds her attractive. He's actually better-looking than Jesse, with that complexion, long eyelashes and soft brown eyes. "No, you're right. He is a dick."

Now he has Maisie on-side and sharing, he gets her to tell the story of how she found out and she unwittingly reveals where to find the workshop. Sitting down with the Italian she tells everything and finds him a very attentive listener. Harry may not find her attractive anymore but she's found a new beau quick enough, she thinks.

As soon as he could leave Maisie without causing suspicion about his true interest, Franco has reported straight back to Gabbini, eager to give him the news. Eagerness is less to do with vengeance but to be in the favours of the boss and take over the vacancy caused by Giuseppe's death. The boss smiles, a wolfish grin. The hitman might be out of reach but the local is still within reach. They can send a message back that they are not to be messed with.

"Good work, Franco. We'll take care of him later and get the girl back. He's going to suffer and tell us where to find the hitman. There'll be payback for Guiseppe and Luigi. But first, we have bigger fish to fry."

His thuggish brain cannot consider what the purpose of the snatch and execution of Guiseppe might have been. He only knows his people have been hurt and his reputation damaged when the word gets out. A boss deals with this and makes pain for others. Tit for tat, but more so.

Dougal has been thinking about Rosie; he's been thinking a lot. He's been back to see her and each visit replicated that first time. He thinks the attraction is more than scratching an itch. After the sexual comfort is the comfort of companionship and the intimacy of a bond. That is why he is not concentrating on his driving. Sean and Mary are in the back seat, holding hands. They are on their way to view an apartment to rent, happy in domesticity. Perhaps, seeing the joy in these two is rubbing off on Dougal. He looks in the mirror at his contented passengers and is slow to react to a truck pulling across the street in front of them to block their progress. He stops hard by reflex but the pause before he thinks to throw the auto into reverse and back away allows two men with tommy-guns to leap out the truck and spray the limo. Bullets tear through the windscreen, peppering the car. The radiator hisses as it is shredded. Pandemonium inside the vehicle. Sitting behind Dougal, Sean is wounded through the shoulder as the auto and Dougal provide a partial barricade. Windscreen glass has cut his head and blood runs down his face. But Mary is exposed, in direct line to the gunmen. Bullets rip into her, jerking her like a rag doll, killing her and her unborn child immediately. Believing they have killed Sean – it must be impossible to survive the barrage of two full drums of ammo – the hitmen climb back in their truck and hasten away. After the noise, the street is unnaturally quiet, the ticking of a cooling engine no longer functioning.

Timidly, adult civilians who had dived for cover at the attack now approach the car to see who was the target. They find Sean, blood running down his face from the cut, bleeding from a shoulder, holding Mary and crying, his face a terrifying mask of pain, coloured and streaked. While the grown-ups take in the spectacle, children rush to collect the brass cartridge cases that litter the street – each worth money. Everyday life in Prohibition Chicago.

CHAPTER 12

The day has slowly passed and evening arrives without fuss, quietly pushing away the sunlight and replacing with shadows. A streetlight comes on, its weak illumination through the dirty window finds Maggie asleep in the double bed, having troubled dreams. Exhausted, Buck is snoring gently on the sofa while Jesse has made up a bedroll on the floor, but unable to sleep with an overactive mind rerunning the events.

Maisie helps her father close the Diner for the day. She is less upset about Jesse now the more handsome Italian has paid her some attention. In her room, she checks her appearance in her mirror and wonders how much her life has changed this past month, unaware what events she has set in motion. She wonders if she could style her hair like Mary Pickford. She needs to let it grow longer first.

Jesse has heard the tinkle of glass, correctly thinking it is a window to the workshop. The door from the workshop creaks gently as someone comes into the stairway up to the living apartment. Jesse, with extreme care, pulls back the slide on his Colt to load a round and, laying on the floor, keeps the top stair in sight. Almost immediately the silhouette of a head comes above the step. Jesse doesn't hesitate, aims at the centre and fires, the flash brilliant in the darkened room and the noise ear-hurtingly loud in the confined space. The .45 slug goes in through the nose and exits at the back of the skull with enough force to send the guy flying backwards off the stairs down to the ground floor. A volley of shots come up the stairs from a second guy who has been at the bottom, smashing into the ceiling above Jesse's head, sending a snowstorm of plaster fragments on to him. When the bullets stop flying, Jesse is confident the guy's gun is empty. Before the guy can reload, looking over the top step with extended arm, Jesse fires off the remainder of his magazine at the shadow, hearing a grunt and watching it slump to the floor over the body of its comrade.

Buck has woken immediately and pulls the double-barrelled shotgun from under the sofa, confirms both barrels are loaded. He sees Jesse is alright and throws open the door to the bedroom. The street light that has been coming in through the window is cut off. Buck fires one barrel, smashing out glass and bits of window frame and knocking the intruder off the roof of the outhouse, flying out to crash on the cobbles below. Woken from her nightmares, Maggie screams.

Jesse reloads his automatic and sticks it in his waistband before collecting a tommy-gun with a drum magazine from the kitchen. He checks quickly with Buck, who nods and covers Jesse as he climbs downstairs. Nothing happens so Buck switches his attention to the yard through the now open window. Maggie has frozen but stops screaming.

Jesse slips through the workshop like a ghost and into the yard, which is empty except for the body of the roof guy shot by Buck. The corpse is splayed across the ground, a big hole in the chest and blood running in rivulets, dead eyes looking up at the stars. Jesse can see that the door in the gate had been the point of entry but also that, along the foot of the large gates which would normally be an unbroken line of light from the street, there are shadows. Knowing that Buck's shotgun is sticking out of the window and his back is covered, he takes a stance, fires the tommy-gun, stitching a line of lead through the gates, not stopping until the drum is empty of its one hundred rounds. Laying the weapon down, he takes out his automatic and cautiously checks the street. Three men holed by bullets and splintered from gate fragments lie dead on the sidewalk. Their car is down the street but unoccupied.

Maggie comes out of her terror once she realises where she is and that Buck and Jesse are alright. Outside, Jesse pulls the bodies into the yard and Buck has gone down to help him move the six gangsters to a corner. The blood on the street and the damage to the gates will be obvious to passers-by in the morning but meanwhile, gunshots have not drawn any attention, Chicagoans having learned not to be noisy.

Buck has assessed the bodies, their appearance and more. "Italians! Smell the garlic."

Jesse takes control. "You'll have to take Maggie away today. I'll give you cash to find a hotel out of town before she's ready to go home."

317

"What are you going to do?"

"I've unfinished business. I'll take care of that and, if I feel it's safe, I'll come home."

"You have to be careful. You've enemies in both camps now and the Irish will wonder why the Italians sent six men to take you out."

"I'll act fast. Right now, they'll be confusion. You must get away though. Get Maggie safe. I'll find a new place to lie up in, break the links. I don't know how they found me here but I must pick up a new identity. If I can take out O'Leary and maybe lay the blame on the Italians, I'll let them fight it out. I'll see what I can take from our friends here, to lay pointers for the Irish to follow."

"Get a wallet off one of them and use their car. Leave both behind when you've done."

"Good idea."

THE BOOTLEGGER

PART III

HOME AND AWAY

"...a curse on both your houses"
William Shakespeare, Romeo and Juliet

Mary O'Leary's funeral is both a sombre and a bright affair. The laying-in required a closed coffin due to the wounds of the gunfight. Four black horses with black plumes pull the hearse with her coffin. The sun picks out the gilding on their traces and the finials. Sean (no one calls him Lucky anymore) follows in a black car, unable to walk properly from his injuries. Unnoticed immediately but discovered at the hospital, he'd taken shrapnel in the leg from a slug that had passed through Dougal. Colour comes from the floral tributes organised and contributed by Dion O'Banion, who sits alongside him. The scent flows invisibly along the street and in through the open windows, cloying. Onlookers stop on the sidewalks. Some feeling sadness at the loss of one of theirs and a woman, others just curious. Only Sean and Dougal know that the coffin carries two bodies, mother and child.

"It was all a mistake, Sean. The wops thought you had put a hitman up against them and he had wiped out family. What do you know about Harry Maguire?" O'Banion talks out of the side of his mouth, gaze firmly fixed ahead.

Sean is surprised by the question. "Maguire? He was your man. I only saw him deliver your beer to the Club."

O'Banion takes a quick look sideways at Sean then back ahead. "The eyeties thought he was your man. I was only trying him out. But they noticed and he was in on the attack on Gabbini's people. And an old guy who was the shooter. He plucked one of their chickens too. Filthy trade and I'd applaud him except for the comeback."

"This is fucked up, Dion. Why did they come after me while Mary was with me? She should not have died."

"I know, Sean. We've been suckered. Was the kid a loner, or from another gang? Or did the Italians set it up to start a war?"

"Whoever he is, I'll find him and he'll wish he'd never been born."

CHAPTER 1

Buck and Maggie had left in the sheriff's car, with enough money from Jesse to pay for a hotel to rest up in, to let Maggie recover. Jesse had handed over all his cash except what he thought he might need, in case he didn't make it – an unspoken realism about the risks he would be taking. Buck had gripped Jesse's hand for a long time while giving an intense look in his eyes. "Don't be reckless. Come home as soon as you can."

Now alone, and daylight approaching, fingers of approaching dawn tickling the cloud cover in the east, Jesse checks. The bodies have been dragged into the workshop. The riddled gates have been pulled open, making the bullet holes much less obvious to passers-by. Several buckets of water were used to sluice the sidewalk, running pink into the drains but generally removing a potential crimson stickiness that would draw attention. His possessions, especially the arsenal now multiplied by the donations from the six gangsters, are back in the truck. It is now time to move off. A momentary thought of "should I set a fire?" quickly forgotten, as are the cases of gin under the covers. He drives the Italians' car away several streets and parks it where it won't draw attention, expecting to use it as a diversion as suggested by the sheriff. Walks back to get his truck.

He drives for an hour and arrives in the suburbs, those in the opposite direction to home. Jesse parks up in a quiet street, still early and only a few residents have set off for work, and goes looking for another vehicle. He no longer needs a truck for his purpose and he wants to ditch this one which could be recognised. Luck was on his side when he came across a private sale while driving here – a car outside a house with a For Sale sign on the windscreen. Far from new but it looks in good condition. It will give him an anonymous car until he is ready to strike. He walks round and checks the tyres.

Having noticed Jesse inspecting the auto, a man comes out of the house. "Hi, there."

"Hi. I'm looking for a car. This might do," Jesse responds.

The owner willingly explains he has hit hard times and Jesse pays the asking price without haggling. As he drives away, he does wonder if he was suckered to overpay and he has depleted his funds. Taking an indirect route, he returns to his truck where, checking no one is around to witness, Jesse transfers the important stuff to the car and dresses in his workman's clothes. Part of his plan is to throw pursuers off the track and instead of dumping the truck he wants some cash now. As he is in the opposite direction to his home town, he plans to sell it and, if found by the gangs, they may assume he continued north. He pulls up at a garage with a "we buy" sign, which he sees as a good omen.

A guy who is probably the owner comes out of an office as he pulls on to the forecourt. "What can I do for you?"

"Selling my truck. Moving away. No work around here. Interested in buying?"

The garage owner rubs a thumb under his chin as he thinks. Not wanting to appear eager, he walks round the truck, asks Jesse to pop the hood and spends several minutes examining the engine.

"Bit worn out. Not worth much. No getting much interest in buying at the moment. It will take some time for me to sell on." A list of negatives to hold the price low.

"Offer me a fair price, you can keep the tools in the back." Jesse wants to do the deal and go.

Haggling doesn't take long; Jesse just makes a show of needing more but gives in. He walks away with a small roll of dollar bills and the owner, immediately Jesse is out of sight, puts a For Sale sign on the truck with a 75% markup and the tools are transferred to his workshop.

It's quite a distance to the car and that will eat up precious time. But Jesse is content. He's unloaded a link, got cash in his pocket, and laid a trail, should anyone be capable of following it, in the wrong direction. He walks a mile before catching a bus to near where he left the car. A cautious approach and, when confident no one is around, he climbs in the back and changes from overalls to the suit he'd bought on his drive to Chicago. He lays the work clothes over a bush for someone needy to find; no need to bin. They were non-descript enough for relative anonymity as Harry Maguire, a jobbing workman and would provide no clues as to his real identity or home base.

He checks his finances. What he kept back from his bundle that he passed to Buck for use and safekeeping. Less the cost of the car, plus the sale of the truck. He has the wallets of the six failed Italian hitmen and figures he only needs two for laying pointers to the rivals of the Irish gangs. Four of them top up his assets and he drops the cash-empty wallets and other contents in a tributary to the Chicago river and watches them sink.

Buck and Maggie have travelled indirectly halfway from Chicago to their home town, so as not to leave any trail. When ready they will dogleg to another route for the final leg. The sheriff had agreed with Jesse where they could meet up if the Chicago mission is finished soon and if he finds them not there, he will realise they have made the homeward journey, Maggie having improved sufficiently.

Maggie had left the workshop only wearing one of Jesse's shirts and an overcoat and it had been necessary to park in one of the suburbs with shops and Buck to go alone, armed with Maggie's measurements. He would have preferred to use several different retailers but, worrying about leaving Maggie alone for too long, he'd purchased from one, explaining to the assistant that his niece had lost her luggage on the railway. The store was also able to sell him a suitcase.

On an empty country road, Buck steps away from his coupe so that Maggie can dress in her new clothes. He spends the time working on the suitcase so that it does not look brand new. Rubbing grit from the road over it, takes the shine off parts, where it would be expected to wear down in use over several months. Satisfied with his work, he rolls a cigarette and smokes it, not wishing to rush Maggie. He ponders over how Jesse might be. He has to trust the young man knows what he is doing as this is way outside Buck's experience. Marshalling in a cowtown and now as sheriff, things have been much simpler. The change in crime, gangs organising on the scale he is aware of in the cities make him feel a dinosaur and maybe he should retire.

Maggie steps out of the car and he throws down the half-smoked cigarette to return to her.

"How'd I look?" Maggie quietly asks.

"Looking great, Maggie. A picture," which is less than the truth, taking into account how pale and frightened she looks.

Maggie is in limbo. Her great adventure in Chicago, starting a new life, had gone horribly wrong. She'd made a huge mistake trusting a stranger and, without the sheriff and Jesse, where might she be now? After what happened to her, she feels unclean; her body was abused. That could have been her life – a slave in a brothel until worn out then disposed of. She's determined not to cry in front of Buck, who has been so kind and she is only partly aware that Jesse has stayed in Chicago and may be in danger. She'd thought maybe he was travelling separately, not aware of his determination to fix things so they could all be safe.

Maggie's parents, Donald and Catherine, had learned from Agnes Buckley that the sheriff has found her but won't be home immediately as they have loose ends to tie up. They can't understand why and are still wondering why Maggie ceased communication. They worry she has been in an accident and had to be treated in hospital. In a coincidence of thought, Buck has come up with that excuse so they need not know of Maggie's distressing misadventure.

With Maggie properly dressed, she and Buck arrive at the hotel. Buck explains to their hosts that his niece has been ill and needs rest. They expect to stay for a few days, maybe a week. The owners say that is not a problem, glad to have some business during a low period.

CHAPTER 2

Prior to the funeral of Mary, Dion O'Banion had met Johnny Torrio on neutral ground.

A deserted warehouse with entrances from both ends and nowhere for assassins to hide. Bodyguards from each faction have checked it out before letting their bosses enter. Both gangleaders have more armed muscle as a precaution against a double-cross. The atmosphere crackles with tension from an inbred hate made stronger by competition.

"What is it you want to tell me?" the Irishman growls.

Torrio turns his hands palms up, in a gesture of openness mixed with a slight shrug. "What happened is bad for business, Dion. We have a good deal between us. I don't want to see it spoiled."

O'Banion is not impressed. Business is business but there is a lot of hate and distrust between the nationalities. "Then why the whack job on Sean? You killed his wife. Did you know she was carrying their child?" O'Banion had learned late of the extra fatality that so affected O'Leary.

Torrio exchanges looks with his lieutenant, Capone, before answering. "No we didn't. But it wasn't an authorised hit. We had one of ours go off territory. He'll be dealt with, by us."

328

Capone nods before speaking. "It makes no sense for us to kill your man, or his family." He turns to the mobster behind him. A silent communication and the man leaves. O'Banion, Moran and Weiss stiffen, touching their holstered guns, ready to draw. There is increased tension in the room, which Torrio senses and pats down air to calm it. The mobster returns, with another, and a third man, hands tied behind his back and his face bloodied from a beating. He is thrown to the floor between the two gang leaders. Capone hovers over him.

"Tell him." The man does not speak immediately and Capone kicks him. "Tell him."

The beaten man is Vincente Gabbini. He tells the story.

Capone provides the epilogue. "We knew you weren't hitting us. Why only kill one man and let two live? It didn't make sense. So we asked questions. This is a personal vendetta. But we didn't authorise it. It's bad for business."

O'Banion concedes this might be true. "We don't know the guys at our end. This Maguire character only turned up recently and we used him as a driver. Nothing more. He's gone."

Torrio leans forward. "We have an address. Vincente here, sent his guys there to take Maguire out. They were handed their heads on a plate. Your Maguire and another guy were tooled up and very professional. We thought they were out-of-towners hired by you then the maths didn't add up. As Al says, it didn't make sense not to waste all three at the house." Points at Gabinni. "We now think this was a

329

personal thing to get a girl his pimps were training." He pushes a piece of paper across to O'Banion. "That's where they holed up. We've taken the bodies away. That's all we have." He stands. O'Banion stands also. They don't shake hands but nod agreement. The Italians leave with Gabbini. O'Banion watches them go before speaking.

"George. After the funeral, take this address to Sean. Stay with him. Whatever he wants to do, help him. Keep me informed." He spits on the floor where the Italians had stood. He doesn't trust them but can't work out what they are up to. He'll keep his men on high alert.

Straight from the funeral, Sean stands in the gateway of the workshop. He can see the signs of the gunfight. The bullet-riddled gate; the glint of brass cartridges left unpicked on the cobbles. There's a cold chill in his heart that his troubles can be down to something plotted here. A happy future lay ahead once. Marriage to the perfect woman, a child, hopefully a son but a daughter would be fine too. Maybe many more children. Move to the West Coast, set up a small legitimate business. Dreams evaporated in a single day.

Bugs Moran watches Sean hesitating in the gateway, his head swivelling to take in the scene and a reluctance to step over the threshold as if in the doorway to Hell. He looks up at the broken window, not knowing that a shotgun blast had taken the glass out and a man too. Shards of glass on the cobbles and bloodstains reveal the truth. Briefly, what with the glass reflecting, the red of blood and gold gleam of brass cartridges, Sean is back in the church being married, the stained-glass coloured sunshine coming through the windows. Bugs wonders whether Sean would stay fixed there and maybe he should go in for him. Then Sean puts one foot forward and starts into the yard The door to the workshop is unlocked, not hindering access. Another door is fully open and the foot of stairs can be seen, the obvious route to the rooms above. Another clue to carnage decorates the floor and Sean steps over to make a laborious, cane-assisted climb to the upper floor. Bugs remains outside and lights a cigarette; there's nothing for him to do inside unless Sean calls him. A police officer on his beat walks by, recognises Moran and takes the hint to keep moving.

Upstairs, in the living accommodation, Sean examines the rooms for clues. Some food left and is going off, a sign of a fast departure. No paperwork, nothing to say who lived here and executed here. He supposes he can find the landlord but he suspects he'll learn nothing from doing so. The guy was clever enough and would have given an alias and paid cash, all too easy in Chicago. This is proving to be a dead end. Probably the Italians had cleared any evidence along with the bodies of their men. Going down the stairs was fractionally easier than going up; all the same, Sean pauses at the interior door to catch his breath. The workshop is empty except for some old tarpaulins in the corner that have a shape. A quick look, especially when here to remove bodies, would have got the impression of being a discarded pile but Sean notices a straight edge that must indicate something underneath. The cane taps the floor as he walks over, grasps an edge and pulls. Under the covers are a couple of cases of gin, missed by Torrio's men. Sean gives a wry laugh to himself. Was this about booze after all? He takes a bottle out, hefts it. Something stirs in his brain. He recognises the label. The same as the bottles that the drummer had brought him. The same as McAvoy had returned with on that first visit to the country distiller. A quick investigation shows that all the bottles have the same label and all have unbroken seals. Illinois Water. Sean does not believe in coincidences.

CHAPTER 3

Jesse has been careful about being seen around. No longer wearing the workman's clothes of his Harry Maguire disguise, he now wears the good suit and hat that he had bought during his original planning, had his hair cut and shaves every day. In a pawnbroker's he bought a watch and a wedding ring. His bearing is more confident. He knows that people look for association when trying to remember faces – what was worn, where seen before, what doing. He now looks like a prosperous married man.

He avoids the areas where he is more likely to be recognised despite the changes. He keeps a distance from the workshop and the Diner, but he still needs to look around the Irish districts so he drives around, getting out for a coffee here and there, and picks up a discarded newspaper, partly to read, partly to hold before himself as a screen. Frontpage is a report, hastily cobbled together to meet the print deadline, of a mob hit on Sean O'Leary and two others, one believed to be his wife. Lurid details of a car riddled by bullets, photo showing the damage from two hitmen with tommy-guns – the people inside reported to have died at the scene. Jesse lets out a long sigh. His mission is over, the threat removed. He can go home. He leaves without seeing a newspaper with a correction. The Italians' car is not needed and two wallets, empty of cash are flipped out on to the roadside.

More relaxed, Jesse enjoys the journey to the hotel where he plans to meet Buck and Maggie. All the bad stuff is behind him, he thinks. He can make a future without fear of law enforcement or gangland reprisal. Weight he hadn't realised was on his shoulders has fallen away. His heart beats happier and the tightness he has felt in his chest has gone. He ponders on what life holds for him now. He knows Moses and Molly would hand the farm back to him if he asks but he has a sense of obligation not to do that. He might get back to his idea of farming co-operatives, leasing machinery to farmers who can't afford the purchase and only need something seasonally. Money was banked in an account for a future, more than enough to set up such a business. But first, check on his friends and meet them at the planned rendezvous, if they haven't moved on yet.

Buck is outside the hotel having a smoke, thinking maybe he should quit. Agnes doesn't like him smoking indoors and if he is to give up his job and spend more time at home, perhaps he should make the effort. Maggie is resting inside, staying in the room while bruises are fading but still visible if she doesn't wear make-up. The day is fine, the air clear. Deer move across a patch of open ground between woods, oblivious or just not caring of Buck. This little country hotel has its own chickens in a backyard and a vegetable garden. With local meat producers, the meals have been wonderful and Buck knows Agnes will look askance at his increased waistline as he seems to have discovered an insatiable appetite post-drama, so he takes a walk up and down the road for exercise as well as keeping a look-out. A pistol resides in a holster under his coat, ready to hand, more in the car should he need them, a legacy from the six hoods. Some farm trucks pass and he acknowledges them with friendly waves at the drivers. He misses home and hopes he and Maggie don't have to stay here much longer. A phone call to Agnes last night to reassure her all was OK but he hadn't been able to share any news on Jesse. Was also good to hear that the town was quiet and nothing untoward was happening. The government men had asked around briefly but left a day after meeting Buck and Wyatt. That seemed to be the end of that. The town was clean of bootlegging and any production still going on was limited to home consumption by those making booze out on remote farms. The clock appeared to have been turned back to safer times, although the brief period of alcohol production and sales had brought prosperity to quite a few. The McGregors had done well from the increased sales of materials for manufacture. When they'd been questioned over the higher number of stock purchases, they'd explained that local people were bottling and pickling more, produce they weren't selling but could be preserved. Money had been spent around the local area and public areas had been made over. Buck contemplated the balance between the good achieved and the bad things associated. He couldn't decide if he had regrets (apart from Maggie of course, but that was not

335

a direct correlation to the prohibition-breaking activities) as the scales seem to tip in favour of good, he'd felt like his younger self for a while and it had been grand reunion with Wyatt and reminiscing old times. His reveries are interrupted by sight of a car approaching from the direction of Chicago and he steps into the shade of a tree so as not to be noticed, grinding his cigarette out under his heel and resting his hand on the butt of his gun.

Jesse spots a figure in the near distance that has the size and demeanour of Buck but who steps off the road into the tree line. It might be innocent and there is now no reason to fear an ambush but all the same, he takes his gun out and lays in within reach on the seat. New-learned habits die as hard as old ones. He slows the car down to pass the hidden man but is ready to accelerate away. But Buck has recognised Jesse and steps out and waves, surprised that Jesse has turned up at the midway hotel so soon. No question but a raised eyebrow. Jesse smiles.

"Not needed. Someone else took the boss out. Gang war I imagine." Jesse turns the engine off and climbs out the car. Relief floods over the sheriff, barely resisting a hug for the young man. "We can go to the hotel and have coffee," he says, "or do you want something to eat?"

"No, I'm good thanks. How's Maggie?"

"She's marvellous. I mean, she is looking more like her old self already. Just being away from Chicago and knowing we're going home seems to have revived her." A pause for reflection on what

336

Maggie had been through before Buck continues. "What are your plans?"

"Guess I need to come back with you. Not sure what I'll do next. I'm not going back to farming. How are Moses and Molly?"

Buck smiles. "They renamed the farm as you suggested. Moses also closed the road in and opened up another route. He's thinking it adds to confusion had anyone come looking."

"He's no dope. I think they will do well."

"He buried a lot of the kit. What wasn't distributed around other farms. It can be dug up for use." Buck looks keenly for Jesse's response.

"No more distilling. It brought too much trouble."

Buck is relieved. "Maybe you'd like to buy into a business. Town is growing."

"Let's wait and see. I need to see Maggie safe and better before deciding what I do."

"A couple more days here and I reckon we can go home. Maggie will be pleased to see you. Let's go down to the hotel." Buck climbs in Jesse's car to travel together the few hundred yards.

CHAPTER 4

"Whom the gods wish to destroy, they first make mad."
Sophocles, Antigone

The Ace of Clubs has stood silent for a period of mourning. O'Banion now lends a manager to open it up again, before too much trade is lost. He supplies a lot of beer here and he wants the supply chain to keep moving. Besides, without his lieutenants, O'Leary is not bringing in the money from other rackets, letting things slide. At the Club, Sean feels the confusion of the staff whenever he appears. How to act around him. The absence of Dougal and Mary. Sean – the ghost who walks the corridors and rooms. He knows he has no desire to run the business anymore. He has a desire for revenge. Revenge that will silence the screaming in his head and hopefully grant him peace.

O'Banion arrives early to check up on Sean, finding him playing idly with a jar of Hinds Honey & Almond handcream of Mary's that he shuffles back and forth on his desk, in a melancholy mood.

"How you doing, fella?" O'Banion flips his hat on Sean's desk, away from the jar, and looks around. No sign of booze, no smell. Sean is on the wagon which is a surprise to the gangboss, who expected a decline. He is surprised by what Sean says.

"I want out, Dion. Do you want my club?" Sean sits forward, letting the jar stop at the edge of the desk before it falls off.

"Sorry to hear that, Sean. You've made a good business here."

"Not without Dougal. I offered him a partnership then he gets killed. He took bullets for me. And Mary.... and Mary......"

"Steady, Sean. I miss them too. Why not take a holiday? Take some time to consider? You built this business up. In only eight years you've achieved a lot. You've earned a lot of respect."

"No use, Dion. When I go out there, I see Dougal behind the bar. When I go to my room, I can still smell Mary's perfume. There'll never be anyone else for me. This place hurts. I must find the bastards who set this in motion. Only then can I rest."

"Well, if you're sure. I know the books; I'll pay a fair price. And if you ever change your mind and return, you can buy it back."

"Yeah. OK. Hold the cash for me. I'll be going away for a while. I can telegraph if I need it. You're safer than a bank."

"You got it. I'll be away then. Let me know when you're leaving. And ask if there is anything, anything, I can do for you."

Sean rises to shake hands and is taken in a bear hug by the other man.

O'Banion has been gone a few hours and Sean is checking accounts prior to handing over full control when the barman knocks and sticks his head round the door.

"Boss. Guy here to see. Got a parcel of something."

"I'm not expecting anything. What's he look like?"

"Oldish. Asked for Dougal first." The barman gives an embarrassed shrug.

Sean decides, "I'd better see him. Send him in."

The barman retreats and seconds later a short, middle-aged man with a long parcel enters, slightly nervous.

"Mr O'Leary. Your man just told me about Dougal. My condolences."

"What is it I can do for you?" Sean is wondering whether the parcel hides a shotgun and whether he can reach his pistol in the drawer of his desk, feeling stupid that he may have let his guard down and this was to be a second attempt on his life.

The man speaking, "I have the leg, sir," confuses him.

"Leg?" Sean is puzzled. "What leg?"

"The leg for Johnny Miller. Dougal commissioned it. It's here," and he proffers the parcel and tears at the paper nervously.

Sean watches the reveal of the artificial limb and steps forward to inspect. It's a rigid leg, replacing from just above the knee, with a cup to go over Johnny's stump, and straps for securing. Carved smooth to represent the patella and calf, down to an ankle and foot. He's impressed that it is not just a simple pegleg.

The man pulls a bandage from his pocket. "He must wear this over his stump to reduce friction."

Sean nods.

Johnny Miller takes careful steps around the yard, still using a crutch but as a walking stick, until he feels more confidence. Gradually, his confidence grows and soon he throws down the crutch and does a jerky run, a sort of hop using the false leg and a propulsion by his good leg. A big smile lights up his face. "Look, Mr O'Leary."

Sean turns to the artificial leg maker, taking out his billfold. "Here's a couple of hundred dollars. I want you to supply any guy who needs it but can't afford one. When that's gone, go to see Dion O'Banion at his flower shop. Tell him you are to have money from my account with him. And that kid is your most special customer. As he outgrows that leg, he's to have another, the best you can make." At least he would be leaving the Ace with one happy memory. He'll phone O'Banion to advise him of the arrangement. He hadn't thought of it earlier, but he also needs cash to pay off the girls. Their new boss-to-be doesn't trade in prostitution, having tried to talk Sean out of it before, and they'll have to find new employment, but he can soften the blow of the change in Mary's memory. There's probably one of his smaller businesses that can be converted to a bordello and he'll set Josephine to running it as a madam, In the short time Mary had stepped away from the role, she had shown a talent for it. The girls can run it themselves and keep the takings. He won't come back. There's nothing in Chicago for him. When he has wreaked his revenge, maybe he'll return to Ireland, run a small bar there, away from sad memories.

341

CHAPTER 5

A few days spent at the hotel and it is deemed time to return home. The owners are sad to see them go, they have been good guests during a lean time. Very quiet people. They'd thought father and niece, as how Buck had introduced them on arrival, and wondered whether the later arrival was son or the girl's boyfriend. They had been a tight-knit group, the girl quiet and spending a lot of time in her room. The older man, who had given his name as Frank Clayton, had explained she had been ill and was recovering in some fresh, country air. Once the young man had arrived, the three would take short walks and return for afternoon tea in the shade from a large apple tree. The proprietors watch the two cars head off in Chicago's direction, assuming they are returning to home in the city.

Several miles down the road, Buck waves his arm out of the coupe's window and they pull off for Jesse to drive his vehicle deeper into the woods, out of sight. All misdirection should they be followed. In time, no doubt, someone would come across the car, but with nothing to link to Jesse. They would feel lucky at their discovery and not talk about it in case it got taken off them. Jesse just wants time to pass and the trail to go cold, although they are feeling confident all is behind them. They've been disciplined in blurring their tracks, leaving false clues should anyone still have an interest in them for rescuing Maggie. As for the bootlegging, the main boss is dead, they think, and perhaps no one knows of the failed attempts to get Jesse to supply.

Now all three in Buck's coupe, they swing round and head towards their own town, taking a longer route to avoid going back past the hotel. The nearer they get, the landscaping looking familiar, the more nervous Maggie feels and Buck stops the car for Jesse to get into the rear seat with Maggie for the last miles, unspoken communication between the two men. Maggie manages a weak smile and Jesse puts his hand over hers to reassure her. He can feel her pulse racing.

Agnes Buckley is in the yard feeding her chickens when Buck's coupe turns in. She looks over and can see Jesse and Maggie in the back seat. Although expecting them, alerted by a phone call from her husband, she is relieved to see them in the flesh. Putting down her corn bucket she walks fast over, first to hug her man then Maggie, then Jesse. The chickens don't care about the reunion as they fight over the bucket. Agnes fusses the trio into her kitchen. Seated round the table, the men drinking coffee and the women drinking mint tea, she is brought up to date with developments, with certain incidents omitted. Buck outlines the plan.

"I'll phone Maggie's parents and we'll take her over this evening. Jesse can stay here tonight then take my car to see Moses and Molly if he wants."

"I'll get dinner on. No sense in doing anything on an empty stomach."

343

Jesse takes Maggie out to the porch seat, leaving Buck and Agnes in the kitchen.

"Tom! What really happened? Something's not right." Agnes' sixth sense in overdrive.

"It wasn't nice, Agnes. She'd been picked up by a gang. Abducted. Do you remember the Wilds? Moved to Chicago some years back. Pete Wild's son, Jimmy is in the police there. It was my good fortune he was at the precinct house where I was making enquiries. He gave me pointers where to look. Without that, I doubt whether we would have seen Maggie again."

Agnes shudders. "That's the devil's own city, Tom. I'm so glad all of you have come back." She embraces her husband as if she would never let him go away again. "Jesse doesn't seem the same. All this has changed him."

"He's grown up fast. I thought the war made a difference but that was only the start. This business with gangsters has given him a toughened core. He doesn't back down from anything."

"Oh, Tom," Agnes says with a smile. "He sounds like a certain young lawman I once met."

Jesse and Maggie sit quietly for a while, enjoying the peace and lacking the words to start a conversation. A bird sits in a tree opposite and sings, drawing both their attentions.

Eventually, Jesse speaks. "Maggie." A long pause before he

continues. "Staying home from now?" which starts her crying and he pulls her in close and lets her rest her head on his shoulder. Jesse can't imagine what she feels. There's a cold anger in him that could see him returning to Chicago and wiping out all the vermin trading in young women. They sit there in silence until Agnes calls them in to eat.

Buck waits until the evening, past the time when all the businesses are shut and people mostly gone home. He'd phoned the McGregors when to expect them then he, Jesse and Maggie set off into town. Agnes had planned to go but noticing how protective of Maggie Jesse is, decides to wait for the two men to return later. The town is quiet except for a radio heard through an open window and the occasional barking of a dog. Buck drives to the rear of the store and finds Maggie's parents waiting by the entrance to their accommodation. A long tearful reunion while Jesse and Buck stand quietly by. Eventually, Maggie is shuffled indoors by her mother while her father vigorously pumps Buck's hand then Jesse's. "Thank you. Thank you. What happened to her?"

Buck spoke. "Unlucky to catch something that put her in hospital. That's why she couldn't write or phone. She's getting better. Give her time."

McGregor wants to know more but a certain look in the sheriff's eyes dissuades him. He feels there is something more, attuned to the demeanour of both men but he thanks them again. "I'd better get inside.

Bless you both."

Buck turns to Jesse. "Let's go." Handing over Maggie to the welcoming arms of her parents seems like a weight off their shoulders. "Agnes is waiting for us. Let's get some rest and you can head over to see Moses and Molly in the morning if you drop me at the office on your way."

"Yes, sir."

Buck watches Jesse walk round the car to get in the passenger seat and feels a twinge in his heart because of memories Jesse raises of his son, Tom Jr. It really isn't that long since he saw him off to enlist and that was the last time they'd been a family. Is he projecting too much on Jesse to fill that gap? Will Jesse stay around or move off once he has checked on his friends?

Jesse is awake early. He can hear the chickens scratching in the yard. He'd slept in Tom Jr's old room. A familiar place as sometimes he had stayed over with his childhood pal and nothing seems to have changed. He doesn't think the Buckleys have kept it as a shrine but he assumes they just haven't had a reason or need to clear it out. An old comic book he remembers lays on a bookshelf where it was last put down, probably by Tom Jr. For the first time he recognises a mirror image of his grief at missing his parents is reflected in the Buckley's grief of losing a son, their only child. Thoughts grow wider. McAvoy was a nasty bully, but his father, the Alderman, had lost his son. Is that right or wrong? If he, Jesse, had not gone into the business of producing alcohol, how many would be alive now? Would he still have the farm though? What has this government done for people like him? Prohibition is a stupid law – it's solved nothing but it has made more crime. And they had abandoned farmers and farming communities after the war, to create cities and industries. Jesse begins to accept he has just been going with the current and, apart from the occasional paddle for steering, he has allowed himself to be dictated by circumstances rather than control them as he had once thought he was doing. If there is a God, what is his plan here? We live, we make choices, decisions are forced on us, we die. Is that it?

Agnes ensures the men have a good breakfast before they leave for town. Buck lets Jesse drive so he can be dropped off quickly and Jesse continue on his way to the farm.

"You'll be surprising Moses and Molly. Never had a chance to let them know you're back."

"I'll drive up carefully. Moses should recognise your car anyway."

"All the same. Pull up short of the house and honk the horn. Moses keeps that ole shotgun of his close by."

"I hope the need for that has gone now. We've nothing to offer the mobsters and the ones that came here are all underground now."

Molly is feeding the old horses, Jesse's dog following her around.

347

Moses was not in sight when Jesse draws into the outer yard and honks the horn. Molly squints to make out who has come but the dog recognises his master immediately and runs over and makes a huge fuss. That's when Molly realises who it is and runs over herself, calling over her shoulder to the barn, "Moses! Moses"! Quick."

Moses comes out and, just as the sheriff had forewarned, he is carrying his shotgun but when he sees Molly hugging someone and the dog leaping around two people, he rests it against the barn door and goes over. His limp is noticeable. He holds out his hand to shake but Jesse moves in and gives him a hug.

"Jesse. Jesse, It's good to see you." Moses is hugely relieved.

Molly wipes the tears on her face with her apron. "Come into the kitchen. I've made biscuits and I'll put a pot of coffee on. My, Lordy. What a turn up."

The farmhouse is brighter and cleaner since Jesse last stayed in it. Molly has worked on it and added their personal possessions now they are living in it.

Jesse takes it all in. "I'm so pleased you've moved in. The house needed a family again."

Moses speaks at a look from Molly. "It's all yours, Jesse. We can move back to our shack."

"Heck, no, Moses. I meant it when I gave the farm to you two and I wouldn't dream of changing my mind." He kisses Molly on her cheek before sitting at the table with Moses. A plate of recently made biscuits appears on the table, along with mugs while a pot begins to boil on the stove.

Moses waits politely for Jesse to take the first biscuit, then takes two, one for himself and one he slips under the table to the expectant and eager dog.

"Moses Freeman! You ain't feeding that hound with my biscuits, is you?"

"No, ma'am. I dropped it by accident and he got to it before I could pick it up."

"Don't you give me that. I saw you pass it to him. Mr Jesse, what am I to do with him?"

"I guess you're stuck with him, Molly."

"I guess I am," and she brought the coffee pot over and filled the mugs. "We got fresh cream if you want some."

"No, this is fine. Thank you. Good biscuits." Jesse is enjoying the camaraderie with old friends, something he'd missed.

Moses takes up the conversation. "What plans do you have now, Jesse? If you're not going to be a farmer again."

"Giving it some thought but I haven't fully decided. Still got plenty of money. Banked quite a bit as well as the cash I hid."

"We done well. Been paying the bank as you said and the mortgage is way down. We got better farming methods due to the modernisation you started. Making some profit again." Moses is proud.

Jesse rubs his chin. "That has given me one idea that I'd like to share with you." Molly sits at the table and he has the attention of both. "Thinking, maybe, to buy more equipment and rent it to other farms. Mechanisation is the way and I did see a catalogue of new machinery while I was in Chicago. Get more crops planted and harvested. Would you be interested in being my business partners?"

"Sounds like something we could do, don't it, Moses."

"I reckon we could. But I don't know much about machinery. I'm a horse and plough man."

"The garage in town has a mechanic. I could talk to him about maintaining our stuff. He'd maybe take on extra hands, go out to the farms to do the work so we don't have to take stuff to him. And don't underestimate yourself, Moses. You did a good job on the distilling. You'll soon pick up how to do things. Besides, it would be more supervising from you, to see what needs to be done and done well."

"Then we up for it."

"That's settled then."

CHAPTER 6

As he gets off the train from Chicago, Sean O'Leary is welcomed by the station cat, which curls round his legs as he stands and thinks. So this is the place where all my troubles started. What could have been a simple transaction between supplier and buyer, profitable to both, became a war because of the stupidity of McAvoy. Well, he's dead now, saved me the trouble of doing it. But also Mary, my child, and Dougal. My future – poof – in a second.

There are no taxis at the station but a man collecting his wife home offers the quiet man with a cane a lift into town.

"Visiting anyone?"

"No. Just taking a break from the city. Do you know of a good hotel or boarding house?"

As usual, Buck puts the bowl of water out on the sidewalk by his office for passing dogs. He looks up at the sky. Weather changing. Could be storm coming. He misses the car giving Sean a lift into town go down Main Street.

The local drops Sean at the boarding house of the Widow Jessup, which he says is a good clean establishment, well-run, omitting they are cousins. Martha Jessup welcomes her new guest, shows him her best room as this new arrival looks more prosperous than her usual clientele.

"On business, Mr......?"

"Dara O'Gill," Sean says, having adopted an alias to keep himself anonymous to anyone who might know his true identity. "No. I had...an auto accident. Doctor suggests I get out of the city and rest up. Take it easy for a while."

"Well, I trust you'll be comfortable here, Mr O'Gill. Anything you want, just ask."

Sean thanks the widow and once she has left him in his room, he unpacks his travelling case and checks that the pistol and ammunition are secure at the bottom. He curses his injury that prevented him driving here, with an arsenal in the trunk, ready for all eventualities.

Downstairs, Martha Jessup checks her appearance in a mirror while she considers the handsome and polite guest. Irish, obviously. Age? Hard to tell exactly. One thinks it's a youngish man, maybe early thirties, then again, he can look older. Some grey at his temples, lines on his face and something in his eyes. That must have been a terrible car accident. There's no ring on his finger, and he's alone here, so unlikely to be married. She primps a bit before moving away from the mirror. She might be 40 but she's kept her figure. Well, maybe, a bit curvier than she used to be, but men like that in a woman.

Sean takes a walk down Main Street. The cane gives some support but he is finding his strength returning and he is less reliant on it now.

Even if he could walk fully without it, he'll keep it. The limp and the stick can give an impression that is less threatening. Besides, the handle is weighted with lead and can make a weapon while he has left his gun in his room for now. He comes level with the Pharmacy- his one link for certain- and enters. The man behind the counter must be Fred White, the only male working here and obviously in charge.

"Good day, sir. What can I do for you?"

"I'd like some tonic and painkillers, please." Sean smiles disarmingly. It's too soon to make a move.

"Leg giving you some pain, is it?" Fred leans over the counter, despite nothing to see other than Sean's trousers.

"Recent injury. It flares up when I've walked on it too long."

"I've just the thing for that. Let me get it."

Fred hands over a bottle of pills with instructions and with the transaction completed by the addition of a bottle of tonic, Sean pays and exits.

Further down the street is the welcome sight of Sid's Diner. Walking in, the bell over the door jangles but two old men bent over a checkers game don't look up. Sid, who had been stood up reading a paper, puts it down. "Howdy. What can I get you?"

"Coffee. Cream and sugar, please."

"Coming right up. Why don't sit over there. Take the weight off. I'll bring it over."

Sean nods and takes a seat at a table. It is good to rest the leg which has started to ache. He takes out two pills to wash down with coffee but Sid has noticed and not only brings the coffee as ordered but also a glass of water."

"Couldn't help noticing. I take them myself sometimes. Arthritis in the knee."

"Thanks. That's very thoughtful."

"No trouble at all. Haven't seen you around before. Arrive today?"

"Yes. Came in on the train. Staying at Mrs Jessup's. Taking a break." Sean stirs the sugar into his coffee and adds the cream.

Sid doesn't go back behind his counter. "You'll be comfortable there. She has some regulars but most of her guests are in-and-out travellers going through. You know, salesmen and the like. What is it you do? If you don't mind me asking?"

"Not at all." Sean figures he needs conversation to flow if he is to find out anything. "I run a warehouse. Middleman between manufacturer and customer. Small, but it pays the rent and a bit more."

"That as much as anyone can hope for these days. It helps when a bit of good luck comes along too." Sid realises he is starting to talk too much, makes a gesture he'd better go back behind the counter. Already spotless, even so he wipes again. "Me and my big mouth," he thinks. "I was about to talk about how Jesse had helped the town."

Sean plans to try again but not right now. The owner is a garrulous sort and a couple of visits could get that tongue going. Meantime, more to see.

"Good coffee. I'll be back for more," and he leaves cash on the counter, nods to the checker players, still absorbed, and steps out on to the sidewalk.

Buck, through his office window, sees a new face in town. A tall, red-haired man coming out of the Diner, walking with a cane, and going down to the General Store. No haste, no need to be anywhere. He locks the office door and goes over to see Sid.

Sean buys Newman cigars from the General Store then spends some time browsing the racks. A pretty young girl had served him and now she is tidying a shelf. He senses something about her, shadows in her eyes. This could be a place to find his farmer; where he comes in to shop for his needs. A sign on the wall reads "Farm and Garden Supplies" and lists spray pumps, water carts, harrows, cultivators and mowers. This looks like the "come to" place in town for all the rural communities. Sean wonders what he might do to get the farmer to come to him rather that a potential wait of days, even weeks, for a chance encounter. It has to be in town as he can't drive himself.

CHAPTER 7

Sunday comes, his first in town. Since arriving on Thursday, he walked each day from the boarding house to the Diner, drank coffee, ate pie, started to chat to the old guys who seemed fixtures there. Sid had still to volunteer any useful information but he had other avenues to investigate. He'd bought a small bottle of perfume from the Pharmacy, also Palmolive shaving cream and Gillette blades to provide a casual opportunity for conversation with Fred White, later presenting the perfume to the Widow Jessup on his return to lodgings. "Just a small token of my appreciation how nice you keep my room and the wonderful meals."

"Oh, you didn't need to do that," simpered the landlady, and made him sit for tea and sandwiches, joining him to chat.

He'd learned about how the church had enjoyed repairs courtesy of one of the farmers, which is why he is now seated at the back, observing everyone. The young woman from the General Store is three pews in front of him. With her, two people he assumes are her parents. No boyfriend. A tall man, seated with a woman, is checking him over. Sean pretends he hasn't noticed the attention.

The minister, a middle-aged man leaning to corpulence and a balding pate, a Pickwick, takes the service. Sean copies the other members of the congregation, being only familiar with a Catholic mass and not this, easier-going ceremony. At the finish, the Minister takes a position at the door and thanks each person for coming. Sean holds back until last so he can have a word.

"Thank you for the service. I've not been much of a churchgoer but I feel I need to make more of an effort now." A generous, modest smile accompanies his speech.

The minister preens a bit. "That's nice of you to say. Have you moved into town? Mr....?"

"O'Gill. Dara O'Gill. No, I've come for some country air to recuperate. I had a bad auto accident and my doctor recommended the trip."

"I'm sorry to hear that, Mr O'Gill, but this is a nice town and people will make you welcome. We look out for each other here."

"I'm beginning to see that. Obviously, the people support the church. It's in excellent condition. That's not been my experience." Sean looks at the interior, all clean, painted and almost immaculate.

"Well, we had a sponsor. Young Jesse Hakerman has been generous. He raised funds for a restoration."

"A good man then. Must be prosperous to afford to do that. What is his line of business?"

"Ah. Oh. He was a farmer. Inherited his parent's farm. Sold up and moved away. Excuse me. My wife is expecting me. I have an appointment to discuss a Christening. Nice talking to you, Mr.."

"O'Gill. Be seeing you," and he walked away, barely using his cane.

The minister pulled a handkerchief from his pocket and mopped his brow. He hadn't said too much had he? No, of course not. Mr O'Gill didn't look like a Government Agent. Quite a nice chap. No, it's alright. Now to deal with the young family and their first born.

Although the town businesses are closed for Sunday, Sid opens his Diner just for lunchtime, to catch those leaving the church who want to meet socially, have a coffee, maybe something to eat. Sean walks in to a fairly busy establishment. He sees the tall man and the woman who must be his wife. The pretty girl is not there, nor her parents. Other faces he had seen in the pews. There is Fred White, sitting alone. Ordering a coffee he walks over.

"Hello, there. Mind if I join you?"

Fred looks up, recognising his customer immediately. "No, please do. How's the leg? Are the tablets working?"

"Pretty much. I'm finding the rest and a little exercise helping." Sean accepts a coffee passed over the counter from Sid, courtesy of another customer, acting as a waiter, who brought it to his table. Sean nods his thanks before turning back to the Pharmacist. "I saw you in church. Good service."

"Well, the minister can go on a bit but he's a good man."

"The church is in such good condition. Looking almost new but I understand it was built last century." Sean probes gently for more information.

"It was in disrepair but funds were raised to make it over. Gave a lot of employment to the trades in town."

"Yes, the minister said a farmer paid for it all. What was his name? Jed..Jesse…?"

"Jesse Hakerman," and Fred is suddenly anxious he's talked out of turn.

"That's it. Jesse Hakerman. Good for a town to have a philanthropist."

"We were lucky." Fred stands. "I have to go. Nice talking to you. Come by if you need any more drugs. Have a nice day."

He leaves, a little too quickly to look natural. The Irish accent and the questions have brought back bad memories. The tall man with an official air has noticed the exchange and is sizing Sean up. Sean is only aware when the man walks over and sits in the chair previously occupied by Fred White.

"Howdy, sir. I'm Sheriff Buckley. Like to say hello to visitors to our little town."

"Sheriff. Dara O'Gill. I'm spending a few days here for my health. Lovely town, lovely people."

"Thank you. We are proud of our community. So not here on business. What is it you do, if you don't mind me asking?" Buck's eyes are quite penetrating but Sean is not fazed.

"I have a little business. Run a warehouse supplying small traders."

"In Springfield, or Chicago?"

"Chicago." The atmosphere across the table has chilled. Each man recognises an inner predator in the other. Buck rises and leaves the

Diner. Sean doesn't want to be revealed just yet. He's making headway and believes this generous Jesse Hakerman is his man. He recalls now that McAvoy had given such a name to Dougal as the source of the gin. He'd had other things on his mind at the time and hadn't paid the attention he should have, thinking it was all under control. It's not unlikely, Hakerman is tied to the assassination attempt by the Italians, triggering their action. Could this tall lawman be the hitman? What were their motives in Chicago? He has a link between the bootlegging and the workshop having found the bottles of gin. Was that a coincidence? An older man, described as tall, good with fists and gun. He'd just this second met such a man. A younger man. Hakerman was described as a young farmer. They rescued a girl. Could she be from this town? Sean said goodbye to Sid and went to find somewhere quiet to sit, smoke one of his cigars, and think.

In his office, Buck sees the red-haired Irishman walking away from the Diner. His instincts shout Trouble. A search of Chicago's telephone directory reveal two Dara O'Gills but no mention of a business. It is simple to phone both numbers and he finds both O'Gills at home. He apologises for disturbing their Sunday but are they associated with a warehouse business. Both men say No. One is a worker on the railway. The other is a stockman in the cattle yards. Neither knows of anyone related to them having a warehouse.

CHAPTER 8

Monday comes round. Jesse has checked in on Maggie every day but skipped Sunday as he knew she would attend church with her parents and, at the moment, Jesse's faith is under attack. Today, he calls in at the General Store first thing, having driven in from Moses and Molly who continue planning their business venture.

Hearing the door open, Maggie looks up and gives him a smile. His heart lifts at this sign of the old Maggie returning. He walks quietly over to the counter and without communication both reach over and hold hands. Jesse hasn't noticed the red-haired customer with a cane browsing in the corner in the clothing section next to housewares.

"Jesse. Missed you yesterday."

Jesse! So that is him. Sean steps behind a display of brooms to be hidden but enabling him to examine the young man and listen to the conversation. His luck is changing.

"Maggie. Stayed on the farm to help Moses. I reckon God will forgive me missing one service."

Maggie! Could that be the woman rescued from the Italians? That could explain her haunted look the first time he saw her. Yet, now she looks blooming. Sean firmly believes he has his man; so many pointers to it being him. When Jesse turns to look out the window, Sean gets a profile and gasps. This is Harry Maguire, the driver from O'Banion. He reaches to his belt reactively then silently curses that he has left his gun at the boarding house. If he has recognised Hakerman/Maguire then the guy can recognise him. He keeps silent and hidden behind stock.

Jesse's distraction, causing him to stare out the window, was Buck on the sidewalk having tapped the glass then beckoning him outside, away from Maggie.

"Maggie. Excuse me a minute. I think the sheriff wants a word. I must be badly parked." They release each other's hands and Jesse leaves the store.

"Sheriff. What is it?"

"Walk with me, Jesse. We have something to discuss." They move further down the street, away from being visible from inside the General Store. "Would an Irishman with red hair have any interest in you?"

"That would be Sean O'Leary. But he died in a gun attack from another mob. That's how I knew it was safe to leave Chicago and catch up with you and Maggie." Jesse's brow is furrowed.

"Are you sure? Only there is such a guy in town and he seems to be asking questions?" Buck holds Jesse's gaze intently. He wants it to be alright, but his senses are telling him it isn't.

"I'll know him if I see him. But, no. It was front page news."

"Pity you skipped church. He was there yesterday. Then in Sid's. I questioned him and he gave his name as Dara O'Gill and his line as a warehouse owner. I checked the phone directories, called two guys, neither him, and no mention of O'Gill Warehouse in the book. Walks with a cane. Claims he was in an auto accident."

"Jeez, Buck. I'd better be careful. That's not stacking up well."

"Let's go to the office. I can phone the Chicago Tribune to find out whether the death is true."

Buck leads the way across the street and down to the law office. Sean takes his chance to leave the General Store unnoticed by either man, just a farewell to the girl. He hurries to the Widow Jessup's to retrieve his pistol.

Buck manages to get through to the Newsdesk and learns the news that O'Leary survived the attack but his driver and his wife were killed. O'Leary hasn't been seen since shortly after the funeral and O'Banion is running the speakeasy.

"That's it then, Jesse. He's here and he's looking for you."

"I don't know why. We finished up the bootlegging. There's nothing for him here."

"Maybe that's not the reason he has come. What if our rescue of Maggie from the Italians is linked to the Italians attempt on his life?"

"Sheriff! Is Maggie in danger again? I'd better go to her," and he rises quickly from the chair.

Buck waves him to sit down again. "Let's think this through and not act hasty. As far as is known, he came alone, on the train. I'd expect a mob if there was to be danger. This is either a coincidence and he really is convalescing or he has a more personal agenda." Buck rubs his hand over his face. The devil has risen again over their community.

"What do you suggest?" Jesse is keen for some positive action.

"We watch him. If you can see him without him seeing you and positively identify him as O'Leary, I'll have something to go on. It might not be him. Maybe he is O'Gill and his business not listed under his name."

"I don't like ifs, sheriff. We can't take chances. God, this is all my fault." Jesse slumps in the chair.

"No, Jesse. You didn't plan this. It was a simple operation to save your farm. I didn't see any trouble from it, apart, maybe, the government getting interested. No. It's as much on my shoulders as yours." Buck pauses thoughtfully. "Are you packing?"

"No, sir. Didn't see the need anymore."

Buck reaches into the drawer of his desk, pulls out a .38, holster and box of ammo. "I'll swear you in as Deputy. Make it legal," and he tosses a badge to lie by the gun.

Maggie is wondering why Jesse is taking so long. It shouldn't take much to move his car if that is what the sheriff really wanted him for. That lodger at Mrs Jessup's sure left in a hurry. I'd forgotten he was in the store.

The Bootlegger

Jerry is back in town, for his regular visit to Fred White. He sees a familiar figure on the sidewalk and decides to keep on driving and give the Pharmacist a miss this month. He still owes money but hadn't been bothered for it. No need to remind his creditor.

CHAPTER 9

The Widow Jessup is cleaning in a backroom when she hears her front door open and close then hurried footsteps up the stairs. When the footsteps sound above her, she knows it is her new lodger, Mr O'Gill. A quick check of her appearance in a mirror and she goes up the stairs and knocks on the door. The sounds inside cease immediately.

"Mr O'Gill. Are you OK? Would you like some tea?" she calls through the closed door.

Back comes "No. Thank you. Just need a rest, Mrs Jessup. Rather overdid it. I'll just take a nap."

Satisfied, the landlady goes back downstairs and resumes her cleaning. In his room, Sean lets out his breath. For a moment, he thought the lawman had followed him, or Hakerman. Relieved it was only the widow, he pulls his gun out from under the pillow where he had stashed it on the first knock, having retrieved it from his case. He now examines it, unloading, checking all parts work, then loading. Not long now, he thinks, until he avenges Mary and his unborn child. Hakerman is going down and he's prepared to kill the sheriff too, obviously his accomplice in Chicago. Hakerman has been his Jonah. Costing him his men at first then the love of his life. They were so close to getting out of the business to start a new life as a family on the west coast. He had nothing to live for now and as long as he finishes the farmer, he doesn't care about dying himself. He doesn't know where his target lives but he now knows where he turns up. The girl will be his tethered goat.

The worry over whether this is O'Leary (and he now thinks it is) is eating Jesse up. Is the Irishman scouting, preparing for his gang to drive in and wreak havoc? He'd better go back to the farm and warn Moses and Molly. He still has the use of the sheriff's car to visit them while he stays with the Buckleys and the lawman says "Go. Of course you must go and warn them. Take some of the guns we added to the armoury and make sure they have enough weapons." The bounty of arsenal from the Chicago adventures provides some heavy firepower, although they are running low on ammunition for the tommy-gun. Jesse can't get to the farm soon enough and Molly is concerned that something is up with the speed he enters the yard.

"Mr Jesse. Is everything alright?" she asks, deep worry lines on her face.

"Molly, Where's Moses?" Jesse can't see him nearby.

"In the top field. Why? What's the matter? You got me scared, Mr Jesse."

"I'm sorry, Molly, but I think the mobsters may have returned. At least, one of them has. We need to be prepared. Take my rifle and telescope and go wait up the ridge while I fetch Moses. Just in case I was followed."

Only pausing to see his instructions followed, Jesse starts the long walk to the top field. Cursing every step of the way at fickle fortune.

Was the farm worth the trouble it has brought down on friends? It is no longer a place of happy memories. The yard is where Moses was shot in the leg. He nearly died there in a knife fight. The creek has the bodies of two gangsters. The ground is contaminated by blood.

He sees the big man before he is seen. Thankful no one else is in sight, Jesse calls out to Moses.

"Jesse. You alright? You look worn down? Here, have a drink of water from my flask."

"Thank you, Moses. I'm afraid I have bad news. The boss man in Chicago has turned up in town."

"But you said he was killed in a gunfight between gangs." Moses is confused.

"That's what I read in the paper but it was misreported. Two died in the car but he was only wounded. I guess he's been recovering and now I think he has tracked me down. If he wants more gin, he's going to be disappointed and angry. He will probably want to know what happened to his men."

"We'll tell him we're not in the business anymore. Let him have all the kit, Jesse. That might satisfy him." Moses wants an easy solution but Jesse has deeper doubts.

"I'm assuming that is why he has come...but he may have other reasons. It's possible rescuing Maggie set off a chain of events that led to the gunfight that killed his wife and his driver."

Moses is suddenly alert that his wife is alone back at the farmhouse.

"I'se gotta go to Molly. She may be in danger."

Jesse puts a restraining hand on the larger man's arm. "No. She's safe for now. I set her up the ridge with my rifle and scope. She can see the road from there and will fire a shot to warn us if anyone comes. I think you should move back to your shack for now. Only a local would know where it is. If anyone comes to the farm, let them find it empty."

"As you say. Let's go and make preparations." He whistles for the dog, which has been hunting rabbits.

On the way back to the farmyard, the two men plan. Molly sees them walking back, stands and waves an All Clear before walking down to the yard herself. All three meet by the barn.

"I'm sorry for bringing this on you. I intend to make it right."

"Jesse. We all in this together. You've nothing to be sorry about." Moses and Molly are in agreement.

Jesse arms them with spare weapons from the trunk of Buck's car. He lets them keep the rifle as he can't see that he would use it in town. Also the tommy-gun – it will give them greater firepower if attacked. The plan he agrees with Moses is to move out the farmhouse, make it seem deserted, and block the tracks in with carts and farm vehicles, so anyone would have to approach on foot. Their shanty is not visible from the yard or even the ridge, so the likelihood of townies trekking round the landscape to find another dwelling is nearly non-existent. However, every precaution must be taken. Satisfied he has done all he can, he promises to be back as soon as there is news then heads back into town, where Buck is waiting for an update.

CHAPTER 10

Buck has stayed in his office, handy to a phone, with a clear view out across Main Street and downaways. A shotgun rests across his knees. Earlier, he'd phoned Agnes to advise her to be on alert and at any sign of a stranger or event she is not happy with, to go out the back and into the trees. Take his home pistol from the drawer in the hallway. If she can manage a phone call to him, he'll be home as if riding lightning. He'd borrowed Sid's car while Jesse is about in his, and parked it outside.

Finishes his instructions to his wife with "I love you."

"I love you too. Be careful," is the response.

Buck has confided in Sid at the Diner and Fred White that Mr O'Gill may not be who he says he is and they have promised to phone him with any sighting. Unknown to them all, is that Sean is indeed napping at the Widow's, saving his strength for the evening. He has a plan.

Jesse comes back into town and immediately goes to the law office where Buck is anxious for news.

"Moses and Molly are moving back to their shack, which any townie won't know about. I've given them some guns."

"They'll be safer there than in the farmhouse but when Moses works the fields, he'll be vulnerable."

371

"The crops are OK for now. They'll take the milk cow with them and the horses. Let's hope we can sort this. Or we're wrong about O'Gill. Has anyone seen him?" Jesse gratefully takes a mug of coffee from Buck, who answers.

"Not a sign. He may be holed up somewhere. Even at Mrs Jessup's, but I don't want to alert her to our concerns. If he is O'Leary, she couldn't carry off a pretence. Fred and Sid know we are looking into him and have promised to ring me as soon as they see him. I reckon we keep this tight for now. No reason to get the town panicked." Buck tries to roll a smoke but the tension in his hands tears the paper and the tobacco falls to the floor. Both men stare at it, as if an omen.

Maggie is finding recent events are fading in her mind. In the comfort of her home and cared for by her indulgent parents, normality seems to have returned. Yet, sometimes at night, she will wake up crying. Jesse has called in every day and spends several minutes chatting to her. They've held hands during the last two visits and a feeling is emerging in her heart that perhaps a future is possible. Jesse now knows more about her then any other individual and they have a shared secret of that night. She can't truly recall events as Buck led her out of the bedroom but there is a memory, like the memory of a movie she may have seen long ago, that a gun was fired and a man, an evil man, died. Then the time at Jesse's hideaway where time had no meaning and she slept a lot and another memory on a cinema screen in her mind, of a gunfight. She only started to have true memories of a time spent in a hotel, with Buck watching over her then Jesse arriving and they all came home to town and safety.

Jesse has been playing thoughts in his mind, over and over. He can't change the past but maybe he can change the future. Maybe he can do something right. He tells the sheriff he is going to check on Maggie, having walked out mid-conversation that morning. Both men scan the street through the window before Buck allows him to leave. The street has locals going about their business but no sign of a red-headed man or other strangers. Jesse crosses over and walks down to the General Store. Gets a couple of "Hi, Jesse. Back in town then?" and waves and smiles, but his eyes are darting everywhere and his lips are tight, creating whiteness around them.

Maggie looks up from arranging a pile of overalls when she hears the door open. She is happy to see Jesse back; he left too soon before and she was enjoying the unspoken conversation under the verbal one.

"Hi, Maggie. Sorry I left so quickly. The sheriff sent me on an errand. Look," opening his coat to reveal a deputy's badge on his shirt. "I'm a temporary lawman while I work out what I want to do with my life."

"That's nice, Jesse. You and the sheriff get on so well together. I think you help him over Tom. But you said 'temporary'. What do you mean?"

373

Jesse stands nervously, seeing some concern in Maggie's face. He hopes it is the right sort of concern considering what he is planning to say. "I'm not sure about what to do now. I'm letting Moses and Molly keep the farm, they deserve it. Molly says they have written wills. It comes back to me at some point. Moses and I have talked about investing in farm equipment and leasing it out to farmers who can't afford to buy outright. Farming needs more mechanisation to be efficient." He hastily adds, "there'll be business for your parents in that."

Maggie waits patiently. "That sounds nice. Are you going to do it?"

"Kinda depends…. Maggie. I stood back because I thought Tom and you were meant for each other. Truth is… Maggie, I love you. Always have. Do you think you could love me?"

"Oh, Jesse. Yes, yes, yes," and she runs into his arms.

CHAPTER 11

Unaware of events in town, Sean has been sleeping. It's the best sleep he has had in ages. He even dreamed. He was walking through a park with Mary, under the blossom fruit trees, and they were pushing a pram. The baby was sleeping. Sean didn't know if a boy or girl and, in the dream, it doesn't matter. That was the dream. Walking as a family in the summer sun, shaded by trees.

When he awakes, he hears the sounds of crockery and cutlery being laid in the dining room and there is a distinct whiff of roast meat coming from the kitchen, the aroma taking the stairs and somehow penetrating his door, making his stomach rumble. Sean decides he does need a good dinner to see him through the evening ahead. While he waits to hear the dinner gong, he strips to the waist and washes himself down. The pot of Hinds handcream has travelled with him and he rubs some on the back of his hand which he raises to his nose, closes his eyes, and smells.

"Oh, Mary. I might be seeing you soon, my darling."

The gift of perfume was a trigger to the Widow Jessup and she went all out to provide a meal that showed off all her culinary skills. This gentle giant was so attentive to her and bringing such a personal gift is surely a sign of some intention. He seems too honourable to just

375

want to bed her, not that she would object, it had been so long since she had had a man in her bed. She finds her body warming at the thought and a flush rises on her cheeks. Earlier she had bathed and used a new bar of Ivory soap, unperfumed except for the natural scent of its ingredients, so that it would allow the perfume the Irishman had given her to flourish unchallenged.

The meal passes quietly, just exchanges of compliments and the two other guests wondering what the special occasion is that provides such a fulsome dinner over a more usual pork chops, potatoes and greens.

"What a shame we don't have wine. Prohibition is so unfair, do you agree, Mr O'Gill?"

"I do indeed, Mrs Jessup. To deny a person refreshment with their meal is a cruelty to the digestion. I will have to settle for a walk instead."

The McGregors are comfortable in their rooms above the store. They listen to a play on the radio and Mr McGregor always pays more attention to the advertisements in case he should be stocking an item. Mrs McGregor is sewing, repairing clothes and Maggie is reading a romance novel. But Maggie's mind isn't on the words of the book but the words of Jesse. She had promised not to say anything yet to her parents but the secret is burning her up. Reflecting on their past history, she is coming to realise she always had feelings for Jesse but Tom was more attentive and to deny she had feelings too for him but not as

376

strong would have hurt him. So Jesse too had been standing back for his friend. How things might have been different without a war. Tom would still be here. Had he proposed, she might well have said Yes. Life is so complicated.

In the Law Office, Jesse has pulled a chair up against the window and is sitting with the lights off, better to watch the thoroughfare unobserved. Looking along the street, he can see the lights above the General Store and he thinks of Maggie, she'll be there, with her parents, and he now has accepted his feelings for her. Ironic, and cruel even, that events had had to take the path they had to reach this position. Before the war, there had been three of them, best friends, then one doesn't come back from the Front. Post-war, his ma gone and the struggle at the farm which led to the early death of his father, already heartbroken at losing his soulmate. Times that followed had added to the change to Jesse. Conflict made him a man much sooner than nature intended and time and events showed him the strength two people could find together. Moses and Molly – childhood sweethearts that had endured then flourished. Sheriff and Mrs Buckley – a loving couple who shared the heartache of losing their only child but who have been there for Jesse. He and Maggie must survive this current crisis and then they can live a quiet, contented life, no more danger, maybe start a family. What will that be like?

A pleasant evening of domesticity for the McGregors is disturbed by a sound of breaking glass. Not sure he has heard correctly, Mr McGregor checks with the others that indeed it is glass and it sounded like it came from downstairs.

"Stay here," he commands, then cautiously descends the stairs to the store.

Mrs McGregor's quiet, timorous voice drifts behind him. "Oh, dear. Do be careful," and she huddles with Maggie.

The storeowner hesitates to turn the lighting on and relies up streetlamps illuminating the store to be enough. There is nothing untoward at the front and, anyway, it wasn't that big a sound, so he goes to check the back. Before he spots the broken window, he can feel the breeze entering. The window is ajar. Whoever broke it, their purpose was to undo the catch and climb in. That means they could still be in the store unless he had scared them off. He pulls the window closed and the cold muzzle of a pistol is pressed against his neck.

A hoarse whisper, "Don't make a sound. Do as I say. Who's upstairs?"

"My wife and daughter. Please don't hurt them."

Brings a tap on the head from the gun. Painful but not incapacitating. "Do as I say and no one need get hurt. Disobey and I'll shoot them both. Now call them down."

"Please, mister. Take the cash. I'll open the safe for you. No need for this." A second head tap, that makes the Scot wobble.

"Call them down. It will be better for you all if you do?"

"Catherine. Maggie. Will you come down here?" Close to tears, fearing the consequences for his family.

The two women timidly descend the stairs and, when they reach the bottom, they see their man standing, shaking, with a thin trickle of blood from a head wound running down his forehead, past his eye, over his cheek, to drip off his chin on to his shirt.

Sean O'Leary steps out of the shadows. "Don't make a noise. I don't want to hurt you."

Catherine McGregor rushes to her husband's side to support and dabs at the blood on his face. Maggie is frozen. Sean allows the little scene to play out, realising the numbing effect of shock on all three of his prisoners. Catherine is the first to respond.

"We have money in the safe. It's all yours if you don't hurt us."

"Do as I say and no one need get hurt." The store provides what he needs. "Get in the storeroom." To Maggie, "Tie them up," and he throws rope over. "Make the knots tight."

Zombie like, Maggie picks up the rope and, with her parents seated on sacks, winds it round and round them before tying it off. Sean waves her to stand back while he checks her work and is satisfied. "OK. Come with me."

He indicates they go back into the main store. Maggie is thinking he has come to take her back to the brothel and she will die fighting rather than let him do that. She'll be compliant until they are further

379

away from her parents and she is checking around for something to use as a weapon.

"Sit down." Sean indicates a bentwood chair he has pulled out into a free space.

Maggie is not near anything she can use as a weapon. The man is so much stronger and towers over her. She mustn't let him knock her unconscious. If she can't fight him, she'll kill herself but she has to be certain of success. She sits.

"Put your arms round the back."

Sean had already prepared a loop and he slips this over her hands and pulls the rope tight. Then he can put the gun down and tie it off. Maggie is helpless. If the man is tying her here and not taking her away, what is his plan?

Jesse returns to his post at the window, having gone out the back to make coffee. He blows on the hot liquid so he can take a sip. A Oh Henry! bar is all he brought for food and his stomach rumbles. It's late now. Probably nothing going to happen. Drink the coffee then settle down on the chairs to sleep. His attention is drawn by a light going on in the General Store. Maybe old man McGregor is retrieving something to use upstairs. He watches to see if it will quickly go out.

The crack of a gunshot, a flash, and the large window of the store shatters into the street. Dogs bark. Jesse drops the coffee mug and sprints out on to Main Street and runs down to the scene, drawing his gun as he does so. His heart pumps.

Buck had dozed off in an armchair, reluctant to change into nightclothes and go to bed. The insistent ringing of the telephone rouses him and he answers a call from a concerned citizen.

"Sheriff. There's been gunfire in Main Street. Something is going down at the General Store."

He wastes no time in running to his car.

Jesse slows down as he approaches the broken window, keeping tight against the buildings. Stooping low, he peers round the edge of the window to look in the interior. Illumination is coming from a single desklamp by the till. It shines on Maggie, gagged and tied to a chair.

Buck curses that his car won't go any faster. He'd made the decision to go home so as to protect Agnes should the need arise, feeling safe that Jesse had volunteered to sleep at the office to keep an eye on the town. Now he fears the worse. Have the mob arrived to pay back for their lost men?

Jesse jumps through the window to present the hardest target and rolls across the floor up to a display stand. There is no sound other than a scared whimper from Maggie, escaping past her gag. He risks a look round the side of the stand to check her out and hopefully reassure her, Maybe whoever did this has left. Who in their right mind would stay after making such a noise? Maggie has seen him and he mimes to indicate it will be alright. Extending his gun arm forward he creeps round the display. Too fixed on Maggie, he is not alert enough for what happens. A weighted cane cracks down on his arm, causing him to drop his gun. A hand reaches down, grabbing his collar and drags him in front of Maggie.

"You came, Hakerman. Or is it Maguire?"

"What do you want, O'Leary?"

"Answers. Just who the fuck are you and how have you ruined my life?"

"What do you mean? You sent men here to take my gin. I didn't invite you. You could have stayed in Chicago and we'd have all been happy."

"You killed them, didn't you?" Sean is putting the pieces of the puzzle together. "Paddy and Spud never deserted. You killed them. And that was you with McAvoy and the guys. Just who the fuck are you?"

"Look, O'Leary. You can go. There's nothing for you here. What's done is done."

"There's nothing for me anywhere." The Irishman removes Maggie's gag. "You're the girl the Italians had, aren't you? Hakerman and, I assume, the sheriff came for you?"

"What if we did? What's it to you? They were Italians. You're Irish."

"It has everything to do with me. Those wops thought I had sanctioned it. They came after me. They killed my wife and child."

"Oh, God. Believe me. I am so sorry. I had no way of knowing they would do that."

"It was all down to you, Hakerman. They'd seen you deliver to the Ace and thought you were my guy. They came after me." Sean is screaming, veins popping on his forehead and tears falling from his eyes. "Now you pay. I take one you care for and you can feel the pain. Then I'm going to kill you."

"You don't have to do this. Maggie is innocent. Kill me. Let her live." Jesse pleads.

"Mary was innocent. My poor sweet Mary. My child was innocent. I would have died in their place but I never got the offer. Say your goodbyes. Mary and I never even had that but you can."

Sean lines up his pistol on Maggie.

Buck takes in the scene through the window. There is no confusion about what is happening.

He takes a double-handed stance with his pistol and prays for a clear shot.

"Goodbye, Jesse. I love you. It's not your fault."

"I love you, Maggie. I'm so sorry."

Residents who had been woken earlier hear a new gunshot.

Postscript

In writing my first ever fiction book, I took a very leisurely approach (no contracts, deadlines or publisher chasing me). So as not to lose the idea, I jotted down some notes as to the plot and some ideas about the storyline. One was that Jesse would be a veteran and have some military skills and Sheriff Buckley would feel beholden to him for trying to save his son.

When I went back to my notes, I decided on an ambush from cover of the gangsters visiting Jesse's farm, so it was logical to make him a WW1 sniper. That was all I had when, in the UK lockdown for the Corona Virus (Covid19), I picked up the excellent Nicholas Rankin's "Churchill's Wizards – The British Genius for Deception 1914-1945 (Faber & Faber 2008). This wasn't research – just my interest in military history. In the first part of the book, the amazing Hesketh-Prichard appeared – an advocate for sniping and founder of the Sniping, Observation and Scouting school. From that piece of serendipity I found (free online from the Open Library) Prichard's own publication "Sniping in France – with notes on the scientific training of scouts, observers and snipers" 1920 Hutchinson & Co. So what had been intended as an explanation for Jesse's skills with a rifle, became a bigger part of the book as I incorporated the SOS experience into the story.

As my writing developed, I realised I needed more on the Chicago crime scene of the 1920s, as writing about Jesse's and Buck's region would not fill the book. Luckily, I found another excellent book "Al Capone's Beer Wars – a complete history of organised crime in Chicago during prohibition" by John H. Binder (pub Prometheus 2017). This helped correct many misconceptions I had from reading books years ago and watching movies. A big surprise was the youth of the mobsters – many in their twenties or only just in their thirties.

I am extremely grateful to Mr Binder for informing me about the Whiskey Rebellion (Western Pennsylvania 1791), the Lager Beer riots (Chicago 1855) and that by 1917 thirteen states had gone "dry" due to the Temperance movement, but that did not mean all were alcohol free, some having a prosperous illegal trade. In 1906 residents of Chicago drank nearly three times more than the national average. It confirmed, for me, that I had a workable plot.

Another book that proved invaluable was "Mr Capone" by Robert J. Schoenberg (pub Robson Books, 1992). Short of going to Chicago (which would have been fantastic) I had to rely on immersing myself in good histories.

I'd finished a draft, the complete story told but still needing the embellishment to keep your interest, dear reader, when I picked up "The Mafia – the first 100 years" by William Balsamo & George Carpozi Jr (pub Virgin Books – Penguin – 1988). Apart from being slightly horrified that the title suggests we'll have the Mafia for another 100 years, I did draw comfort for Sean O'Leary's actions at the end with this:

"It is axiomatic in some sectors of the underworld community that revenge is sweeter when it is not taken against the person who committed the harm......the theory is, it is better instead to take the life of someone near and dear to him."

To keep me in the period, I noted the big events of each year on a page before the action and decided not to delete when I completed the story, as I felt they added background, especially for you, the reader, who may not be versed in American history.

While working on the drafts, I was also reading the excellent "Forensics – The anatomy of crime" by one of my favourite authors – Val McDermid. I do recommend this to any fan of crime fact or fiction. It is so superior to the memoirs I had recently read by a pathologist. It jogged my memory about Edmond Locard (who first came to my notice in the Lincoln Rhymes series of books by Jeffery Deaver) and also Song Ci, whom I had read about in a fictionalised story of him, plus an episode of BBC's Silent Witness. That gave me material to fill out more of Jesse's back history and his skill at deleting evidence.

As a postscript, I wonder if "whisky chasers" originated during Prohibition, the legally produced "near beer" being boosted by neat alcohol in a process known as "needling." Just a thought.

As for the ending…. well it is whatever you want it to be. You'll be right.

I hope you have enjoyed my humble efforts.

Keith Lawson
Dorset 2022

Printed in Great Britain
by Amazon